FAMILY AI
No. 13

ALSO BY S.D. MONAGHAN

The Accident

THE FAMILY AT No. 13

S.D. MONAGHAN

bookouture

Published by Bookouture in 2018

An imprint of StoryFire Ltd.
Carmelite House
50 Victoria Embankment
London EC4Y 0DZ

www.bookouture.com

ISBN: 978-1-78681-447-0
eBook ISBN: 978-1-78681-446-3

This book is a work of fiction. Names, characters, businesses,
organizations, places and events other than those clearly in the
public domain, are either the product of the author's imagination
or are used fictitiously. Any resemblance to actual persons, living or
dead, events or locales is entirely coincidental.

To Anne – the white on every page.

PART ONE

CHAPTER ONE

THE DAY OF

CONNOR

The blood welled up as a desolate cold crept into the wound like a ghost. Connor stared down at the corpse. It had a face he recognised; a face he knew too well. Then he nodded, his shocked body agreeing with his composed mind that – *yes, a knife will do this to flesh*. Connor gripped the camouflage-green handle, looked at the steel and then down to the injury as if finding it difficult to believe that this same tool had only moments before knifed spinewards through reefs of ribs. For a moment, the blade glistened under the suburban street lights of St Catherine's Hill before the shadows of the trees swallowed it, turning the bloodstain into an oily smear.

Connor delicately lifted the head, hoping to find a hint of life to comfort and yet also wanting to look, for a final time, upon that face that he had become so familiar with. He needed to keep the weight steady, not wanting to jolt it, as if there really was an expectation that a bleating whimper of hope would be detected. But there was also an acceptance that this was the heaviest type of burden anyone would have to lift. Blood as thick as paint had already spilled across the driveway in a circular motif, while further away more of it was splattered about like an angry Jackson Pollock.

An upstairs bedroom window opened in the neighbouring house and a woman leaned out to the usual quiet of St Catherine's Hill. There was a stretch of silence as her brain processed exactly what she saw – and then she screamed, a penetrating and dismayed acknowledgement as to what lay, cruelly mutilated, on the driveway of number 13.

Connor stared up and intended to shout, but only a whisper emerged; 'No. It wasn't me. I don't know what happened. I wasn't here.' Despite the rising panic, a flash of bullet points riddled a neat line across his brain: *I've been set up. From the very beginning. Now no one will believe me. I'm completely and utterly fucked.*

The woman once again shouted out to St Catherine's Hill, this time making words. 'Oh my God! Police. Someone call the police!'

Connor looked between the two driveway pillars topped with flashy stone griffins to the road outside. In a matter of minutes they'd be putting all their resources into finding him as quickly as possible. They had to. They knew that when a person killed once, they entered an existential realm where life was revealed to be nothing much and so to kill a few more would make no difference. Lights brightened the hallways of a few nearby houses. His time was already running out.

CHAPTER TWO

THREE DAYS BEFORE

MARY

I flick the outdoor switch and the spotlights turn off. A blackness settles on my garden and the lawn becomes a dark lake. Overhead is a moon so thin you could get a paper cut off it. Leaning on the rail, I take my usual position on the patio about ten feet above one of the many landscaped gardens of St Catherine's Hill.

Behind me, my reflection is mapped on the glass. It's a new hairstyle – dark brown, shortish, with a sheen to its edges that makes it look carefully shaped. I was worried that it might make me look too formal. But I think it makes me look confident rather than arrogant, controlled rather than severe, a chic forty-year-old rather than 'mumsy'. When I said to my husband, 'Well?' Andrew had regarded me in silence; almost as if I'd lost the last of my looks in just under an hour and he didn't know what to say. But slowly his face lit up with the correct expression and he said that it took a decade off me, and since I already looked like I was still in my thirties, people would now think that I was his daughter. On the rare occasions when Andrew says things like that, it makes me beholden to him as if he's some monarch and I his royal guard.

I *love* this new haircut.

Closing my eyes, I begin the ritual of my favourite part of the day. There it is – the metallic snap of my husband's old lighter followed by a deep inhalation of smoke into my lungs. Behind shut eyes I can positively feel the tip glow. When I see others smoking outside offices, in their cars, blocking pub entrances, it seems to be something needy and contemptible. But when I do it, secretly, once a day, just before midnight in this same spot, each inhalation feels as if I'm slipping into a perfect bath.

Ashing the cigarette on the deck, I stare across the lawn to the back of Brona and Zachery's house. The flowerpots on the rail hide me from her sightlines above the bushes and trees at the end of the garden. It wouldn't do to have someone like Brona know my secret. Secrets are only enjoyable when they're secret.

As usual I've a perfect view of Brona fifty feet away as she walks by her living room window on the middle floor and out the slider to her balcony patio. 'I see every part of you,' I whisper, as if that was a good thing. Brona's strange vaporiser glows green. What's the point of that? Surely the joy of a fag is that they're dangerous, forbidden, bad. She inhales the electronic cigarette, smoking the technology, and exhales the dense steam to the night air. The cigarette burns down to my fingers and I realise that I'm gripping the patio banister like it's the rail of a sinking ship. I stub it out in one of the heavy decorative urns.

My phone vibrates but I don't answer. The odds are high that it's bad news. Only bad news comes late at night. I wait in dread for the arrival of a message and eventually the phone vibrates again. The screen is inches from my face. Finding the voicemail, I listen warily.

YOU HAVE ONE UNPLAYED MESSAGE. THIS WAS LEFT AT. ELEVEN FIFTY-ONE. PM.

A quiet, polite but urgent girlish voice speaks. She sounds like something from history recorded in wartime rather than someone who's spoken just two minutes ago. It's as if the voice is afraid a guard might hear; which, of course, is entirely possible considering where my sister is.

'Mary, it's Emer. So, you believe time is the great absolver. You've convinced yourself that the further into the past the deed – your dirty deed – sinks, the easier it is to live with. And you hope that one day it'll get to the point where you'll barely be able to believe that you did it. That it happened. You're my older sister, Mary. You had responsibilities. You *have* responsibilities. You're the one accountable. I'm here because of you.'

Emer pauses to control her breathing which has sped up with the tumble of words.

'He wasn't meant to be. That's where I fell down. Trying to hide that truth. Trying to ignore it. Trying to pretend that I didn't feel it. He wasn't meant to be.'

My sister likes to talk about her feelings, which is understandable when 'feelings' are the only thing that important people will talk to you about; the only thing that'll get you out of your hell and back to the real world. Emer can't help but be self-obsessed. Though I'm glad she's chosen me to cling to. We have so much in common; so much history. I want to help her more. I need to. I just don't know how to yet.

'Mary… there's something new. Something I haven't touched on before.'

I doubt it.

'Mary… I wish it was you in here instead of me.'

That is new.

'Mary, I can't help it. Today and other times… recently… I hate you.'

The phone moves a few centimetres from my ear.

'I do hate you. And I resent you. I… I face you and I get small. I am small. You make me like this. I've got to *grow* now. But I'll be in touch. Very soon. You'll feel it.'

I save the message and it joins Emer's other twenty-two stored missives-from-the-brink. Andrew isn't aware of any of them. I can't tell him. Being an ex-army man, he's very protective – especially with regards to all of this. He takes action. It's the only way he knows. And this situation does not require action. Not yet.

It's past Brona's bedtime. The lights in her living room switch off and blank out my garden with an ebony splash. Since I stepped away from the travel agency, this garden is my reason for making plans; my never-ending project. It's like having the countryside in your city home; a manageable size but big enough to trickle my green fingers over it. My degree is in literature not botany, but all the facts I have – all the academic specifics I now possess – are about trees, bushes and flowers. This garden has the effect of making me aware of nature; the teeming, flourishing, unremitting explosions of birth and rebirth through the seasons.

Suddenly there's a noise in the darkness of the garden below. It quickly grows louder – like the dull sound of a clenched fist pounding moist meat. I squint into the black. Everything about that ugly sound frightens me. I know it's not an animal down there. I know *exactly* what it is. Aware of what's about to happen, it's very odd to know that I really could've walked away.

'Oh dear God,' I hear myself whisper. 'Not again…'

CHAPTER THREE

TWO DAYS BEFORE

CONNOR

It was a bright morning beyond the ground floor office window – an early milky hue that made the polluted city air seem fresh and nourishing. Connor ran his hand through his dark hair, mussing it up further, and shut his eyes. *The absolute worst-case scenario.* He clenched his fists. It was no use – in the darkness behind his shut eyes he could still hear his immediate future; it sounded like a bottle bank being pushed off a ten-storey roof.

For three years the Fitzgerald Building had been unadulterated perfection. Who would complain about only having to take an elevator ride from their bedroom to their office every morning? But then two things happened in rapid succession to petrol-bomb his world.

First, an Airbnb opened three months ago directly above his apartment. Connor duly complained to his landlord – a Chinese pension fund – who said that they would deal with it. A month later they told him that they would not be offering to renew the lease. Apparently, they too had decided to turn as many of their downtown units into Airbnbs as possible. So just two weeks ago, he'd been given notice to vacate both his apartment and his office by the end of the month.

Of course, the irony was not lost on Connor that it was *he* who was being tortured by Airbnbs, because it was beginning to look extremely likely that within the next year Connor would be heading up the new Committee of Mental Health and Noise Pollution. This committee would have powers to penalise inconsiderate neighbours and close down clubs and bars that exceeded healthy noise levels; plus the power to write new legislation to govern the Airbnbs materialising all over the city.

But that was still months away. Until that happened, Connor needed somewhere to live and somewhere to practise his counselling therapy. He needed the Health Board to see that he was a professional worth investing in, worth listening to, worth believing in. However, he'd been so busy putting together his final proposal in collaboration with universities in London and Finland *and* running his practice, that he'd had no time to deal with such fripperies as eviction notices. And suddenly Connor found himself with less than two weeks to sort it all out.

From behind the desk of his ground floor office in the Fitzgerald Building, Connor soaked up what his clients saw: the mounted awards, the 'shouty' and vainglorious degrees and letters of congratulation on the walls. There was a digital frame on top of the cabinet, the image changing every thirty seconds, sliding and corkscrewing through photographs of Connor with a famous actor on the set of a TV show about therapy, to one of him shaking hands with Angela Merkel, to another of him shoulder to shoulder with an ageing rock god. There was no sense of clutter in his office, no distractions to be seen. Pens, pencils, notepad, leather-bound diary and a stapler were all neatly arranged on his desk next to the closed laptop. The walls were white, the carpet an unspectacular beige.

It was 9 a.m. and the first of six scheduled appointments was due. Connor's clients were generally of the same upper-middle to upper-class clans, communicating the same confessions and anxieties: abortion trips amalgamated with shopping jaunts in Paris; gender reassignment fantasies; fears about Iran nuking the West; or the banks collapsing and all their lovely money disappearing along with their hopes and dreams. They were educated, anxious professionals trying to win the struggle to find enough hours in the day to enjoy the fruits of their workaholism; a breeze. But once his project with the Health Board was up and running, then he'd finally be in the financial position to refer on his therapy clients and instead devote his entire private practice to actually helping make the city and then the country and maybe, eventually, even the world, a better place.

Right on time Zachery D'Silva took the seat opposite, his coat thrown onto the spare chair as if to a butler. He had the dark looks of a tortured, handsome poet and the smooth, tanned skin of a thirty-year-old man who was half-Dutch and half-Moroccan but he was actually born Canadian and grew up all over North America.

'Connor, you look exhausted.'

'I am exhausted.' Early last night – Sunday evening – he'd watched in dismay from his balcony as a stretch party limo, complete with internal disco lights and thumping sound system, pulled up before the Fitzgerald Building to deliver a group of Welsh hens with buckets of champagne and their own DJ. Connor reckoned he'd managed to grab about three hours' sleep in total.

Zachery was a youngish millionaire managing his own property portfolio, but he wasn't in the first division of wealth that some of Connor's clients occupied. He wasn't the type of man who said, 'Let's take the yacht out this weekend.' He was middling Division Two. However, he was still rich. Where Zachery really differed from the others was that he'd been a session musician in the 1990s and had toured with famous pop singers, played prestigious festivals and had stood on the stage of Madison Square

Garden plucking chords on his bass. But that was then and this was now.

In therapy, Zachery often voiced his curiosity as to what his younger self would've thought of how he'd ended up at thirty – administering an investment portfolio for a Dutch bank that was an engine of pure profit. Despite the fact that Zachery would take every opportunity to remind Connor of his original God-given talent – to hold it up and marvel at it like a precious jewel – Connor didn't think Zachery's younger self would've been too disappointed. Connor had yet to meet a liberal with a knack for making money who, under their *Guardian*-reading polish, didn't have conservative instincts. For example, whenever Zachery forgot about his past, he would end up pontificating about the almost magical entity that was The Market. 'You know green stocks?' Zachery had asked only last week. 'Green stocks are nice. But not smart. And the markets only reward smart. So, I bet against them and people in Harvey Slings noticed – I was doing a jingle for them. And, just like that, I got a new career. See? I always believed that this whole starving artist thing – it's not really necessary.'

Connor reckoned that Zachery struggled with masochistic tendencies that were beginning to be played out in their sessions. Zachery would demand, demand, demand until Connor had no alternative but to blatantly reject him. These masochistic tendencies were probably the core of his unhappiness but Connor couldn't touch on that. His remit was simply to reorganise his wealthy clients' lives to maximise their fabulousness.

However, recently the transference that Zachery was emitting – the imaginary friendship or attraction to the therapist on behalf of the client – was getting out of control and impeding his progress. He was becoming too intense, wanting more sessions than he needed, was fascinated by even the minutest detail of Connor's life that he picked up on during their sessions, and had started to overstep the mark with regards to his personal life.

'Connor, did I see you in St Anne's Park on Saturday afternoon?'

Connor hadn't realised he'd been seen. 'Well, it sounds like it.'

'You live nearby?'

'I grew up on the north side,' Connor replied, answering a question he hadn't been asked. He preferred his clients to know as little as possible about his private life – that is, when he'd time for one.

'But do you live near the park?'

Connor paused just long enough for it to begin to feel awkward. He was used to imposing emotional gaps between the client and himself. 'There must be a park out near you?'

'There's several, actually. But I decided to bring Brona on a road trip. We took in the beach too… out on Bull Island as the sun set. It was beautiful.'

Connor thought of his last girlfriend. The very final time he'd been with her was out on Bull Island, parked in his Saab on the promenade. That was almost a year ago. Time flies. Since then, work pressures had forced him into trying a platinum dating site but he'd failed to gel with his weekly matches. More recently, Connor had taken the advice of an *Irish Times* article and tried the free Tinder app, but despite his online profile stating 'NOT INTO HOOK-UPS', each of his matches had been *only* interested in hook-ups.

'Connor, I look at you – my judge, my jury, my sentence – and I envy you. However, I do wonder if you have everything you want.'

If I had what I wanted, I wouldn't have had an Airbnb over my bed for the last three months and I wouldn't be about to be evicted from my home and business premises… Instead I'd have a nice house, a quiet garden and someone who loved me as much as I would love her…

'Zachery, let's not focus on me. Remember "the work". Turn your curiosity inwards.'

Zachery smiled broadly, reached inside his suit jacket and removed a neatly folded sheet of paper. 'Look, man, I'm not going to beat around the bush any more. I *have* what you *need*. For once, *you're* the prayer and *I'm* the answer.' He placed it on the desk between them. 'You're welcome.'

'Is it a present?' Connor always asked this when his clients brought him something. It was a trick from psychoanalysis; forcing the client to openly acknowledge their craven transference. Usually their shy pleasure at the expectant gratitude would crumble into embarrassment, then resentment before, finally, via the extraneous emotions, lowering their guard and saying something useful that could be seized upon to make them better. It was 'tough love', basically.

'No, it's not a damn present.' Zachery scanned his immediate environs. He always enjoyed looking around Connor's office. It was his only chance to see into his therapist's mind.

Connor unfolded a colour printout of a page from an online property brochure. There were two pictures; one of an exclusive apartment block, a second one of a fancy living room. The rent was underlined. It was one hundred more than he was currently paying but just about manageable.

'You need to leave here, Connor? Then that's where you should go. There's office space on the ground floor, too. Just like here. I'm sure the rent's in the same ballpark as what you're currently paying. Totally doable. You're sorted, man.'

'How do you know—'

'Again – you're welcome. Who told me? No one. I just overheard you last week. Remember? I had to sit here while you were outside on the pavement talking to someone on the management board who you'd just seen walking by. Goddamn Airbnbs, right? Great in theory. Great from the landlord's POV. But live near one. Sheesh, man. Nightmare. Total damn nightmare. I don't envy you, dude. Not one bit. That's the problem with these older blocks.

They don't update their tenant policies. Some of them don't want to either. Depends where the money's coming from. If it's Russian or Chinese? Then forget it, man. You're looking at Airbnb central.'

Connor pushed away the printout. The mere mention of Airbnbs was causing his breathing to become an effort. It was as if the Airbnb had become his illness. 'Thank you, Zachery. I do appreciate the thought. But—'

'Nah, no problem. I just came across that rental in a neighbourhood rich in potential investment opportunities during the week. I know the area well. And so I thought of you and, well, there it is.'

Bullshit. You all think of yourselves first. He could read Zachery's thoughts as easily as opening a text. 'It's inappropriate, Zachery. You can't develop an interest in my personal life. No matter how well intentioned.'

'Jesus, Connor, I'm just trying to help a buddy out.'

Connor watched as Zachery smiled like the winner he'd always tried to believe himself to be and he could almost hear Zachery's brain changing gears as he searched for the great one-liner to come into his head and make everything better. It didn't come.

'I'm not your buddy.'

Silence.

'I'm not your friend.'

Silence.

'I'm your therapist. Shall we continue?'

Zachery had paled. His countenance was one of narrowed lips, frown, glacial stare, a quick swallow. However, Connor was comfortable with silence – aware that he could make it stop at any time. But he still didn't like having to make such plays. He got no satisfaction from making other men cringe and he was aware that the power imbalance almost made it an act of bullying. But with Zachery, he was certain that he had no choice. The transference problem was too obvious.

Zachery asked, 'What's the game plan, coach?'

'Go on. Begin where we left off last week. Home life.'

'Well, the real interesting thing that I realised is that…'

And quickly Connor lost interest, his exhausted brain finding it impossible to stay focused and instead, once again, he began worrying about his eviction notices. Those Airbnbs had literally smashed a hammer through his life – just like his older brother had done with his drum kit and mates when growing up in the family home. If the Health Board found out about his difficulties it could put the entire Committee of Mental Health and Noise Pollution at risk.

Zachery said, 'So, coach, you with me?'

'Uh-huh.' *Pay attention. Be a professional.*

'Brona.' Zachery's face always coloured while talking about Brona – it was as if she was a form of sustenance. 'That's all I end up talking about – Brona.'

Brona, Zachery's girlfriend, was a bit of a mystery. From how Zachery described her, she didn't stack up to much; she assisted him occasionally in his business affairs but outside of that she just seemed to be a trophy girlfriend that he had become obsessed with. In their first session together, Zachery's calm voice had said, 'You never wear a suit as good as the one made for you, and Brona was made for me.' Connor had not met Brona but had seen her several times outside on the street, leaning against her car, smoking an electronic cigarette. And while Connor had certainly not put any great store in Zachery's shallow description of his girlfriend, as Connor had watched them together through the window, he'd had to reluctantly agree; on a purely superficial level, Brona certainly did have the fashionable edge that made Zachery walk that little bit taller. He'd looked better next to her.

'Material wise, I've given her everything she wants. I mean, Jesus, the inside of our fridge is like an organic farmer's market. Her walk-in is better stocked than a Prada showroom. So, like everyone in the history of ever, she wants something more than money. And I give her that too. Well, I offer it.'

'You offer what, exactly?'

'To be honest, I offer me. I'm available. I'm accessible. My work life is not behind a locked firewall. She's welcome to come along on the ride. And I mean that literally. Like, she's welcome to come away on business, but she won't any more. She says it tires her... even though, you know, at a certain income level air travel is just another form of hanging out at home. Get me? So basically, she won't come with me on business and she thinks I go away too often. To be honest, I'm doing it for her. For *us*. It's as if she wants me to be some type of superhero who can give her the life she deserves with me permanently available for her. How can I make her realise that the payoff for the good life is that for a lot of the time, I won't be around – unless, that is, she agrees to travel with me? To be honest, Brona sometimes feels like a stranger to me.'

I wish he'd stop saying 'to be honest'. Connor's brother had always used it when he was lying; therefore, it was one of his brother's favourite sayings.

'Like a dangerous stranger. It hits me outta the blue. Just this morning when I was shaving, I opened the bathroom cabinet and ended up looking at Brona's face replacements, her desire replacements, her hope replacements, her drive and love replacements. Beneath the products, is there anything left there any more? Sometimes I think Barbie dolls bleed more than she would. To be honest...'

That phrase again.

'It was like... I don't know. You tell me. That's your job.'

'It's like you're losing control of her?'

'No way, dude. Connor, I'm not a cruel partner. Fine, she still needs me for everything, but maybe Brona has begun to realise that she *is* in a cage. But it's not so small that she can't fly in it. In fact, it's big enough to let her *think* that she can fly in it.'

'Maybe you're more controlling than you think. Maybe what you believe to be normal is not so normal to her. Maybe she's talking to friends or observing other relationships and reaching the conclusion that—'

'No.'

Connor's lips narrowed. Interruptions were a direct challenge to his role as judge and jury. Therapy wasn't a democracy. 'Maybe all this drama makes you happy?'

'Are you serious?'

'Without the drama you'd just be… ordinary. Ordinary and happy. Is there anything more boring?'

'Again – are you *fucking* serious? My relationship with Brona is Sisyphean. I get up. I try to make her happy. I grow exhausted. I sleep. I get up again. I try to make her happy. You getting the picture? Want me to draw it for you? On a sheet of paper – the back of that unappreciated fucking present I gave you?'

'And yet Camus says that we must imagine Sisyphus as being happy.' Connor sat back in his chair. *So tired. So… fucking… tired.* 'Zachery, a few weeks ago we began to touch on your idea of parenthood and Brona's idea of… well, *not* having a family.'

'Look, man, I never put myself forward as dying to be one of those papoose-wearing asshole dads. But she always knew I wanted kids. Preferably girls, by the way. I know from particular experience that teenage boys are complete and utter dicks these days. Anyway, she'd never said no. She'd said, "Some day. Just not now." I'm beginning to… think of her dead. Like, killed in a crash or something.'

Wait. What's he saying?

'Wishing my girlfriend dead makes me feel powerful and guilty at the same time.'

'So, you imagine… *murdering* Brona, right?' Despite himself, Connor felt a tourist's thrill. But at least it woke him up.

'As the Russians say, "You can't make an omelette without killing people".'

'Know what'll happen if you kill her?' Connor felt silly even asking. So he phrased it hypothetically and answered it himself. 'They'll send you to jail. You'll get life. You'll never get out.'

'Yes, Connor. That's generally what happens when you kill someone. But it sometimes feels like all that would be nothing worse than if I don't kill her.'

Connor nodded and tried to look as if he'd expected that answer.

'It frightens me sometimes. But if I was imagining killing her because I hated her then I would simply leave her. But I don't want to leave her. Definitely not. So obviously I don't hate Brona. It's the opposite. When I imagine killing her, it could be anyone. It's just killing her 'cos I know her best. When I feel anger, you know?'

Anger. I'm familiar. He saw himself at 3 a.m. that morning banging on the door of the apartment above.

'Embrace the darkness, Zachery. But don't be the darkness.' It was time to put this macho-posturing to bed. Zachery can resent his partner. He can belittle her. But he can't pretend to want to murder her. 'You know, stating man-of-action wishes such as killing are usually the same as wishing to fix and build. Like, how do I cross this bloody river? I wish I could build a bridge. It should be so simple. But, of course, it's not so simple. You just wish the solution was so simple and you focus on it being so simple so as to hide your real issues that might have nothing to do with the roaring river itself – but more to do with how you came to be standing, stranded, on the bank of a roaring river.'

Connor leaned back in his chair, as he always did at the end of a session and joined his hands together before his face. 'This is all good stuff, Zachery. It's the feelings behind these thoughts that you're to focus on when moving forward. Which brings me to… us.'

It was time to send Zachery on to another therapist. And the new therapist, if he or she was any good, would quickly reach the same conclusion that Connor had, which was that Zachery wanted kids and Brona didn't. In other words, Zachery had unconsciously chosen to fall in love with a woman who came preloaded with a *fatal internal error* for their particular bond. Relationships don't survive that. However, their inevitable separation wouldn't necessarily be the fix-all of this situation. When Brona finally left Zachery and he moved on, what would he move on to? All too often a man's embrace of freedom was his undoing because his partner had been the Wall of Jericho protecting him from all the world's fantastic vices. There was every chance that once Zachery disentangled himself from Brona, he'd begin down the well-worn pathway in which he keeps getting older, the girls keep getting younger and the drugs keep getting harder.

'You've gone as far as you can in here. So, I've taken the liberty of approaching two excellent therapists who are available to continue the work with you. Of course, you're welcome to find your own. But I strongly recommend these two. Especially Dr Costello. An interesting woman. PhD in philosophy before becoming a Lacanian scholar. You'll *dig* her, as they say in 1975.'

'What are you saying to me?'

'I'm saying that we're done.' *Christ, I shouldn't have said that.* But Connor's exhausted mind was blank. *I need to take a walk. I need air.* 'What I mean is, Zachery, I can't help you any more. It's in your best interests to move on. See, "move on" is the term. It'll be furthering the progress.'

Zachery's forehead creased as if he was thinking too hard. 'Christ, you're such a vile, entitled cock, it makes me depressed at humanity. Not because humanity produced such an utter cock as you, but because it obviously produced so many people that, for whatever reasons, have actually queued up to indulge such an utter cock. I mean, where else would you get that type of arrogance?'

'Chill out. You've got to learn to know how to let stuff go, Zachery.'

'You have to learn to *not* let stuff go.'

'You need to calm down.'

'You need to go and fuck yourself.'

It was a solid point and Connor knew it. He had made a complete mess of concluding the session. It was important never to make a scene. And if there was an outburst, then it was important to take no part in it. Power was always more effective when it was quiet.

'Take a deep breath and calm down,' Connor said, trying to get the balance right between being authoritative without encouraging violent escalation. 'Then think about what I said to you and why I said it. And then reflect on your immediate response to that.'

'Stop telling me what to do.'

'Keep acting like a child and I have to tell you what to do.' *Did I just say that?* Connor blinked and rubbed his eyes. It was amazing how a personal crisis plus just three hours of sleep could reduce a doctorate to a struggling fresher.

Zachery stood and rounded the desk. Connor pushed back his chair and stepped up to him. Taking a deep, reassuring breath, he told himself to rise above it all, to stay calm, to deal with this drama efficiently. However, he also felt a chill wash over him and it made him feel weak and older than his thirty-six years. It was the lack of sleep. It was the pressure.

Slim and lithe, Zachery had the physique of an athlete. Connor kept his gaze on his fiery glare. There was something about it that reminded him of his older brother. Zachery's hand landed on his shoulder with just enough weight to communicate the impressive and, currently, controlled strength that lay behind it. 'Fuck. You.'

Calmly, Connor asked, 'What are you going to do?'

Zachery blinked. Apparently, he didn't know.

Connor nodded. Life was a series of decisions and reactions and then it was over. Zachery's inability, his stasis when it came to making major decisions, was another rock on which he was doomed to perish – just like Connor's brother had.

'Think about why you're acting like this. Surely you can see that this is evidence – Jesus, even proof – that you need to move on from me?' Connor wanted his calmness to be a contagion and so spoke slowly, the way assertive men do; the way men do when they know that they're the ones with the power.

'What you've just said, about me moving on, is *not* fucking relevant.' The words came out in fits and starts, the way someone with a punctured lung might speak. 'I'll tell you why I'm angry.' Zachery paused and inhaled, drawing in his emotions like they were strands of rope. Then, with a sincerity that eclipsed vulgarity, stated, 'Because you're a fucking prick.'

'Where is this aggression coming from?' Connor asked, knowing exactly where it was coming from, knowing that it was deserved and hating himself for coming out with North American soundbites that meant nothing but sounded like something.

'You know, Connor, I believed – I mean *really* believed – that you were the first person I'd met that didn't even *know* how to be a jerk. I know you guys do your own therapy. Once a week, isn't it? Just to clean us all out of your hair.'

Connor vaguely nodded. The fact was, only certain therapists had to go to their own shrink or group meetings. Connor certainly didn't.

'You know, you're drawn to this *not* because you're the type of man who indulges the weak, or because you're kind, but because, underneath it all, you're just one of us. And that disgusts you. You, Connor, hate yourself more than I ever could. You're not an almighty god.'

Stellar observation. 'Ah, come on,' Connor said, for a moment his accent becoming more hardened Dublin, as it always did when feeling threatened. 'Whatever I did to—'

'You did nothing, Connor. Absolutely nothing. You know, you were my last chance to get my life in order – to lock it away in a secure bond that paid a regular happiness dividend worthy of what I've done since I've been on this earth. But nah, it hasn't worked out. It's over for me. I see that now. I'm done. My day is over. But I don't mind. Seriously. I don't. It was a good day. Better than yours, if you don't mind me saying. Actually – fuck you, I hope you *do* mind me saying.'

Zachery whipped out his wallet, pulled six fifties clear and placed them on the table. 'And there's always more.' He took the rest of his money out – about two hundred in twenties and tens – and let the notes flutter to the carpet. 'You know, Connor, I'm delighted you've finished this. I'm free now. I can see this therapy for the horseshit it is. And you know, tonight when you're still here, storeys up above, alone in your hellhole of an apartment, killing another hour on Facebook bitterly hating people with "likes", I'll be back in my lovely quiet three-storey house wanking off into some caviar.' He took out his keys from the pocket of his Crombie coat and they tumbled to the floor from the jelly that was usually his hand. Picking them up, he added, 'One day, I'm gonna make you feel like me.' And with that, Zachery was gone.

Connor walked over to the window and watched him cross the road. Calmly and with a resignation that only deep fatigue brings, he thought, *Let him go. Let him cool down. Then call him later. You get to be the big brother this time. You get to do it right.* On the other side of the glass, two uniformed boys ran by, late for school, the day stretching ahead of them like a huge playing field. Boys always seemed to be running. *When did I stop running?*

Connor's brain was beginning to race, his pulse quickening. He wished he didn't understand exactly what was happening to him. Knowledge in this instance was worse than ignorance. For the past six months he'd been communicating almost daily with a doctor of neurophysiology from the UK Medical Research Council who had been supporting his presentation to the Health Board, and so now Connor knew everything there was to know about sleep deprivation. *Dearth of REM has forced my orexin to remain switched on. Which means the sensory gate of my thalamus is jammed open, which in turn ensures that my dorsolateral prefrontal cortex won't turn off and therefore I'm stuck like this for another FULL seven hours.*

Regulating his breathing, he tried to forget that people over the age of thirty-five who sleep less than six hours a night are two hundred per cent more likely to suffer a heart attack. *It's just a panic attack. Relax.* Connor had to fight the urge to leave and find a park that would offer him the space in which he needed to breathe. Between the stress, the lack of sleep and being evicted, it had felt like his childhood stammer was about to return, which totally threw him, as until now, he hadn't even thought about it in years.

Connor returned to his desk. If this had happened last week he would've already been on the phone leaving Zachery a message. But that could wait until later because suddenly he saw it; Zachery's printout neatly folded at the side. He picked up the sheet and looked at it again. The outside of the building was impressive and there were shopfronts lining the ground floor, some with To Let signs. With this sheet his current business might not only be saved but improved, along with his living arrangements.

Taking out his phone, Connor keyed in the number. Alas, the call was unspectacular – they simply took his details and said they'd be in touch later in the week. But then, a few minutes later, they called back; the apartment was gone but there was a bungalow in the same area for a similar price that also contained a home office. There was a viewing right now and it would definitely be let today.

'So, Connor, can you come and view this lovely bungalow at number twelve St Catherine's Hill immediately?'

Connor paused to ponder the unfairness of using Zachery's gift before answering, 'Yes.'

And just like that, Connor made the biggest mistake of his life.

CHAPTER FOUR

MARY

It's a gorgeous August morning – perhaps the first café-patio-day of the summer. So, I breakfast on the balcony.

The garden is so peaceful now. It's almost impossible to think that it's the same piece of land that was home to such utter pandemonium only eight hours ago. It's perfectly quiet, with just birdsong and the rustle of leaves carrying on the breeze. My long-sleeved cashmere wrap cardigan hides the welts – though I'm lucky in that I have delicate arms that wear bruises nicely.

Looking up through the parted curtains of my hair, I scan around the other houses, which look just like ours. We have the same balconies on the middle floor, the same tennis-court-sized gardens separated by neatly cut young hedges. We all face a row of similar houses, as if opposite a mirror – our lawns ending at ten-foot-high bushes separating our land from theirs.

But somehow an air of exclusivity has been retained rather than a cookie-cutter vibe; somehow the variations in the landscaping and patio furnishings manage to project a clashing yet interesting disharmony. It's the natural gully running between the two lines of houses that allow St Catherine's Hill to be so special, permitting all the houses to drop down sharply at the rear with the natural ascent of the original inclines. In effect, from the front all the houses – besides the bungalow next door – appear to be two-storey structures, yet are three-storey from the back.

On my right, a tall hedge blocks the odd house out in this corner of St Catherine's Hill; the bungalow, which is attached to our 'real' house. It's been empty six months, and I've been promised that there will be lots of advance warning before it's put up for rent. I just hope that whenever someone does move in, they are understanding of our current… needs. The previous owners – an old, unobtrusive couple – disappeared to a retirement home. They sold quietly. No sign. No advertisements. No noticeable viewings. Not that you'd expect to have to do much to get rid of a house in this area. People would kill to get into St Catherine's Hill with the large gardens, the architect-designed homes and the wide, self-confident but discreet roads that smoothly unfurl into the nearby metropolis. Even the trees lining them seem pleased with themselves.

Someone is standing at Brona and Zachery's large kitchen window. The reflective glass makes it impossible to see the details, except for the white coffee mug floating upwards to be sipped. It's probably Brona herself. What else would a beautiful playgirl have to do on a Monday morning besides take a slow breakfast while working up the strength for a power shower before heading out for a facial and eventually – but only when *she* is ready – putting in an appearance at the office?

What's wrong with me? I shouldn't be so cynical. Especially about others who seem to understand me, support me, sympathise with me. I don't need any sympathy – but God, sometimes I love to soak up Brona's soft, pitying gaze.

It's 8.40 a.m. and Andrew will be leaving in ten minutes. As usual, after breakfast, he's in the basement – doing whatever he does down there – storing away tools or shooting pool or admiring his wine collection or… actually, I've no idea what he spends his time doing beneath my very feet. All I know for sure is that it's *his* space and I'm not welcome down there. Though it's not really a basement, because it leads directly out onto the lawn. I leave the raised decking and walk through the kitchen.

I tell myself, *I need Andrew.*

I tell myself, *despite everything, we are a good team.*

I tell myself, *there are some things he knows better than me.*

There's nothing sparkling new in our house – nothing flash or stylish. Everything has a 'will do' quality. Glasses are chipped, paint is flaking, light fittings are ordinary. We have as much money as our neighbours – maybe even more – but we don't live the life that they do. We don't go on winter cruises or disappear to Italy for June. We never cared about such things – because a simple marriage and the quiet life was all we'd wanted. Anyway, outside of our honeymoon to Australia, I don't travel – which people consider strange, since I used to be a top-range travel agent.

In the front hallway, a small staircase drops to the basement. Before I descend, I remove from my cardigan a tube of lipstick, extend a little rose stump and apply it quickly. The lights are on down there because the morning sun doesn't rise over Brona and Zachery's until after 11 a.m. My feet make no sound as I sink down and down into my husband's den.

With the window shut, the room is close-smelling with dusty air. The basement is supposed to be a type of gentleman's room – claret leather sofa, reading chair, table lamps, built-in bar, expensive music centre. Unfortunately, there's also a pool table. Then, further ignoring my advice, Andrew got freestanding floor lamps akin to miniature pitch floodlights. The effect is less gentlemanly and more frat house games room ambiance. But it makes him happy.

And there my husband stands in profile, seven years my elder, unaware of me, impressively pillar-like and muscular, a pale visage where the razor missed large swathes of its duty, leaning over his well-stocked bar, proud of how it all looks, as if it had never occurred to him just what all that booze is for. Andrew certainly likes a drink, but luckily for him – and me – he's far too controlling for it ever to become an issue.

Appropriately, in the farthest, most shadowy corner of the room is a large framed picture of his late father in full military regalia, the chest medals polished and shiny like they'd just been cast in silver.

I'm about to clear my throat when Andrew turns away from the bar and approaches the sliding door that leads directly to the lawn. Set up on a tripod just before the glass is a telescope. He leans forward like a brawny professor, closes one of his slate-grey eyes and squints through the lens with the other. I know what the telescope is glassing – or trying to. But from the way he's jerking the aim of the telescope left and right, up and down, it appears that this morning he's too late. I can almost feel the loose skin of my husband's chest hanging down, his pelt drooping from his body like an old tracksuit.

Notice me.

Andrew sighs loudly, stands back from the telescope and places his hands on his hips. Then he sighs again as if it's the instrument and not Brona's absence that has disappointed him.

I'm suddenly back at the top of the stairs. I'd reversed, without consciously electing to do so, rewinding myself to the kitchen, silently in my slippers.

That bloody telescope. That bloody basement.

It reminds me of my father's shed in the backyard of the family home, where he'd fix the neighbourhood's bikes in his spare time. I'd never liked the way those strangers in the back lane would steal him away for each free minute of every weekend. Dad's shed in the backyard had been like an embassy in a foreign country – we didn't enter unless we were summoned.

Andrew should be back up any minute now to give me a kiss before he goes. He has a primitive daily urge that makes him hone in on his desk by 10 a.m. He could wind the business down. He could bring in a manager to run it for him. But he doesn't. Andrew loves his warehouses. Men like Andrew *need* to work. Hard work contains the type of truth that can't be learned from all the downloaded self-improvement podcasts that he was once addicted to.

Now, though, I have to do my duty. My feet pad down the corridor towards the front door and the guest bedroom. I'm running ten minutes late. It isn't a coincidence of habit that I've begun to wear my gold Breitling against my wrist, right on my pulse.

Gently I turn the handle and edge the door open. Inside the curtains are drawn because they *have* to be drawn – always. There's the white dressing table. Nothing is allowed on it. Then there's the base of the single bed. A person lies beneath the covers. That's good. That's very good. My eyes run along the covered body, from the feet to the legs, waist, torso and the bare arm resting on top of the duvet. Then I see the hand; its pale, soft skin. My eyes widen because all I feel is a sudden dread. I stare at the hand. The forefinger is moving. Like a pulse. A regular drumming against the side of the bed. Tap. Tap. Tap. It can only mean one thing.

I turn and face the passageway back to the kitchen. I open my mouth and call out. I call out one word.

'Andrew!'

CHAPTER FIVE

CONNOR

Connor cruised along the broad, neat, tree-lined avenues of St Catherine's Hill. His Saab coasted by three grown men gathered on a front lawn worrying over a lawnmower like field medics. It was a lovely neighbourhood, only ten minutes' drive from the city centre and easily accessible to his clients – probably even more so than his docklands base. When his 10 a.m. client had arrived – the chief executive of a whiskey distillery – Connor had told him that there was a family emergency and that he had to cancel. He'd then sent texts to the rest of that morning's clients stating the same thing.

Counting down the house numbers along the winding broad avenue, Connor turned into an entrance between two pillars. A gravel driveway was aligned with flowerbeds like daubs of paint on an artist's palette. It swept around in a graceful swan's neck that led to what appeared to be a flat-roofed Spanish-style villa.

He parked between a black Merc and a red Porsche. The front door was slightly ajar so Connor let himself in. Standing in the hallway was a tall, trim and pinstriped young man who was a spectacular throwback to that ridiculous era when estate agents imitated lawyers and no one laughed.

'And you're Connor. So that means I must be Tim.' He winked. It was supposed to be friendly. But like most men, he lacked the panache to pull off such a difficult manoeuvre and he just seemed sinister.

'Thanks for meeting me,' Connor said.

'Go on through. There's a couple almost finished checking out the rest of the property.'

Connor walked by a few closed doors before entering the back of the house. Despite the fact that it was just a bungalow, the building's footprint was pie-shaped, spreading out towards the garden like a fan, allowing room for architectural flourishes. He found himself standing in a living room that opened up into the bespoke kitchen. It was like stepping into the vault of a bank – it felt like money. Spacious and luxurious, it was furnished to a high spec but was also somewhat expensively bland, like a hotel suite: all neutrals and top-drawer fixtures. Dotted about were featureless lamps, chosen to supply just enough reading light for the business traveller. There was even a show house smell of fresh flowers – though none were in sight. An impressive wraparound glass wall looked out to a covered decking area and a nice-sized garden. Connor skimmed open the sliding door and walked out.

Folding his arms on the rail, he was immediately enveloped by an almost Sabbath-like quiet. The garden was about half the size of the others but enough to remind you that even in the metropolis a person's natural instinct is to have land.

Connor listened to the quiet, thinking of his recent paper for the *Nautilus* journal on Bernardi's experiment that showed how people were most relaxed in the silences between soothing music rather than during the songs themselves. That work, combined with recent research demonstrating that quiet actually helps to grow the brain and increases productivity, had been crucial for Connor in gaining the support of Dublin's Chamber of Commerce before his presentation to the Health Board. It amazed Connor that these facts still surprised people. All they needed to do was to stand somewhere like here in St Catherine's Hill and feel the deep wonder of quiet, peace and lack of stimuli.

A white cat took refuge in the shade under the dense hedge. It stared up with calm curiosity, as if deciding that, 'Yes, he'll do. He won't disturb the neighbourhood. He won't change things.'

But I won't do. I won't do at all. Because I can't afford this. 'Similar price' to what I was looking for? Yeah, right. Thousands of feet above, a jetliner made an airy downward glissando towards the international airport five miles away. It was a threatening sound. *They know my budget. What were they thinking, sending me here?*

Connor looked over his shoulder. A handsome black couple were talking to the estate agent in the hall.

'It's perfect. We want it.'

'Excellent. I've registered your needs and enthusiasm.'

'It's near the hospital, too. We'll pay two hundred a month over the highest offer – so can we sign now?'

'No. It doesn't work like that, Dr Gill. We have your details and references. Call the office in the morning. We'll let you know.'

As the couple left, Connor looked at the agent and realised that another day was about to pass without him having found new accommodation and business premises. Not only that, but he'd just lost a morning's income. *This is it. The moment of fake hope that bursts my final bubble. The moment when I finally get what's been trying to come to me all week.*

'Jesus, Tom—'

'Tim.'

'*Tim*, I'm busy. I've got a life. I took time off work. Why did you drag me here? I can't afford this. What was I even thinking about, viewing something in St Catherine's Hill?'

'Easy, easy.' Tim laughed in a false, front-of-house manner.

What was it about this week? Every passing hour offered something new and unusual, the type of novelties that were the dark side of interesting. *I'll be basically homeless. I might have to call my brother – that hateful prick. My business will be ruined before I even have a chance to head up the Committee of Mental Health and Noise Pollution.*

Tim placed a document consisting of about ten stapled sheets onto the counter.

With a sigh Connor flipped over the first page, scanned it and then did the same with the second and third. Without going any further, he looked up and said, 'It's the rental agreement for this bungalow.'

'Yes. Number twelve, St Catherine's Hill.'

'So?'

Clearing his throat, Tim began his sales pitch. 'St Catherine's Hill is the suburbs but it's not the suburbs. It's the burbs, but they're so close to the centre of things, it can't be the burbs. Know what I mean? It's for those that want the city centre without having to actually live in the city centre. Out in the real burbs everything is in the This-oplex or the That-oplex. But this area is actually cool.'

'What is the *matter* with you? I don't have the money for this.'

'Did you see the front bedroom overlooking the street?' Tim asked as if introducing an important new subject. 'It's a great prize – I mean size. And the living area here next to the kitchen, the way it steps down... well, I don't need to tell you it could also be a great office. Like the one you're looking for. A...' He flicked over a page on his clipboard. 'A therapeutic office near *or in* your home. And what a view for your patients, or clients, or whatever they are.'

'Once again, let me state the obvious, Tim – I can't afford this.'

'But you're interested?'

'I. Can't. Afford. It.'

'Connor, in this townhouse-slash-mews-slash-ground floor penthouse, you can—'

'*Bungalow*. And I can't afford it.'

Tim chuckled. 'True, St Catherine's Hill is the type of neighbourhood where a few million euros has a very limited lifespan. But if you're interested, it's yours.'

Connor opened his mouth to say something, but only silence emerged.

'Yeah – when you're younger, all that matters is a fashionable apartment with a view and elevators that break the sound barrier.' He observed Connor, trying to work something out – his age – and decided to risk the potentially insulting. 'But eventually you grow up and want more. Life's always late at lowering its anchor for people with no children… I offer that in a good way.'

'Accepted in a good way. What's going on, Tim?'

Tim sat on a stool beside Connor at the kitchen counter, the contract spread out before him. 'I'm sorry to rush you. But the owner wants this closed by lunch, and if you don't sign now, then Dr Yuvi Gill and his wife and baby will get it. No doubt about that. And there's five other interested parties. I mean, who would turn this place down?'

'But…' *Shut up. Shut up.* 'I heard the doctor say he'd better the best offer by two hundred a month.'

'Uh-huh.'

'And…' *Shut up. Shut up.* 'You're offering me the same price as the budget I mentioned on the phone?'

'Uh-huh.'

'You're basically tailoring it for my finances.' *Shut. THE FUCK. Up.* 'You're giving me a massive discount. You're making sure I can afford it.'

'Yes. We *want* you to have it. You're perfect. We want someone for the long term. Unlike Dr Gill, you have no kids. You'll suit the neighbourhood. As you saw, it's a very quiet area. And we want a professional, single occupant who appreciates that and who will give the place the respect it deserves.'

'Yes, but…' *Please God, shut up!*

'Look, Connor, I see dozens of prospective tenants for high-end properties every day. It's not just about the turbo-power of their credit cards. It's about personality. I know what I'm doing and I know what tenant is best for St Catherine's Hill. And it's you. That's why we're the best high-end agents on the market. That's why our clients trust us completely. We know what they want. And we deliver. Obviously number twelve St Catherine's Hill is one of our cheaper properties. It's just something on our books that we want filled quickly and effortlessly and most importantly *specifically* to our client's instructions. Money isn't important to them. But the type of tenant is. And bingo – here I am, filling it effortlessly, with the perfect tenant.'

'So I just sign and—'

'Wait.' Tim nudged the contract along the counter back towards himself. Connor, in turn, immediately edged towards Tim and the estate agent sensed his desperate need. His previous demeanour had departed from his bearing and now they began to converse as if equal alpha males. 'Connor, you look worried.'

'Well… I'm worried that things are becoming…' he looked around the shining kitchen, living area and sunken work space '… too extravagant for my needs.'

'Well, stop worrying because when things become too extravagant you'll immediately know it. How? Because you won't be able to afford it – that's how. Now, before we move on, there are just two stipulations.'

'Name them.' Connor shut his eyes.

'The first stipulation is that you have to pay the full twelve months in advance. Today. On signing. You have till close of business to transfer the money.'

Connor kept his eyes closed. He could just about afford to make the transfer. It was basically all of his personal savings. 'Yep, I can do that. Today by close of business the entire amount will go *ka-ching* into your account.'

'Plus a month's rent as deposit, of course.'

'Of course.' Connor, his eyes still closed, readjusted the figures and realised that it was *barely* doable. 'What's the second stipulation?'

'The vendor wants it occupied as soon as possible. He hates it being empty.'

Connor's eyes snapped open. 'But I can move in immediately. I mean, like, today! If that's possible.'

Tim laughed and clapped his hands in triumph. 'See? You really *are* the perfect tenant! I'll call the office and set in motion all the bills etcetera to be switched over to you instantly. So, Connor, we're good?'

'We're really good.'

Tim then signed the contract, his pen twirling and twitching over the paper like an elegant lady whirling and swaying across a ballroom. The nib got to the end, did a jump and stopped. Then he passed the pen to Connor and Connor hoped that there was a God so that his mother could be somewhere up there, looking down, witnessing the son to whom she'd gifted speech, moving forward, moving on, refusing to let crisis stop him, and about to make the world a slightly better place.

Connor returned to the Fitzgerald Building and spent the afternoon stuffing his car with stationery, manuals and wall hangings to decorate his new workspace. Then, while packing in his apartment, he listened to the footsteps that had begun to pound above his head, the thump of suitcases being dropped, the squeal of a woman's laughter followed by a baritone call from the upper balcony. New arrivals, and they were drinking already. Soon they'd go out and at two or three in the morning they'd return, louder and drunker and more menacing, and life would get depressing the way life can at 4 a.m. Sometimes it felt like he'd been awake for every single jostle, vibration, toilet flush and scraped chair that had ever occurred in the apartment above.

After squeezing the last of his personal possessions into a large holdall, he hurried to the door as if, should he not make it out in time, the winds of fortune would change direction.

*

By five o'clock, Connor was settling into number 12 St Catherine's Hill. In the sunken part of the room, a study desk stamped the space as an office. His computer bag was open on it, resting there like an exhausted dog, handles flopped by its sides, the zipper hanging out like a tongue. Next to it was his printer, already set up and loaded with A4 paper.

At the kitchen counter, Connor clicked open his briefcase. Inside were a few recent copies of *American Psychology* and a printout of about a hundred pages of an article he was to edit for their website. In theory, he carried them about so he could steal time throughout the day to do some editing. But today the material had just served as protective padding for the vodka, Galliano and orange juice he'd packed.

Removing the bottles, he twisted the vodka cap with a flick of his thumb. The seam split like an oyster being opened. It was one of his favourite sounds in the world – that and the cracking fissures of ice. Beeps began to sound behind him, like those of a reversing truck. He'd left the fridge door open and when he turned about, the light from it played on his eyes like sunshine. Through the haze he noticed that the fridge had a built-in ice dispenser. It was as if the bungalow could read his mind.

After making the Harvey Wallbanger, he stepped out onto the decking and took a deep, cool sip. *This is it – I'm free.* He hadn't lived in the suburbs since being at home with his father and his brother; the brother who, he'd last heard, was standing on a conveyor belt somewhere down the country, slicing up dead chickens day in and day out.

Looking out into the valley of space and luxuriance that was the row of back gardens, Connor felt like a man overboard who had just been washed up from the high seas to the shores of a very perfect island. He looked out at the teasing peace and quiet, the prissy politeness of all that space, the green spread of nature that filled in the gaps between the buildings, and he loved it all. The air had never felt so clean nor had the blue sky ever looked so beautiful.

He remembered his previous view of bustling lunchtime suits, wandering addicts and excited tourists, circulating on the current of other shoppers. It seemed to be the ugliest memory in the world.

'To a new beginning.'

He toasted the garden and wondered what this new Connor would be like. He pictured him as more studious, more successful in both professional and private life; he imagined this new Connor with more of everything that had been good in the old Connor's life. He pictured this new Connor in which the bad times were just memories – memories so vague that he couldn't be sure they'd even happened in the first place.

And just as he felt fully sated by what this new world could offer him, there appeared something else, something beyond quiet and space; something tangible. A woman stood on the middle floor decking directly opposite the house next door. She was staring at him. He was sure of it. She was less than two tennis lawns away – next door's garden and hers. If he squinted, he could almost see her clearly – or clearly enough for his brain to fill in the blurry bits. From behind the plants hanging from the lip of his kitchen roof, Connor admired her sun-drenched forearms the colour of toast, and convinced himself that her cheeks were flushed shiny like apples. Whoever this woman was, she looked great, even from this distance. She was smoking a vaporiser, the luminosity of each pull signalling something positive, like a traffic light unbarring passage to her mouth.

She had turned away from him, her back leaning against the balcony rail. In a navy sleeveless shirt and a red skirt, the clothes tight and fitted like those of an air hostess. Exhaling steam from the electronic cigarette, the sun glinted off the glass in her other hand. Then she turned about, her head lowered, leaning over the balcony to the lawn below. Connor enjoyed watching her body, her muscular bronzed legs supporting her as she leaned over the patio rail without a care of who may be watching, while the weight of her breasts pulled inside the half-buttoned shirt.

A figure moved behind her on the balcony. A man. He squinted again and exclaimed, 'Jesus,' before stepping backwards as if pushed. *It can't be.* Zachery was beside her – which meant the woman was Brona.

Zachery was holding a small plate, forking its contents into his mouth. *Probably caviar.* Suddenly he looked towards Connor. Could Zachery see him behind the hanging plants? His heart was beating holes in his chest. Connor looked again. Brona had gone indoors; all that was left of her was the dark shadow of her against the glass. Zachery remained, looking at an angle towards Connor, holding himself tall and stately, the way certain men do when everything was going their way. Then, he too turned and followed his girlfriend back indoors.

Connor returned to the kitchen, walking slowly, with a sense of dread. *What's going on?* Was this a coincidence, or was Zachery messing with him? *Cool it. Work it out.* Connor flicked through the pieces of information in his brain. He'd received the estate agent's brochure from Zachery, who knew of an apartment that would be suitable to his needs. If Zachery knew of the apartment, then it was likely to be near where he lived. Then when the apartment was no longer available, the estate agent recommended number 12 St Catherine's Hill instead. Therefore, it was probably just a coincidence that Zachery was living almost directly behind him.

Coincidences are rarely just coincidences. But what else could it be? Zachery would hardly have arranged for Connor to live across from him just so he could... what? Look over at him at five o'clock after work each day? He wasn't that obsessed. *Anyway, if he had arranged it, just so he could be near his ex-therapist, then so be it. Because this bungalow is a dream!*

Connor picked up his Harvey Wallbanger and drained it. Then he heard something. A dull, ugly, muffled sound like… *human cries*? Bizarrely it seemed to be coming from inside the house. He closed the sliding door and the room was immediately suctioned clear of all outside noise. But the muffled moans continued, as if Connor now lived in a castle and the sound was coming from the far wing of the keep.

Slowly he approached the living room wall, walking around his desk and tapping his laptop and printer as he went. He brushed his fingers along the smooth white paint, as if feeling the bark of a tree. Yes – it was coming from next door. There was a voice – it was shouting but unintelligible, as if a fading echo floating across hills and valleys. Then there was a louder thump. Or was it a muffled slap? Then the voice again. Then the thump.

Placing the rim of his glass on the wall, Connor put his ear to the base and listened.

CHAPTER SIX

THE DAY BEFORE

MARY

I've finished putting on my make-up. Despite what happened yesterday, despite the physical aches, I'm feeling fresh and alert. Probably because I've just brushed my teeth. I only use a specific toothpaste that burns my mouth. If it hurts it must be effective.

Andrew's clothes are all across the bedroom – including my side, the neat side. When Andrew goes to work, I simply gather most of his things together, shunt them over the invisible line and kick them under the bed. I do hang his shirts, though – in colour sequence – just how he likes it. I handle them all softly – the way I had once, for a brief period, enjoyed touching him.

Looking at the bed, I feel the weight of it; the symbolism of it. All that bed really is is a blanketed cell for us to sleep in every night. Nothing happens beneath the covers. We both have a customary rejection roll – now completely institutionalised from indifference rather than outright dismissal. When did Andrew stop opening his mouth to kiss me? I can't remember. For us, sex was never that important. Not even in the early days. The last time we made love was at Margaret and Steve's anniversary down in Carton House over six months ago, a week before my sister's breakdown. We had both drunk a lot. Before that, we hadn't made love in nearly a year. What had it been like? It had been just like the other times over the last two decades – few and far between. It had begun when we'd both least expected it, usually after a party or get-together; and before we knew it, we would be doing it silently, making love surgically, or like bank robbers patiently cracking a safe. When it happens it just happens, and when it doesn't neither of us notice. It was never the physical thing that drew us together. It was always something else. Something more cerebral. We're at peace together. We just simply *work* together. Whatever it is that we have, it clicks.

Downstairs on the patio, the *Irish Times* is on the table where Andrew left it twenty minutes ago. Next to it is the morning's mail. The bills and statements have already been opened and left for me to file away. But there's also an unopened, plain white envelope. It has no stamp and on the front a black biro has scribbled *FAO Mary Boyd #13 St Catherine's Hill.*

Probably another book club starting up on the road, or a new 'charity' coffee-morning-gossip-fest. Whatever it is, it's an invite I'll probably decline. Though, of course, I won't see their cause short a few euros. It's just that I hate the idea of those polite parties either at my place or someone else's – blithely accepting someone's hospitality or dishing it out, paying no heed to who's filling my glass, or whose glass I may be filling.

Inside the envelope is a letter spewed from a printer. As I begin to read, I realise that this is no invite; this is something else entirely, something very horrible.

YOU SELFISH BITCH,
YOU SHOULD BE ASHAMED OF YOURSELF. SELFISH. BLIND. DEAF. IS THAT WHAT YOU ARE? THIS NEIGHBOURHOOD SHOULD BE SO BEAU-TIFUL AND PEACEFUL. BUT YOU DESTROY IT ALL. YOU'RE WRECKING ALL OUR LIVES. YOU'RE

*RESPONSIBLE. KNOW THAT WE'RE ALL WATCHING
YOU. WE'RE ALL HEARING YOU. AND WE'RE ALL
WAITING FOR YOU TO GET WHAT YOU DESERVE.*
THE NEIGHBOURHOOD

I carefully place it back into the envelope. Halfway through the letter I'd wanted to believe that it was from my sister, that Emer had fast-tracked from melancholic voice messages to hard copy hate mail. But she can't post letters from where she is. Anyway, Emer has no idea what's happening in this house.

I should be angry but I just feel sorry for myself. I know my near neighbours. They've all been supportive about what's been happening. How could one of them write that? And to make it anonymous? It's so cowardly. They want to upset me. They want to march into my house and tell me how much they hate us and to do so without my having a chance to reply, to justify what's going on – even if I understood what was going on.

Apart from Brona and Zachery's, only the vacant bungalow on the right and the Kellys' house on the left have a direct sight line into us. The Kellys have been so kind and helpful of my situation. They've an Alsatian that doesn't bark and two boys that are charming and mannerly. If Andrew and I had ever had children, they'd be the kind I'd imagine us having reared.

Furniture suddenly moves on the decking of the bungalow next door, which is on the same level as our basement. A heavy table or chair drags across the wood. The large sun umbrella spreads beneath me next to the hedge but the flat-roof lip of their kitchen is blocking whoever opened it. *Has someone moved in?* But Brona promised that she'd let me know if there was going to be any movement on renting the bungalow. She swore. I don't understand.

Beyond the tall hedge, the bungalow's kitchen door slides shut with a *whoosh*. It seems like there's new people. If so, how long have they been in? What do they do? Have they kids? What do they look like? How wonderful is their life? After last night, what do they think of us as neighbours? And again, *why* didn't Brona warn me? If it has been rented then Brona has let me down and that's almost impossible to imagine. I'll talk to her later. I'll find out what's going on then. But if it is rented, then… then it could've been *them* who wrote the letter.

I'm jumping to conclusions – it was signed 'The Neighbourhood'. It could be anyone in St Catherine's Hill, not necessarily someone who directly borders my garden. They just need to be near enough to hear. A window slams in the bungalow. Are they doing that on purpose? Are they aware that I'm sitting here, reading this?

'It's a violation,' I whisper, while slipping the letter into my pocket. An anonymous letter – its purpose is manifold. Of course, it's there to silently make a shrill point: to lecture without interruption; to communicate blunt facts that the author would never have the courage to say in person. But there's another *latent* intent to the anonymous letter. The author knows that it will make you paranoid. It will send you spiralling into your thoughts. It prods at your unconscious, at your secrets, whatever they may be, however irrelevant to the letter. Because the letter is conveying that, unbeknownst to you, you have been watched, judged and found wanting.

'The garden is beautiful,' I mutter in a ridiculous attempt to *be here now*. A wasp arrows low and dangerous across the lawn. There's a tear in the corner of my eye. I collect it on my forefinger and wait for the morning breeze and summer heat to vaporise it. How can I let a stupid letter do this to me? It's nonsensical, but my entire psyche is reacting as if the letter writer somehow knows my truth. It's *that* intrusive. It's *that* much of a shock. Why can't I just rip it up, tear it into pieces, bin the bloody thing? I smudge another tear and decide that this one will be the last one leaked.

Andrew needs to see the letter. He'll know exactly what to do and he'll say what I need to hear. While Andrew certainly isn't an intellectual, he isn't stupid. Stupid people rarely become rich unless they win the lottery. However, despite his lack of degrees, he *is* clever – the way certain people are when they're aware both of their limitations and of what they're good at. And what Andrew is good at is organising people and things and then taking decisive, effective action. That's why we live here in a mortgage-free house in St Catherine's Hill.

I go through the kitchen, into the hallway and down the narrow staircase to his den. He's standing next to the telescope and I can't tell whether he's just used it or was about to use it. But he is surprised at my presence, and his height stretches towards the low ceiling.

The tall figure of my husband is no longer as darkly handsome as he had once been. He's a big man, broad-shouldered, the type of build that means he always has to watch his weight. He stands there in his wrinkled shirt, brown tie at half-mast and a frayed collar – the way a shirt gets when there's no woman in his life to look after him. A pang of guilt jolts through me. *I have to look after him.* Andrew always looks after me. Hanging his shirts isn't enough. I should buy new ones. I should make sure they're always ironed.

He appears tired and drawn – like a hostage in a recorded YouTube message. Nevertheless, after twenty years of marriage I still like to gaze at him: his big shoulders, his loose gait, a man who knows who he is. In all those years his eyes have never changed. They're still the same. When I look at the hall portrait of us that was done by a renowned Connemara artist just after we'd married, I always notice the few details that have remained the same rather than all the things that have changed. His eyebrows in the portrait were done perfectly – charcoal for charcoal.

I look at the envelope in my hand and hold it up as if not sure where it came from.

'What's this?' He takes it off me.

My eyes have widened and my mouth has opened and because I rarely exhibit such guileless behaviours, Andrew's shoulders and chest barge forward and he repeats, 'What… is… *this*?'

Before I can reply, he slits its resealed throat with an index finger and withdraws the neatly folded page inside. He gives a wintry smile and immediately the tension in the room begins to spike.

This won't end well. Usually there's a place and time to share bad news with Andrew. My preferred choice is a restaurant. His temper needs managing. In a quiet restaurant he has to behave. On the table next to him, I move an empty glass out of his reach.

He starts reading, his eyes moving from right to left and back again. I can almost hear a typewriter's *ding!* at the end of every line. Then he lowers the letter and gently holds it out to me. I take it and sigh.

'This is the first?'

'Yes.'

'When did it come?'

'This morning.'

'Who sent it?'

'I've no idea.'

Andrew stares at me, examining the lie. After a few moments he seems to tell himself to accept it. He smiles, gently, and softly runs his fingers over my cheek. But then he asks again, 'Who. Sent. It?'

'Well… there's new people in the bungalow. I don't know who. They've just moved in. Brona never told me. She never gave me any warning.'

'New neighbours, huh?' For a moment he knuckles his eyes before looking towards the bungalow where he seems to have no doubt the letter's author resides. 'They are shit on my shoe. No. Less than shit.' Andrew points out to the garden. 'Shit can fertilise. What the hell can they do?'

When his temper flares, my instinct is to keep quiet. Andrew is convinced we've been victimised and he is made of a special substance that, like copper, grows harder the more it is hammered upon. You push Andrew and he will shove you back with twice as much force. And then he'll do it again and again until he's sure you'll never push him again. Should I ignore my instinct and try to stop him? Should I attempt to cool him down? Should I let our new neighbours get away with what they've done? There are simply too many choices, and when there are too many choices it's difficult to make one.

I say, 'I don't want you to be aggressive. I don't want you to do anything stupid. Remember the golf club. Remember what happened. If you're angry, don't go in there. Are you angry?'

'Of course not.' Andrew smiles at me, but the smile is made with only the left side of his mouth which is one of his tells for when he's lying.

A door closes upstairs. Alarmed, Andrew and I stare at each other for a moment before realising that it's just Elena arriving and now walking about in her soft slip-ons, getting ready for her morning chores.

'Andrew,' I say, 'I'm going out to the shops. Let me leave first, OK?'

Without waiting for an answer, I climb the stairs and meet Elena in the hallway. She has a short Slavic blonde bob and black librarian glasses. Elena smiles as I approach. I also smile – but just for a second – before my lips straighten. Nothing about her gait is communicating that she's late again. But I'm not in the mood to just roll with it today. Punctuality – the courtesy of kings.

Elena says, 'So sorry. I missed the bus,' in her hard, Eastern European accent. When people lie in their second language, it's more obvious, more insulting.

'Today is the last day you miss your bus – understand?' The way I say it – without looking into her eyes – it's a conversation-ender.

She looks shocked because I've never spoken to her like that before. But so what? If she doesn't like it she can leave. I can get another 'Elena'.

'I'm sorry,' she mutters.

I pick up my light jacket and pull it on and then choose a pair of shoes from the vast array lined up in the hall, all busy-busy, as if I had not said what I'd said. With each passing second the tension grows, the atmosphere stiffening against her.

I say, 'Right, see you in two hours. Thanks, Elena,' and close the door behind me with a little more force than I usually do. But my irritation is aimed at myself, not Elena. I shouldn't have spoken to her like that. There are nicer ways to point out that I won't be taken for granted. I'll make it up to her. Definitely.

In the driveway I point the dongle at my silver SUV next to Andrew's black Land Rover. The hatchback pops open so I can check that Elena put back all the shopping bags from last week. She did. Though there isn't much room because my husband's golf clubs are still in there because he thinks my storage space is less important than his. I make a mental note to finally take them out and maybe give them to charity, as they've been unused in almost two years when he'd joined the local club to try and fit in with the neighbourhood alphas. It had seemed a good idea, as the general routine appears to be work hard for a decade, until all that time on the golf course pays off and you get promoted from private practice to criminal court judge, or from managing director to chief executive of some worldwide cabal. But for Andrew it didn't pan out. Last year, after a 'flashpoint' at the club's Christmas party, he'd had his membership revoked. But he isn't really one of them – the local men. You can tell straight away. Andrew may have money *now* but generations of poverty lie bone-deep within him. However, that's one of the things I like about Andrew; his time in the army showed him what airs and graces are – simply airs and graces.

I click the dongle again and the driver's door unlocks. There's movement in my peripheral vision. Someone is looking at me. I turn to the bungalow. There's a car in the front drive – a blue Saab – five years old according to the reg. And then I see him sneaking around in plain view. He steps away from the bedroom window, his face fading to shadow but not before leaving a little oval of condensation on the glass. The man next door – so there you stand, watching me. Did *you* enjoy writing the letter?

He's still there, to the side of the window, a shadow falling on him so that he thinks he's hidden, and I propagate this belief by pretending that I don't see him. Instead I look up at the solitary tree standing next to his front pillars. Suddenly the-man-next-door steps into the light, directly in front of the window, pretending that he's just entered our little play and has, what? Opened the blinds? Started to wonder where his 9 a.m. pizza is?

I smile at him. A big friendly smile that all us neighbours in St Catherine's Hill give each other. And I wave. He nods and smiles back. He's youngish and presentable but obviously on the wrong side of the glass for the shoe-and-watch check. There's a stylish look about him that implies he's not married or at least has no children. He's a ladies' man. Definitely. But there's something about his eyes. Even from out here at the partition wall I can see that they look haunted, constantly suspicious – either that, or he doesn't like me very much. I can sense it. I picture him writing that anonymous letter. I can see him smiling as he does so, getting it off his chest, putting his neighbours in their place, letting them know that there's a new sheriff in town, that there's a new line in the sand that must not be crossed.

Well, Mr Handsome, my husband is about to cross it before rubbing it out of existence.

I wave my farewell as the dongle flashes the SUV's yellow lights. He kills his smile and retreats back into the shadows to judge me in private.

Judge away. You're about to lose your stupid game.

Getting in the car, I spin the wheels on the gravel as I circle the centre of the drive. I can't wait to get out of St Catherine's Hill. I can't wait to be able to look in the rear-view mirror and not see my house and all that's hidden inside it. Before I hit the road I glimpse Andrew exiting the house, shoulders spread, arms swinging. The man next door is about to get what he deserves.

CHAPTER SEVEN

CONNOR

Ten minutes ago, Connor was having his coffee and porridge on the decking. While attempting to read the morning news on his phone and wondering what exactly had caused that weird noise through the walls last night, Connor's attention kept slipping towards the house at the end of his neighbour's garden.

Where are you, Zachery? He'd already tried to phone him first thing that morning and had left a message asking Zachery to call him back, but he was obviously ignoring Connor's entreaties. Apologies from the therapist to the client were taboo in his profession – but this was a unique occasion. Connor had used Zachery's 'gift' to secure this home – it required an explanation. Particularly since Zachery actually lived opposite.

During the night he'd woken a few times, the way one does when staying in an unfamiliar hotel. The first time he'd stared at the ceiling waiting for the footsteps to start, the bass to thump, the laughter to shriek. But there had been just silence; an eerie quiet that didn't even contain regular house noises like tanks bubbling, pipes moaning. And then he'd remembered where he was and he'd effortlessly fallen back into a deep, solid, unbroken sleep.

It had been the first good night's rest he'd had in months, and Connor felt so reconditioned it was as if he'd returned from a long, lazy holiday. As he relaxed on the decking, he imagined that what he was experiencing was something like the relief of being given the all-clear after a health scare. As his colleague, the neurophysiologist from the UK Medical Research Council, had kept warning him, the actual percentage of the population who could get by with less than seven hours' sleep without having their biology scathed, was zero. And by having their biology scathed it meant cancer, diabetes, obesity and devastated mental health. Dr Hughes had been basically telling him that, like thousands of others, he was allowing modern living to patiently kill him.

Connor walked through the bungalow and stood next to the bedroom window looking out the front, eager for the arrival of the day's first client. It was interesting to have neighbours that you could see throughout the day coming and going. For most of his life he'd lived in flats and apartments with so many people around that you ironically learned the knack for being alone. Apartment dwellers appreciated a certain tact for privacy, passing your neighbour on the corridor with the quick smiles and nod of two isolated walkers drifting by each other on a high mountain trail.

Suddenly the parking lights of the SUV in the much larger drive next door flashed three times.

'And who have we here?' Connor muttered as he picked up his electric razor from the bedside table and ran the metal foil over his stubble.

She was wearing a light summer jacket and cream wide-leg trousers, with a red leather tote shoulder bag. From the back, her dark hair was cut short and tight above her neck and into the sides. She turned in his direction, thumbing through her keys, and Connor retreated from the window into the shadow of the bedroom. He didn't want to seem like a snoopy neighbour. That wouldn't be a good way to start a daily 'Good Morning – Let's Comment on the Weather' type of relationship.

But she'd seen him and waved. Awkwardly he took a quick step forward, returned the wave, and then retreated back into the room as his neighbour seemingly lost interest and ensconced herself in the leather and walnut of her SUV. A moment later, the huge car fishtailed around the gravel drive and accelerated out into St Catherine's Hill, tracking behind another SUV, the two of them in tight formation.

Whoever that woman was, she seemed friendly enough. Connor made a mental note to drop in with wine by the end of the day. He really wanted to find out what was the source of last night's disconcerting noise. Plus, he wanted to start in this neighbourhood the way he intended to continue in it – by belonging. He felt a thrill at the idea of settling into St Catherine's Hill. *It's like I'll soon know the first name of the local headmaster. I'll have an opinion on the litter situation of my main street. I'll be a regular at the best restaurant in the area. I will believe that every lone male passing a playground is a paedophile. I will remember to never pass a playground on my walks.*

Connor then noticed a second person – a tall, athletic man – walking down the neighbour's driveway. He reached the road, swung left and entered Connor's drive. *Excellent – I don't have to wait till this evening for introductions, and there's just enough time for a coffee before Fergus arrives.*

Connor opened the door and smiled warmly like the great neighbour he intended to be.

'I'm from next door. Could I have a word, please?'

'Of course. Come in, come in.' Connor walked through the hallway, past the bedroom door and into the kitchen. 'Just close it after you.' He leaned against the island counter and watched as the tall muscular man approached slowly after leaving the front door ajar.

'Can I get you anything?'

The man didn't respond. Instead he was looking over at the sunken dining area which was now an office. He seemed particularly interested in the printer and next to it, Connor's computer bag which was opened up like a toolbox, revealing his laptop and a chunk of A4 printing paper. In profile, the pallor of the man's skin emphasised the old acne scarring on his cheeks, as if he'd been sandpapering his face, while his two-day-old stubble was silver and patchy – the kind that actors grew to look less handsome.

As the man moved away from the sunken office space, Connor cleared his throat, extended his hand and said, 'So, you're the next-door neighbour? I'm Connor.'

'That sounds like a hardman's name. You're not a hardman.'

'Em…' Connor's mind was suddenly blank. He literally had nothing to say. Was his neighbour trying to be funny? He decided to laugh lightly and asked, 'What's your name?'

The man still didn't extend his hand.

'Andrew. Ex-army.' He measured out another tense silence and then asked, 'Why did you write this letter?' He waved the envelope at him.

'I never wrote any letter. What is it?' Connor gestured for it to be passed over.

Andrew folded it and returned it to his back pocket. 'It was very cowardly. And now that you're caught, you still can't face up to what you've done.'

'I don't know anything about a letter.'

'Admit you wrote it.'

'I think you'd better leave.'

'Tell the truth. And that'll be that.'

'Leave.'

Andrew leaned forward until his head was almost touching Connor's. 'One thing the army knows is that with every setback is an opportunity. Every defeat is simply a chance to reorganise your borders and defences. So, now I've got to take the good out of this situation.'

'I have no idea what you're talking about, Andrew.'

'This letter… this has brought me in here. I've now met you. Weighed you up. Taken you into consideration. Judged you. Seen what you have to offer. And none of it measures up to much.' He turned away and retraced his steps into the hallway in a tense, jerky, restless type of walk. At the front door, Andrew paused, before saying over his shoulder, 'If you think last night was bad – well, let's just say you won't believe what's waiting for you in ten minutes' time. Welcome to the neighbourhood, you fuck.'

CHAPTER EIGHT

MARY

Making my way through St Catherine's Hill, I slow down and drive the way one should in a friendly family neighbourhood. The SUV, heavy and powerful, cruises with the smooth motion of a ship along these quiet, leafy suburban roads. I inhale as if taking the first drag of my nightly cigarette. I'm free. For two hours. When I worked in the travel agency I used to spend my days off getting morning massages or an entire afternoon at the spa. God, I miss that; the silence that came with lying face down on the upholstered table, cheeks and forehead pressed into the tissue shield. But these days, when I have free time I just slip away to the local supermarket and a quick visit to my secret place.

By just going out, driving, to the shops, or to my secret place, it feels that I'm taking action. That I'm being the protagonist. That I'm moving this thing, my life, forward. It feels like I'm in charge. That there are choices. As Anatole France said, 'To accomplish great things we must not only act, but also dream'. Remembering quotes from my university days – it reminds me of how smart I once was. They remind me how smart I *can be*.

The phone rings. I Bluetooth it to the car's speakers and say, 'Hi, Brona.'

'Mary. Coffee. Ten minutes. Your place.'

I love her voice; those smooth rhythms, mellow and confident, the smartest voice in the room. It's the voice you want to hear in an emergency. The voice that calmly tells you the way out from the dark laneway.

'Mary, sweetheart – you're there, right?'

Coffee with Brona. That would be nice. And I want to find out about the man next door. Why wasn't I told? Why wasn't I warned? But I can't get into that now. If I don't use this time out of the house there will be no escape for another two days. This is my only chance to get to my secret place. This is *my* time.

'Ah, I can't, Brona. I'm out at the shops. Just parking now.' Guiltily I check the pavements rolling by as if she could actually be on them.

'Well, come home. We need to talk. And we'll call it tea but it'll be wine. It's *basically* the afternoon – we're allowed. Come on, Mary – I want this to happen.'

It's so tempting. Her chosen words are demanding but the tone is cajoling. Everything she says is coaxing. In terms of cold will and captivating extroversion, she's in the top one per cent of the top one per cent. But even she can't swing this transaction. She wants to talk – I don't want to talk. I win. Simple.

'Doing a shop. Getting messages. Sorry.' I'm captivated by lovely Brona, but I'm not sure if I actually like her. I do try, though. She seems like an open book. However, it's difficult to trust someone with no secrets. There's no give and take. She can't reveal something and in turn, I can't reveal something back.

'OK. Maybe tomorrow. Hey, how's things? Everything OK? How's life, you know?'

'Right now, it's…' Shitty? Catastrophic? Disastrous? 'Pretty good. I'll talk to you when I see you.' Now is not the time to mention the bungalow. I've enough going on already with that awful letter. I'll wait till we're face to face.

'Cool. See ya then.'

We disconnect and the lights are red at the next intersection. Across the road is the local gym and outside it are all those teenagers that look like little Bronas, killing the days of the summer until school starts up again. When I'd been their age, only professional models looked like they do now. Today, muscle tone is as important as listening to the correct bands. Their bodies – I can't stop staring at them. I wonder how Brona does it: to be thirty and *still* look like them.

The lights turn green and I drive by the travel agency that I'd worked three days a week in for almost ten years; just something to pass the time with. Well, it was more than that. I loved my job; finding the right country, beach, hotel, for the right people – it was like my inbox was stacked with peoples' wishes and my outbox was filled with dreams about to come true. My desk was by the window looking out at the busy main street and at 5 p.m. I'd watch the buses pass, packed with all those exhausted people, stop-start-stop, a slow journey ending for most of them at a cold, empty flat, and I would be so content and grateful for my peaceful, easy life. But then Emer went off the rails.

They were nice to me in there, impressed at how I did my job. Some of my colleagues called my attention to detail, my perfectionism, obsessive. But I don't. I call it the opposite to what lazy is. I was so busy. People around St Catherine's Hill travel *a lot* – hopping from one country to another, treating international airports the way most people treat railway stations. And they were amazed that I didn't travel myself. But why would I have travelled abroad when I'd created the perfect world for me? Leaving it behind would have been the pursuit of imperfection – even for just two weeks. But suddenly – six months ago – everything changed. Now I'd give anything to get out of here for even just a weekend.

Despite all those people on the streets in short sleeves, and the sky being blue and the sun blazing, I'm suddenly freezing. The bruises beneath my clothes begin to throb. When I was seventeen, I'd learned how to drive. My parents didn't teach me. I taught myself and paid for the lessons. Then I passed my test first time. And my favourite thing was to go driving on the motorway on Saturdays, where I'd close my eyes to see how long I could tolerate the darkness. My best was five seconds. Five seconds is a long time to drive with your eyes closed on a motorway. And suddenly I have an urge to do that again – like the way other women download an old 1980s song to briefly feel how they'd once felt *all* the time. Everything has changed forever. My good mood is gone already.

The phone rings. Good news or bad? Why do I even *think* that question? Have I ever known anyone who won the lottery? But how many do I know who've already contracted rare diseases and deadly cancers? It's Elena, but by the time I press the green button, it's gone to voicemail. Pulling into the side of the road, I count the seconds to the bleep: 'Message received'. When it does so – twelve seconds – I play it.

'Well…' The word is long and drawn out as if she's just run up a flight of stairs and is about to announce something of great gravity. Catching her breath, she repeats; 'Well, I'm afraid—' There's a dramatic shift in tone. 'Mary! Mary! Come back now… *Fuck!*' It's the first time I've ever heard Elena curse. In her Latvian tongue, it's sharp and effective. 'The new man next door. It's the new man next door. *Oh my God!*

And then the phone goes dead.

CHAPTER NINE

CONNOR

Connor watched from his front door as Andrew marched back up his driveway. *What the hell's going on? What happens in ten minutes?* He felt like a child again – the unfairness of being denied the ability to communicate with the world as an equal.

Then, just on time, a wine-coloured Mercedes drove right up to the bungalow.

A few minutes later, Connor settled into his chair in the sunken study area. Stalagmites of journals already grew from the desk and cabinet. It was perfect; the type of therapeutic space that his wealthy clients would appreciate and feel at home in.

Fergus sat opposite. He was a TV executive in his sixties and it was easy to imagine him strolling through the town square, doffing his cap, lord-like, to the locals. Though his recently restored hair looked like a nuclear disaster. So, there really were some things that money could not buy.

'With me thus far?' Fergus asked, running his hands over his catastrophic implants.

'Yeah,' Connor said, answering a question he hadn't heard. His mind had been elsewhere, engaged in a countdown to some mysterious calamity apparently hurtling his way. *Five minutes to go.*

Fergus wiped his eyes. He'd been crying. Connor stiffened. His father again; real men don't cry. *A crying jag first thing in the morning? Jesus, poor guy.*

'Talk to her. Talk about *her* feelings. Talk about how you hurt them. Talk about how the houses and the cars and the suits and the restaurants and your eighteenth-century Parisian baroque antique collection is all just "extra stuff" without some *real* meaning in your life.'

Fergus bristled at the words, the implication that the money he'd made, continued to make and would always make was somehow worthless to Connor. His eyes had already dried.

'Fergus, maybe you're a workaholic who prefers being a TV producer than—'

'*Executive*. TV *executive*.'

'Maybe you love your work more than your wife and she knows this, even if—'

'You don't know what you're talking about.'

Connor was used to hearing that sentence. People always spoke it whenever they'd just been told a truth about themselves. There would now be the inevitable flash of anger. Rich men don't like unnecessary truths. What's the point in having money if you have to face that shit just like everyone else?

Connor opened his mouth to speak but a horrible cry screeched from the garden.

'What the hell was that?' Fergus said, and looked over his shoulder.

Connor positioned his hands over the armrests, readying to stand. He saw the face of his watch; nine minutes had passed since Andrew had left. Another gurgling roar sounded out to St Catherine's Hill. Then a text sounded. Connor ignored it. Another one arrived. Then another. All in rapid sequence. He looked down to the screen. The three of them were from Zachery. He opened the first one. Then the second. And finally, the third. They all contained the same message.

This is the story: I own you now – The End.

CHAPTER TEN

MARY

The message ends and I put the car into drive. There's an emergency at home. Elena needs me. She's never needed me before. What the hell is going on? But a second message begins to play. At first Emer's voice is distant, a distracted murmur as if she isn't aware that the phone has connected.

'… there goes the doc now… Oh! Sorry, Mary-Contrary. Not just for that. But for what I said last time. I went on a bit, didn't I? Must be the pills they're force-feeding me. But I have to be honest – of course I'm going to resent you, even as you charge into the field of battle, salvaging my life. I mean, just what is charity? Isn't it taking from the powerful and giving to the pitiful? I mean, why do I *need* you to do this for me? Why should *you* be able to do this for me? Do you know how that makes me feel?'

My thumb hangs over the disconnect button. *Go home. Go home. Go home.*

'Especially since you are *so* cold. You hide it so well. People really don't have a clue. But I know. You're the coldest person I've ever known. And I know you better than anyone else. Including poor Andrew. Jesus. I saw you – and I *still* see you – as someone who considers friends in need as pro bono debtors on your time account, so why would you—'

I lower the phone to my lap. I don't want to hate her. That's not me. But she broke our mother's heart and literally killed our father. There's also regret. Regret that my self-righteous and self-absorbed sister doesn't know exactly what I think of her. She has zero inkling.

Holding it back to my ear, she's saying, '… I can't put my finger on it, but there's something about your relationship with Andrew. It's a sick life you've constructed for yourself. How you deny the past. What you did. How it affected me. How you, my big sister, weren't there. You're probably pretending that you don't know what I'm talking about. Christ, you are so sick, Mary-Contrary. You're the one who should be in here. Ha – you're living vicariously through me! You never fixed yourself, Mary. And you could have. But instead you decided to break me too. Break me worse than you. Here's something that only a sister can say to another sister – I don't respect you because I know that only an idiot suffers when they don't have to.'

Hanging up, I stare down the road. I have to go straight home. There's a crisis. Elena needs me. But I can see my secret place. It's so close. Just up ahead. *I have to go home.* Putting my foot down, I swing a left. The driver facing me swerves out of the way, gesticulating madly through the windscreen. He doesn't scare me. My fingers slide on the gear stick's leather covering because my sister has caused my pores to seep. Breathe. Breathe easy. Don't let her do this to you. GO HOME. GO HOME. GO HOME.

A sharp pain pangs across my jawbone. It's happened before because I'm oversensitive to somatic discomforts. I grind my teeth in my sleep and sometimes during the day my jaw tenses up to remind me that even in dreams I'm not relaxed. My entire life can be mapped out by listing physical pains I've become overfamiliar with during certain junctures. Even when I've been happiest the memories are physical – the sting of a wasp on our honeymoon. I know where it comes from. Part of me will always be fourteen in that damn bloody laneway.

*

I'm back there now – childhood memories perforating my brain. It was about 5 p.m. and I was on my way home from an after-school hockey match. Night had already fallen. As I walked down the laneway that went by the back of the parish church before emptying out into my estate, I saw a man ahead and thought nothing of it. Why should I? I'd had a nice life like most girls in the area. The world was good. God was loving. My parents were caring. Bad people always go to jail. The man had leaned his bicycle – a racer – against the old church wall. Stained-glass windows towered twenty feet above. The man – he could've been twenty-two or forty-two; I've blanked it – the man was examining his front tyre and asked if I could hold something for him. I remember seeing his member. It was the first of two I've ever seen. He showed it to me the way a flasher shows it to children in a park. It stuck out all veined and red and dog-in-heat, like the most repulsive animal part in all of nature, and he'd smiled while glancing down at it and I'd said something like 'Oh', and a part of me dropped through my body to the ground like an anchor cut loose to rust in the depths. And just like that I was facing the cold blocks of the church, the side of his hand jammed into my mouth as if it were a knife and he kicked my legs apart like a frisking cop. I always dread that cliché on the TV shows. My bunched skirt exposed my knickers and my bottom and my initial reaction was not of fear but of mortification. But then he shoved the knickers aside and his finger really hurt when it burrowed inside. I sank my teeth into his hand, not out of resistance but from the pain, like a patient in a medic tent biting on a rag. Unbelievably, I still managed to stop myself in case I damaged him. I was such a thoughtful girl. How innocent were we in those days? He spat a lot. He spat on his hand and he spat on his member. And when he shoved it into me I tried to cry out because the pressure was so sore. But his hand was still in my mouth and I nearly bit him again but remembered not to because my teeth could damage someone really bad.

It was brief and agonising. I didn't even register that it was sex we'd just had. With my background and education, I'd believed sexual intercourse was called 'making love' for a reason – one had to be 'in' love to make it. When it was over he just pulled out and I don't think he even zipped up. He just said, 'That was sweet,' as if he'd taken me for an ice cream. Then he'd jumped on his bike and off he went in the direction I'd come from. I don't think he ejaculated in me. There was blood, of course. Not too much. And there was his moisture; his spit. I don't remember any sperm; not that I would've known what it looked like. All of that – the contents of my vagina – were only discovered in the privacy of my bedroom when I got home ten minutes later. I only told my mother. But that was much later. That's another story.

But I have to remember that it could've been worse. I could've got pregnant, though that had never occurred to me at the time. I was just concerned with the pain from my torn and slashed privates. And the utter humiliation. And by being swamped with disgust. My vagina stopped bleeding after a day but it took over a week for the pain to fade completely. Plus, he'd infected me with his grime. I'd got an obnoxious, stinging, putrid discharge. To get rid of that, I had to go to the library to reference an encyclopedia of medicine because the nearest we got to meaningful sexual health advice at the convent was simply – DON'T.

After taking that shortcut home by the back of the church, I evolved into an interesting teenager. I became the classic morose goth-child. I didn't paint my bedroom black – that would've blown my cover in a very religious household. But I began reading authors like Hermann Hesse, Ballard and Amis that my parents had never heard of; listening to Bowie whom they heartily disapproved of; and I distanced myself from the girls in my class because they were just like everyone else and were therefore invisible. But *I* could be special. I could be cool *and* be an 'A' student. Everyone wanted to be my friend and I wanted to be no one's friend. My classmates would've queued up to touch the hem of my garment if I'd let them, which I didn't. And I allowed my hockey skills to evaporate. I didn't need therapy to work out why – hockey practice happened after dark.

Now I'm driving too fast, replaying in my head Elena's expletive, wondering just what on earth caused it. The air is suddenly heavier. I HAVE TO GO HOME. What has happened back at St Catherine's Hill? For just two hours, I was supposed to be allowed to be normal.

And then I hear a voice; loud and clear. I know it's just in my head. But the words are distinct. And I know who's speaking them. The man on the laneway. I'm not insane and it's not a ghost. It's a memory. A crystal-clear memory. I've always believed he'd said nothing while doing it to me. But now I remember his words as if I'd never forgotten them.

Are you OK, angel? You look so beautiful when you cry.

I turn the radio on to the people eater that is the twenty-four-hour news cycle. Just the headlines: thirty-five killed in a Baghdad suicide attack. Priest pleads guilty to molesting eight-year-old twin boys. A young man has been stabbed to death over a parking space. I turn the radio off. And then I'm driving into St Catherine's Hill and I wave like the queen at a neighbour. I spin the wheel and, churning up gravel, rush the SUV into the drive.

And there's Elena, standing at the front door. She's shouting, her mouth going, 'Quick, quick, quick', like the words are bubbles bursting all around. I calmly step out of the car because the house is not on fire, the police are not here and there's no sirens in the air. As I walk towards her, the voice from the laneway speaks more of his words.

It's fun. Stop crying. It's fun. Everything will be the same tomorrow. Stop crying, or I'll rip you to shreds.

I say to Elena, 'Calm down. Take a breath. And then tell me what's going on.'

'Quick, quick, quick,' she continues. 'He's attacking him. Out the back. Quick.'

'Oh. My. God.' I don't even realise I've dropped my bag until it hits my foot. 'Attacking? Who's attacking?'

'*The man next door!*'

CHAPTER ELEVEN

CONNOR

Connor joined Fergus by the window of his study area.

Again, the gurgling roar sounded. Was someone dying horribly? Was there a man being slowly mangled in some piece of industrial machinery? The noise was coming from next door. A large trampoline had been dragged into the middle of the neighbour's lawn and jumping up and down on it was a young man with long, thick, blond hair. Each time his feet left the canvas and he was propelled high into the air, he screamed as loud as he could. It was a disturbing sound: animalistic, guttural and full of angst.

Fergus looked at Connor and then back to the sight below on the other side of the hedge. 'What's *that* all about, Connor?'

I have no idea. 'Oh, don't worry about it. Just the neighbours… He's only visiting.'

'Make it stop,' Fergus ordered with the authority of a man who, whenever he wanted a wish transformed into reality, would just summon an assistant.

'I… I…' Connor closed his mouth and tried to make his brain think.

'Really? I'm disappointed. I didn't say that I wasn't happy to have to come out here for our sessions. I was willing to give it a try. But what type of therapist changes location with zero notice?'

'I told you, Fergus, it was unavoidable, and it is an—'

'Don't say "improvement". Do *not* say "improvement".'

Connor failed to meet Fergus's clamped gaze. 'Fergus, I'm sure it's going to stop.'

Outside, the noise kept coming – the screaming, the pounding of the trampoline mat, the squeak of its springs. The blond teenager wore black skinny jeans, white sneakers and a T-shirt with a heavy metal band emblazoned across it.

'Connor, we've never had a cross word. Until now. But this is unacceptable.' Fergus's impatience to leave flowed around him like a cold draught. 'And I don't like the way you spoke to me.'

Connor sucked in his lower lip so as not to tell Fergus to go and fuck himself. Like all of his clients, Fergus was too well connected, too rich and too crucial to Connor's career to be put in his place. So instead he said, 'Fergus, trust me when I say that this interruption could not have come at a worse time.' *Don't apologise.* 'I'm sorry.' *Well done. Now your power's gone.*

'Peaceful? Improved premises? And then you don't even treat me with dignity? And you expect me to sit here and take it for an hour and then, what? Pay you?'

'Jesus, Fergus, this is my first day here.' Connor was pierced by that mix of anger and sorrow that can make a person give up. 'If I was—'

'Enough.' Fergus pulled in his stomach and fastened his jacket. Then he left, Italian shoes clicking on the few steps that rose up to the kitchen area. As Connor watched him, he thought of Fergus's nuclear-powered credit card and how he'd really needed it to blast some numbers into his own diminished account. But that wasn't going to happen. That may never happen again. And Connor needed money now in a way that he'd never needed it before.

The front door slammed as Connor remained at the window staring down at the young man bouncing on the trampoline, facing the house and screaming as if trying to see just how loud and shrill a teenager's voice could get before it broke. But it wouldn't break. His lungs were made of iron.

This can't be the norm. People in a neighbourhood like St Catherine's Hill don't tolerate something like this. But who else was around? Who else worked from home? *Maybe it's only me?*

The young man kept bouncing and screaming and Connor spun away from the window. He marched to the kitchen and slammed his hands down on the marble counter. He couldn't have left the Fitzgerald Building for this. It wouldn't be fair. It wouldn't be right.

Connor took a deep breath. He could just call in to Andrew. Tell the big, angry, army man that he had a business to run from home and could his son stay indoors, or at least be quiet, during normal working hours? *Is that too much of an ask? It probably is when Andrew is an aggressive, delusional nutcase.* It then occurred to Connor that this was suburbia and one of the attractions of suburbia were the gardens. These houses were family homes. What was the point of having a garden and a family if the kids couldn't play in the garden? Especially during the summer, the long, hot summer. But this wasn't a kid. How old was he? Fifteen? Was he high?

The screaming continued – as did the rhythmic creaking of the trampoline springs as he bounced and bounced and screamed and yelled. It was a high-pitched, constant screech now, barely lowering every ten seconds as he drew in more breath. Sometimes it sounded like a garbled word. Was he singing?

Connor walked back to the window. He had earphones on. Could the guy even hear himself? Is that what the problem was? Was it all just a misunderstanding? Did he not realise how loud he was?

Connor stared across the garden, over the hedge, above the bouncing, screaming young man to Zachery's empty balcony. But Connor knew he was up there, somewhere behind the glass, looking, listening, smiling.

I've paid a year's rent. Up front. I've moved my office here. My clients won't tolerate it. Why should they when even I can't tolerate it?

He looked down on Zachery's texts. The cursor blinked at him like a satellite, waiting for his reply. He had nothing. And then the noise stopped. The room was filled with glorious silence. Had the screaming been an anomaly? A one-off? Had Andrew called his son in and was now lecturing him on how to behave with consideration to others? Of course he hadn't. Andrew had warned that something was going to happen. Andrew, like Zachery, was loving this.

The trampoline was empty, though still vibrating from what had just left it. Connor opened the kitchen door and stepped out onto the raised decking. He felt nervous, as if, should he be seen, the screaming would kick off again, like a siren.

Connor spotted him. The blond teenager emerged on his hands and knees from beneath the trampoline canvas. He crawled the few feet along the grass to the base of the six-foot wall bordering the far side of his garden. There was something small and round in his hands. A ball. Except the ball was squirming and twisting and trying to squeeze itself from the boy's vice-like grip.

Jesus, it's a cat.

The boy rose to his feet and, clasping the cat's snowball body as its head twisted and turned, threw it into the air and putted it forward like he was playing volleyball. The creature's four legs parachuted out as it came down on the far side of the wall into the other garden.

'What a jerk,' Connor muttered.

Suddenly there was barking followed by a high-pitched feline screech. The teenager folded his arms across the top of the wall.

'Oh my God!'

Connor jumped over the decking banisters straight to the lawn and ran to the weakest point in the hedge where the leaves were most sparse and he could just about see through to the other side.

'Hey! Stop! Jesus.' As if shouldering a locked door, Connor barged through the branches and twigs. Before him was the trampoline and beyond that the back of the young man with his long blond hair. The terrible screeching of the cat continued from the far side of the wall broken only by the Alsatian's snarling.

The cat suddenly reappeared on the wall next to him and behind it, briefly, the Alsatian's huge snarling head as it leapt up into view. The cat jumped just in time to avoid the dog's gnashing jaws but landed once again into the hands of its tormentor.

The boy was staring at Connor. He was handsome with thick hair, smooth, tanned skin and clear blue healthy eyes. His black T-shirt sported the red letters of a metal band. He said, 'Who the fuck are you?'

'Give me the cat.'

'Uh-uh,' he said, shaking his head. 'What ya doing in my space?'

'What's the matter with you? You're Andrew's son, right?'

'I'm a future McDonald's Employee of the fucking Month.' He took a bow, his loose hair sweeping forward. 'At your service.'

'Give. Me. The. Cat.'

'Again – what you doing in my space?'

'You're screaming your head off mid-morning and torturing a cat. You're lucky I don't—'

'Yeah. Uh-huh. I get where you're coming from. But ya see, the morning's best – people let down their guard. They think they're safer in the daylight. So, they're not looking out for people like me and what I do.'

'Give it here.'

The boy sighed. 'OK.' He held out the trembling white ball but when Connor moved to take it, he snatched it back.

'Uh-uh,' he said again. 'Look but don't touch – stripper rules.'

Connor stepped forward but the boy held the cat up, as if it was a sacrifice, before flinging it back over the wall. The cat screeched, the Alsatian barked and what sounded like hooves charged across the neighbours' lawn.

Immediately Connor hauled himself onto the six-foot-high wall. The boy clapped his hands and said, 'Up, up and away, Captain Fantastic.'

Then there was a second voice: female, Eastern European. She shouted, 'Hey, you sir! You sir!'

But Connor didn't have the time to look at her because the cat was cornered, bunched into the crook of the garden between the far neighbour's wall and Zachery's hedge. The Alsatian crouched, front feet stretched out, fangs bared, drool spilling. In turn, the cat's back arched as it too exposed its much smaller fangs.

Connor shouted down at the dog, waving his hands. The Alsatian looked up, its tongue hanging over his teeth, sending out little puffs of breath to the warm morning. The cat made its move. It ran across the grass and leapt into the air towards the wall. But Connor's heart took an alpine plunge as the Alsatian chomped its salivating jaws tight onto the back of the cat's neck and rapidly shook the poor creature from side to side. The smaller animal whined a terrible moan and Connor watched as the grass rose up towards him and his feet landed next to the Alsatian. *What the hell am I doing?* Up to now he'd had a rule concerning cats – anything smaller than a lion was vermin.

For a moment, the dog was confused – there were suddenly two bags of warm meat that it needed to burst. It dropped the cat and, snarling, tried to bite Connor's leg. Connor, who only knew one aggressive manoeuvre – the headbutt – had to quickly come up with something else. He kicked out, missing the Alsatian entirely but causing it to retreat a few inches. It snapped at the air a few more times, glaring up at its foe, contemplating its worth. Connor was suddenly very aware that skin was just a sack to hold a person in. Then the huge dog suddenly darted to the right, chomped into the cat's hind leg and flipped it over.

Connor kicked the dog in the stomach. It howled and the cat fell to the grass, panting and shaking. Despite the danger, Connor couldn't bring himself to hurt the animal a second time. Instead he waved his arms, advancing like a lunatic. But it was enough to make the Alsatian back away a few metres as it calculated its next attack.

Plucking the wounded feline from the grass, Connor tucked it beneath his arm and with his free hand, hauled his weight up onto the concrete wall. The Alsatian lashed forward but Connor managed to swing his legs to safety and landed on the other side of the boundary with the cat bloodied but alive.

Suddenly pain shot through Connor's back. Someone had hit him with a powerful punch to the base of the spine. Connor dropped the cat and as he spun about, received a second punch into his shoulder. It was the teenager, his long blond hair swishing madly behind him, his cheeks red, all the while screaming the type of guttural roar that belonged to a much older person being burnt alive. Within wide eyes, the blue pupils floated in a pool of raging white. Despite being seemingly all limbs and no muscle, his skinny rage was conjuring up brute force behind his swing.

As the cat limped across the lawn, the young man took another jab but Connor parried it as he stepped to the side. His shoulder collided with his aggressor and he tumbled backwards onto the grass.

'Calm down,' Connor snapped. 'What's the matter with you? Are you tripping?'

In one deft movement, the teenager flipped back onto his feet.

'Get out! Get out! Fuck you! Get out, you fucking fuck!' His arms were already windmilling and from the back of his throat another deep guttural roar was dragged from the depth of his lungs as if by meat hooks. And then the fists pounded into Connor's chest – one, two – thump, thump – as if the young man was a weather system that was aimed directly at him; roiling, furious and loaded with the weight of very bad news about his future.

'Stop it, kid,' Connor shouted. 'Enough.'

But still the arms windmilled, still the punches landed before suddenly knuckles collided against Connor's nose and a white, excruciating pain shot through his brain. Connor grabbed the teenager by the shoulder and swung him around before linking his hands together at the base of his neck, effectively imprisoning him into a full nelson.

'Jesus Christ,' Connor said. 'You're crazy.'

His screeching grew in ferocity while the Alsatian's snarling head appeared and reappeared as it leapt up against the wall with a fearsome bloodlust that begged to tear something to pieces.

And suddenly, within all the bedlam, a woman shouted, 'What are you doing? Leave the child alone. Jesus Christ, are you mad?' The voice wasn't Eastern European but upper class, big city and *very* annoyed.

Maintaining the full nelson hold, Connor faced the voice. It was the woman he'd seen from his bedroom earlier. Up close, she was a slim forty-year-old with a chic haircut that belonged to a woman who never had to work hard at being attractive. She had probably once been a real beauty judging from her bright blue eyes and pronounced cheekbones. Her face was angular, the skin tight to the bone, a broad forehead and lips painted with an elegant rose-red lipstick. But the lines around her eyes were heavy and definitely not the kind that came from too much laughter.

'He's out of control,' Connor gasped as he swayed with the struggling teenager.

'Leave Finn alone!' she demanded.

'Look at him,' Connor said. 'He'll kill someone or himself.' Unconsciously he tightened the hold. 'Who are you? The mother?'

'I am Mary Boyd.' She had a genuine natural authority – the type of person who could silence the room with a whisper. 'And you are now in serious trouble.'

PART TWO

CHAPTER TWELVE

THE DAY OF

CONNOR

Connor needed to leave the corpse behind. He needed to run. On the driveway, blood crawled like a long finger pointing towards the wall separating Mary's driveway from his own. Slowly it found its way.

Windows all along St Catherine's Hill were lighting up. *Run. Run. Run.* But Connor's body refused to get adrenalised. It was as if his wired brain had soaked all of that chemical up. Part of him denied that this could be happening here. This wasn't TV, where there were hundreds of murders every day to give people's staid, streamlined lives the injection of blood their primal needs required.

Suddenly the eyes of the body opened. Teeth gritted and a pool of saliva overflowed from between the lips.

'Jesus, you're alive,' Connor said.

A right hand reached up and tried to touch his cheek.

And suddenly sharp pain ripped through Connor's side. The attempted touch had been an act of misdirection. The left hand had picked up the army knife and jammed it upwards, aiming for Connor's stomach. Connor looked down at the rip in his shirt, the blood staining the white linen. With the knife back on the ground, Connor mashed the flat of his palm against the wound. *How deep is it?* His blood was mixing on the drive with what had already been spilled. Tracing the gash with his fingers and seeing how the sliced skin arced from the side of his stomach to his back, Connor decided that it was a flesh wound. *No internal damage. There can't be.* But it hurt hot, like the wound was poisoned, like he imagined a snakebite would feel. It would need stitches. But not yet.

For a moment the victim's eyes wandered and then suddenly locked onto his. The body was dying fast and gently. And then suddenly, all its remaining life was just gone.

From two or three houses away, there was the sound of voices and marching steps on gravel. *Nothing has changed. Except you're now wounded. Run. Just run. And don't stop.* Connor knew he had about an hour. He thought of all he had to do and of where all of this was going to culminate. This was going to end where it was always going to end.

CHAPTER THIRTEEN

THE DAY BEFORE

MARY

'I am Mary Boyd,' I snap, before adding for good measure, 'and you are now in serious trouble.'

The threat is supposed to have the immediate effect of springing poor Finbarr free. It doesn't. I move in close and, pointedly ignoring the brute from next door, look sternly at Finbarr. He stops screaming. It's like a valve being shut off. He's embarrassed to be crying in front of me. But his struggling continues. His embarrassment is feeding that awful temper.

'Finn, calm down. It's OK, honey. Count to three. Remember what we said? Count to three.' As he continues to wrestle against the hold, I steadily continue, 'Finn, let's go together – are you ready? Three. Two. One. There now.'

As simple as that, Finbarr stops struggling. The man can barely believe it but he still maintains the hold.

With a sudden ferocity that surprises even myself, I shout, 'My God, will you release the child?!'

'*Child*? He's a psychopath.'

'Fuck you! Fuck you! Fuck you!' Finbarr screams, tears and snot pouring down his face, but he maintains physical control and doesn't start struggling again.

'He's not a psychopath,' I hear myself say, almost beseechingly.

'Then what? He's suffering from a medical condition called total-utter-stupidity?'

Finbarr shouts, 'I'm going to fucking kill you, motherfucker. I'm going to kill you. Kill you. Kill you, you fuck. You fucking fuck!'

'Yeah, just like you tried to kill a little cat,' he says, finally risking a slight slackening of his grip. 'You might find me a different sort of proposition.'

'What!' Finbarr exclaims, and looking at me says, 'He's mad. He attacked me. I was bouncing and the wanker attacked me. From nowhere. Talking about noise and shit.'

'I saw it happen,' the man says. 'That bloody dog could've savaged me, too.'

On the other side of the wall, Bairbre Kelly's Alsatian is pacing the length of the border, sniffing around, tail wagging, wondering what the fuss is all about.

'So, the *dog* tried to kill a cat?' Making a *pish* gesture, I fold my arms.

'Yes. Obviously. Jesus.'

'So, the boy *didn't* try to kill a cat?'

'No, you don't understand.'

'Let me help you: A or B? Pick a line. It's really that simple.' My pulse is banging but I will not let this bully see that I'm intimidated.

'He threw the cat over—'

'Excuse me, Mister Whoever You Are, but for the last time, release the child.'

'Stop calling this psycho a child. And the cat didn't do that to itself.' He gestures to the middle of the lawn where there is no mauled cat present. On the other side of the wall sounds the heavy *ploff* of falling faeces as if there's a horse in the Kellys' garden rather than a dog.

'Yeah,' Finbarr shouts. 'Where's the cat, Captain Fantastic. Where? Point to it. Go on. Let me go, and point to it. You asswipe!'

I say to the man, 'Can you just forget about the phantom cat and concentrate on the person in front of you that you are clearly restraining against their will? For God's sake, where is your empathy for your fellow human being?'

'My what?'

'So, like so many men, violence against animals outrages you more than violence against children and women?'

'*What*? He tried to kill a cat. I saved it. Jesus.'

'Can you remember how angry you could get at that age?'

'Wow, you're putting it down to what? Adolescence? Trying to feed a cat to an Alsatian is not normal. And I know what's normal. I've a master's in psychology. I'm a therapist.'

'Then I shouldn't have to explain this to you, as it should be flaming obvious to anyone who hasn't got a screwdriver embedded in their frontal lobe, but I'll do so – slowly.'

He bites his lip.

'Imagine you're Finn's age. You're angry. Now imagine all those hormones pounding through your body and you've no idea, no ability to put them anywhere.'

'You put them where every other teenager puts them. Into games and adventure and girls and football – whatever. You *do not* put them into torturing cats. What is the matter with you?'

Finally, he releases Finbarr and Finbarr lurches away from him and then turns about and spreads his slight shoulders and his bony arms and stretches as tall as he can and says, 'Any time, dickhead. Any fucking time.' He's doing it for face. He's doing it just for me. I press my hand soothingly onto the flat of his back. Quickly Finbarr nuzzles his head into the side of my arm before suddenly realising just what he's done and immediately snaps his blond head away from me. Poor Finbarr – he's a cauldron of contradictory wants and needs. He's had such an unstable upbringing that part of him craves physical affection and yet the other part of him finds it mortifying and unsettling. He runs off to the steps of the house, pauses there and spits. A glob missiles to the ground. He then ascends, two steps at a time, and disappears inside to where Elena is gawking through the kitchen slider.

'How did you bring him up like that?'

'He's *not* my son.'

'If you can't handle him, then why is he here?'

With raised voice, I reply, 'Because what's the bloody alternative?'

He takes a step back.

'Was I just supposed to leave him in a giant basket on a doorstep outside a stranger's house? Jesus Christ!'

'OK, take it easy. I didn't mean to upset you.'

And just like that I'm calm again. 'You haven't upset me. You've upset Finn.'

'Really? Look, I don't know anything about your life. And—'

'*And* you think I've something to hide?'

'What? No. Look, I'm genuinely sorry. I just wanted to move the cat to safety. That's all. And that young man… well, I'm sorry but he really was trying to kill it.'

'Are you finished? Do you want another minute?'

His eyes widen. 'Why, is there something I'm missing?'

'Just the entire point.'

'And that being?'

'Finn obviously has problems. He's seventeen but he looks, what? Fifteen? He's had a difficult upbringing. In fact, he hasn't had an upbringing. Not in a conventional sense. So, patience is required. And a bit of heart and empathy. All the neighbours know this. *All* of them.'

'I'm sorry,' he says, matter-of-factly. Then he stretches out his arm and his hand hangs there, waiting to be shaken. Pretending not to see it, I turn my attention to the kitchen, as if I'm checking on Finbarr's whereabouts. This man is attractive. Very attractive. He takes trouble with his appearance, the desired result being that it looks as if he didn't. He's like a sexy, relaxed schoolteacher – the type of male schoolteacher that should not be allowed to teach adolescent girls, no matter how talented he is.

'My name is Connor,' he says to my profile.

Turning back to him, I say breezily, 'Well, hi there. My name's Mary.' He hasn't withdrawn the hand. He even gestures to it, in a friendly, goofy way. My eyebrows arch as if I hadn't noticed it until now. I shake his hand. His warm skin is on mine. His grip is strong but not unpleasantly so.

'Mary, I just saw him throw a cat over the wall… to that dog. I had to do something. I hope you understand.'

Connor has a pleasant manner. He keeps eye contact but not in an over-sincere way. He also seems like the kind of man that would write an anonymous letter – because everyone in the world is that type of person. Plus, everything points to it being him. The letter arrived as soon as he'd moved in. What has he been told about us? What has he already heard through the walls, through opened windows, from patio to patio?

Connor says, 'I really didn't mean to upset Finn. I just thought… well, he was hurting the cat. And I had to act fast.'

Why does he persist in lying about the cat? As an excuse to confront Finbarr and rough him up? To let off some of that steam from having to listen to him? No – Connor's not a thug. He lies about the cat so he can cause an emergency and then sell the rescue. Connor would like to arrive into his new neighbourhood as the wonderful hero he isn't.

'You say Finbarr has had a tough upbringing – how tough?'

Connor effortlessly portrays himself as someone who finds others remarkably interesting. It makes him charming. Which makes him dangerous.

'He's had an extremely difficult life. You can't get much more extreme than what poor Finn has gone through. No half measures with my Emer.'

'Emer?'

I wave away my sister's name. 'Finn's mother.'

Now he knows me. Now he knows Finbarr. Now he thinks I trust him. But what's his endgame? Can he use anything he's experienced today or learned from me to do something like report me to the social services, or to the council? Is that what all this is about?

I explain, 'Finn's highly intelligent. High IQ. But his education is a mess. Homeschooling to poor schools to worse schools to dropping out altogether after being expelled from everywhere. But he's lovely, actually. But he… because of his upbringing he has issues that were never dealt with. When he was in school they reckoned he had Oppositional Defiant Disorder, but they threw him out before he was officially diagnosed. He certainly has discipline and temperament issues. But he knows what things he needs. And he usually needs them straight away.' I grimace, thinking of all the times he didn't get the things he needed straight away and the damage he caused.

'I don't know much about kids, Mary. I just deal with adults. Particularly high-functioning overachievers. The complete opposite to…' he stops himself just in time and corrects himself with '… the complete opposite to kids. But I do know that many kids, while not academically gifted or socially skilled, instead have huge emotional intelligence.'

I keep my friendly smile on to stop my jaw actually dropping. *Emotional intelligence?* What does that even mean? And if it means what I think it means, then is it not a precise oxymoron? *Emotional intelligence* – Jesus. 'Finn can do anything with a computer. If you saw him on it, you'd assume he's a genius.' Quickly I pick something to move the conversation on. 'So, you're our new neighbour?'

'Yes. I just moved in. It was all very sudden.'

'Sudden in a nice way?' I'm now so sure it's him, it's almost a disappointment. Clearing up a mystery is boring compared to starting one.

'Oh yeah. You'd know better than me how great this neighbourhood is, Mary.'

Instinctively, I like how he casually uses my name. I must be careful of that. It's such an obvious trick of his trade. He knows that most women like it when you use their name out loud. But not too often, as that would be possessive. Just the right amount of times. If he wrote that letter then he's a very clever, devious liar – which most psychologists have to be.

'Well, welcome to the 'hood,' I say, and laugh good-naturedly.

'That's something Andrew said to me when he called in. Andrew's your husband, right?'

'Right.'

'He accused me of—'

'We received this… letter.'

'I heard. I didn't write it. Or send it. Or whatever. I can't remember the last time I wrote and sent a letter.' He speaks quickly – the way all guilty people do.

'Yeah, there's a "ye olden days" feel off a letter. It should be cute. It usually is.' Quickly I then ask, 'So it wasn't you?'

'Was what me?'

'The letter.'

'I'm sorry but… *I told you*.' His cheeks have reddened. I'd love to feel his pulse. He opens his mouth and the most snivelling and lamest of life's lies – blatant denial – comes tumbling out: 'Of course I didn't.'

'You can tell me. It doesn't matter any more. I'd understand it if you did.'

'Seriously, Mary, I don't know anything about a letter. Honestly. Just like I told your husband.'

Honestly – the word all liars use. It wasn't me, guv. *Honestly.*
'What is this letter?'

'It's just something silly. A mistake someone made. Sent a letter to the wrong person. It's funny, really…' I smile brightly

'Andrew didn't think it was funny.'

'Forget about it. Seriously. Let's start again. Letter-schmetter!'

He has that empathetic trait that makes him feel sorry for people who are trying to be funny, which makes him laugh too loudly at their jokes. The best thing to do with men like Connor – men that are attractive and charming and have already demonstrated their manliness by pretending to save a cat from a savage Alsatian and who are educated and possibly wealthy – is to focus on the flaws. And Connor's flaws are there, even if you have to look closely to spot them. He's past his peak. He's begun disintegrating. It's all about to wither. And he *knows*. Without a doubt he's doing things like testing his charm on baristas and waitresses and has slowly come to accept that beyond the leeway afforded a well-dressed, handsome man, he is losing it.

'It's just you?' I ask. 'In the bungalow?'

'Oh yeah,' he says, quickly, as if a pause would allow two or three of the over-scheduled and tutored children of St Catherine's Hill to move in with him. Connor then asks, 'Finn – is he just visiting?'

'Finn's my nephew.' He really doesn't *seem* to know anything about us and Finn. So, they allowed the bungalow to be rented, not only without warning me but without warning the tenant about Finbarr? But Brona would've known. She's meant to have my back. It's not like her. As for Connor, anything he knew he would've learned it himself after moving in. And he would've responded the only way he could – by writing a letter.

'Right,' Connor says with blatant relief in his eyes, because he clearly thinks that Finbarr will be going back to where he came from sometime soon.

I say, 'My sister had been pregnant with twins. One died midterm and had to be carried full term so as not to harm his brother. That's Finn. He survived.'

As Connor blabs words of consolation towards my absent sister who wouldn't tolerate them even if she had been here, I think of the time when Finn was born. He was the tiniest shred of life I'd ever seen. His skin was so translucent. His chest a tiny balloon pumping up and down in rhythm to the wonderful life-giving oxygen that was driving into his lungs. The moment I saw Finbarr, he became my favourite thing in the world. The only time I'd ever wanted a child was the moment Emer placed him into my arms. The memory is so clear – as if it'll be my last mortal thought.

I begin talking about my sister as if we're close. 'Poor Emer is thirty-two now. But she's had a difficult life. But… they were her life decisions. Her choices.'

'Alcohol? Drugs?'

I try to keep it brief about Emer's and Finbarr's tale of woe, so I rattle off, 'God, no. Emer was, is and always will be a very good girl. It's religion. She was devout from a very early age. But she made a grave error in her early life and became pregnant at fifteen. Just one of those things that can happen. A mistake. Albeit a crucial one. A silly thing, really.' It's extremely irritating that after all these years, I still have to explain away Emer's life from nearly two decades ago. It's incredible that after all this time she's still never managed to take control of her own existence. But one day, soon, she'll get it together. One day. 'And so she was a single mother in a religious evangelical sect. For the first ten years of Finn's life he was homeschooled.'

'Is it that easy to do?'

'Well, unfortunately parents have a constitutional right to educate their children at home. It's ridiculous – you don't even need a formal teaching qualification or curriculum. Parents are allowed to choose the approach they feel best suits the needs of their child. I mean, you can indoctrinate them into the Flat Earth Society as long as they sit the state exams. Sure, they do have a vague law to ensure that your child receives a certain minimum education. But they allow parents to do this without teachers of any kind. Just as long as the children sit state exams until they're sixteen.'

Connor puts his hand on my elbow, commandeering the conversation once again. Is that something he learned at his turbo-powered university, that cast-iron ability to impose his will on others?

'Never realised that,' he says, making a thoughtful face, as if he could've actually helped.

'But having said all that, Finn did very well being home educated. They found that he was way ahead of other kids his age when he eventually went to real school.'

'So your sister changed her mind on homeschooling?'

'No. He had to go because Emer was having mental health problems. She was becoming emotionally exhausted and needed frequent rests in care homes, shall we say. So, like I was telling you earlier, Finn went to school, where they discovered he was super-smart *and* had a form of ODD. At first they thought his disruptive behaviour and violent outbursts against other kids and teachers were because he was bored and because of his isolated upbringing… Well, that's what they blamed it on at first when he was quickly thrown out of two schools.'

I can feel myself becoming more fascinating to Connor and so I continue, actually enjoying getting some of it off my chest. 'During this time they were moving all over the place. It started when Emer's rent went up one hundred percent. Pretty quick, Emer was broke. Proper broke. To this day she literally has not got a bean.'

There's a brief flicker in Connor's gaze. No doubt he's thinking, *Why didn't you help her out? You've money and a big house.*

Why didn't you sprinkle some of that magic her way? I'm tempted to tell him the truth – that she refused all my entreaties. That Emer would accept nothing from her family, no matter what was offered and how much she needed it. But I don't have to justify myself. I let him think what he wants.

I explain, 'And when she had to move, Finn had to change schools even if he wasn't yet thrown out of it. And the moves were obviously disruptive on top of all the rest, and he was mixing with questionable kids. Of course, he wasn't being influenced by them. He didn't want to be them. But he was being bullied. And his temper made him fight back and he was being beaten all the time and ostracised and singled out and the poor thing... can you imagine?'

'Poor guy,' he offers.

'By the third and fourth school – each one worse than the last – they suspected he had ODD on top of general "weirdness". But he was fourteen by then and just another problem they neither wanted nor cared about. As far as they were concerned, his mother brought him up like that and it's legal, so therefore he was basically just another case of a child being forgotten by, or at least disregarded by, the education system.'

'But a civilised state can't treat a mother and troubled child like that. No way.'

I look at Connor carefully. He seems to actually care – like he has a vested interest in Finbarr's well-being. He said he was some sort of psychologist – does that make him an excellent mimic of an empath?

'Yes, you're correct. Not right, but correct. There is a difference. But by the time he was in his last school, they were surrounding him with autistic children, kids with learning disabilities. It was crazy. He doesn't have that type of problem. He has... historical issues. That's all. And yes – maybe some ODD. He has no patience. When he needs something he needs it now. And his temper is explosive. I mean nuclear. Uncontrollable. You saw it yourself. But it's all associated with his past. I mean, who wouldn't be odd with his upbringing? When other children were at playschool, he was praying and reading the Bible. When kids started playing rugby and hockey, he was stuck in the wrong type of school for him – you know, the type that focuses on woodwork and skills rather than academia – so he ends up fighting in the yard and punching teachers and being chased down the street and God knows what else. He's never had friends. Other boys were either scared of him or wanted to kill him.

'He's seventeen now and no other school will have him. Not with his record. He was legally required to be educated until he's sixteen. So, that's it. The state has washed their hands of him. So since last year he was back to being Emer's full-time problem – not that she didn't have enough problems of her own already. She bred him. She pays for him. She looks after him. She deals with him. Totally. As I keep saying, no half measures with our Emer. Not ever.'

Connor nods quickly because I've now got to the point that *really* interests him. It's obvious from the way he keeps glancing up to the kitchen, searching out Finbarr as if he were a nascent criminal. Then he turns his attention back to me, the person he probably regards as Finbarr's overeducated guard. Connor's looking at me kindly. And then I realise why – my eyes have watered. Withdrawing a tissue from my pocket, I dab and soak up the tears.

I say, 'It could be worse. As in, I suppose it's never boring. That's one thing.' My own words surprise me. Sometimes fear and dread is superior to a life of tedium. People do die of boredom. People who live in fear and dread usually do their best to survive.

'Mary, I know it's difficult. But you've such a cool attitude to it all.'

I laugh as if I'm grateful that he's just judged me aloud and ruled in my favour. I laugh as if I don't know it's he who wrote the letter. 'Well, this too will pass eventually. And we'll then get on with our wonderful lives. I just have to remind myself that happiness is overrated. It's just the overstimulation of specific nerve cells.'

The start of a grin tugs at the edges of his mouth. 'Well, Mary, I'm so sorry about the misunderstanding… I mean, I obviously had to save the cat.'

Looking around the garden, I silently emphasise that there is no bloody cat.

'Wherever it's gone…' Connor adds, recognising the point I'm making. 'But, hey, when I'm settled in, it would be great to properly meet my neighbours. So hopefully yourself and Andrew will pop in sometime for a glass of vino and proper introductions, yeah?'

'Sure,' I reply agreeably, thinking, NEVER.

'And I hope things get better for you soon. You and your sister and Finn, of course.'

'It is what it is,' I say with a shrug. '*Altiora peto.*'

'Huh?'

'"I seek greater things".'

'Actually, it would be great if you could ask your sister to call in to me so I can explain what happened with Finn and apologise in person.'

'Emer? Call in to you?' I can't help but snigger like a child.

'Yeah. When's she picking him up?' There's hope in his eyes. He so wants to hear the opposite of what I'm about to tell him.

'You won't be seeing Emer any time soon. Emer has had… Emer is taking a long break. Her biggest one yet.' Dropping a light cough into the hollow of my fist, I then rattle off, 'Emer has had a breakdown. The mother of all her breakdowns. And until she's better, we're looking after Finn.'

Connor glances up at the house, no doubt recognising it as the totem of money that it is.

It's time to spell out his new reality to him. 'Of course we'd have him in his own home if we could. But he's too young. As I was telling you, Finn is seventeen now. The state finished with him a year ago. Without us, he'd simply be homeless. So he's staying with us until Emer is discharged. And they're taking it a month at a time. Money's not the issue. It's Emer. She expects to be out soon. But you know how things are. Things get delayed. There are setbacks. Which isn't surprising – not after all that has happened in the past. So, with all the delays and setbacks, we've had Finn for six months.'

I can't quite believe what I've just said. *Six months*. Jesus Christ. The days of my life have been machine-gunned down in front of my eyes and I didn't even duck. Talking to Connor about my life is actually therapeutic. Like, when I talk to Brona. But different. Brona steers the conversation away from all this drear. She listens for a bit and then at the first opportunity we're roaring laughing about something else entirely. But Connor, by just asking blunt questions, makes me see how things really are.

For him, the worst is beginning to dawn. 'But he's seventeen. He has to go to school, right? Surely a boarding school—'

I actually guffaw. 'After everything I've told you? After everything you've seen with your own eyes? Look, Finn's great but... he's nothing like any other child.'

And there it is – plastered all over his face. The realisation that he's lost. That the letter had been pointless. That Finbarr is going nowhere. Connor tries to say something but the words get caught in his throat. He swallows and tries again. This time he manages, 'Monday to Friday. The working week. Finn is here?'

Despite the letter, I still feel sorry for him and so there's a slight downward droop in my tone as I say, 'Yes. He lives here – for the time being. The only external relief available to us is Elena, who you briefly met before I got home. She's our maid but she also helps out with Finn when Andrew is at work. She can manage him.'

'He's out here every day?' Connor's eyes have widened with what? Fear?

'Yes. He loves the trampoline.'

'Is he not too old for it?'

'Look, do you really think Finn had stuff like trampolines to grow out of when he was growing up? Anyway, it's good for him. We were advised to get him a punching bag as he would need to work out his frustrations and offload some wired energy. But with his violent history and temper… well, I don't want to encourage that. So Andrew went out and got the trampoline. Best thing we ever got him. And thank God we have this big open garden. It's where he spends all his time that he doesn't devote to his laptop, doing what, I don't know – flaming Tokyo, maybe.'

'Yes, but *every day*?'

'Yes. Of course. He's usually just like any other teenager. Running around. I'm sorry if occasionally you'll have to close your windows against the noise. But he needs to let off a lot of steam, pent-up whatever, testosterone, like lots of teenage boys do.'

'In the morning and afternoon?'

'Of course. Whenever he likes. In that way, he's just like any other adolescent. Burning that energy. Fine, sometimes he's noisier than a group of ten-year-old boys. But at least he doesn't actually have friends like all the other boys growing up. I remember the Kellys on the other side of me when their boys were little guys. There'd be ten or so lads out the back there charging around screaming all day. But that's the great thing about this neighbourhood. The gardens. And how family-orientated it is. Bairbre Kelly next door – who owns the Alsatian – she says Finn reminds her of her boys back when they were seventeen. She thinks Finn is keeping her young.' I laugh, trying to make it sound real. 'She's even sent me private messages on Facebook with pictures she's taken from her kitchen of Finn.'

'You see, I work from home,' Connor mutters. 'My therapy. It's in the back of the bungalow. To the side of the kitchen. The step-down part. There's only my bedroom out the front. And even before the cat, he was... he was shouting a lot. When he was on the trampoline. Jumping up and down. Roaring, in fact.' He says this as if teenagers making noise outdoors in the back garden of a family neighbourhood is some type of bombshell. 'The windows were closed and it still just filled the room. The noise, you see?'

Gently I explain, 'Connor, it's a family neighbourhood and everyone in St Catherine's Hill have always let their children play in their gardens. That's what the gardens are for. These are houses. Not business premises. Finn likes his earphones and awful music and with his ODD condition – fine, unofficially diagnosed – he needs to blow off steam and let it all out.'

'But—'

'But what?' There's always a 'but' with men like Connor.

'But—'

'There are no buts,' I snap, before resummoning friendly, nice Mary. 'Connor, you've just moved in but I imagine you did your research before deciding to base your business in St Catherine's Hill? I mean, surely they told you about the area, and presumably you had questions too? All before you signed? Like, if it doesn't suit then surely you can get your month's deposit back, right?'

'Month's deposit? That... Yeah.' I can almost see his brain churning.

I try to picture him writing the letter, hunched over the keyboard, pondering how to disguise his real voice and yet make his point with succinct darts of words. To send an anonymous letter to a neighbour in a tightly knit community like St Catherine's Hill – and get away with it – requires certain characteristics. He must possess low levels of guilt, if any; surely he realises the hurt and paranoia it will cause. He must be immune to post-event angst – otherwise, what's the point? The objective must be clear – to make things better for the writer. He must be an excellent and effortless liar, because no doubt he will eventually be face-to-face with the addressee and perhaps the addressee will even tell the writer about the letter that she has received. In short, the successful writer of the anonymous letter must have a toughness of character.

Connor says, 'I think I'd better go now.' But he's not looking at me. He's looking beyond me to Brona and Zachery's house. I stare into Connor's face – has he a toughness of character? Of course he does. He invaded a stranger's garden and openly wrestled a hysterical seventeen-year-old boy into submission. And he never stood down when challenged by me.

Lowering his gaze, he says, 'Sorry for the drama.'

'No problem. Like I said, let's start again.'

Connor begins walking back to the hedge that surrounds his bungalow's patch of grass and raised decking area. There's still part of me that can't see him writing the letter: the part of me that likes him; the part of me that would value being taken for granted by him. The part of me that is stupid enough to ignore Occam's razor, because if it wasn't Connor who wrote the letter – a letter that was written just after his arrival when he had no idea just what would be waiting to spoil his life – then who did?

I wave as if he's looking at me but it's his back I'm facing as he squeezes through the hole in the hedge. A moment later his shoes clip against his decking, and then the top of the bungalow's kitchen door is visible over the bushes as it opens.

I suddenly call out, 'That cat. What colour was it?'

Don't be white. Any colour but white.

Connor shouts over the hedge, 'White. A white adult cat. Not wild.' Then the top of the kitchen door closes over.

Brona's cat is white. It's the most regular cat, that roams and sprays its way through the gardens. Could it be true? Maybe he just saw Brona's cat passing on its rounds earlier and that's why he chose a white cat to lie about rather than a black one, or a ginger one, or a tabby or whatever. Retreating up to the house, I slip off my shoes.

Back inside Elena tells me what had happened when she heard the screams from the garden. Elena never saw a cat – just Connor arguing with Finbarr, which of course instigated an immediate code-red, level-10 meltdown. She said, 'Like the bad guy in American wrestling. The big guy beating up and cheating against the small hero.' I let Elena leave early after tipping her big and thanking her profusely.

With Finbarr immersed in the computer, I stand hidden on the decking behind the hanging plants and light up. After the day's excitement – and it's not over yet – I break my 'night-time only' rule and inhale gratefully. But I regret it as soon as I exhale. The smoke coming off the cigarette seems greasy. But I persist while banging out a text to Brona, asking about her cat – whether it's missing or even just shook up. I tell her that Elena glimpsed the neighbour's dog chasing a cat.

The text is a nice excuse to contact her, to mention my new neighbour. I want her to acknowledge that he'd arrived without my being warned. I want her to know that I feel she has an unspoken obligation to me. That we have obligations to each other. I press 'send' while staring down the garden, over the hedge to where her balcony is wide and Brona-less. After two minutes, there's still no reply and that means there will never be a reply because she's out and busy with her life, because she has one.

As Finbarr stomps through the kitchen, I stab the cigarette out bitterly and kick it off the decking to the grass below. He emerges onto the decking, wearing his grandfather's brown peaked cap, music blasting in his headphones. I gave Finbarr Dad's cap a week ago. He's family and he needs to feel part of the family. Plus, some cool kids are wearing them in some HBO show he likes. Of course Finbarr never thanked me for it but I know he likes it. He wears it indoors a lot. He wears it to pull down over his eyes when he's on the laptop and doesn't want to be looked at.

Before he heads for the trampoline, I ask, 'What really happened out there, Finn?'

He pulls back the cap and looks at me with deep blue eyes. He's contemplating pulling off one of his more infuriating manoeuvres – responding to a question by simply putting on his earphones and turning the volume up – but this time decides against it.

'I told you.'

'But why did he say—'

'I never went near Brona's cat.'

If Finbarr had tried to feed Brona's cat to the Alsatian, what does that make him? Is he some type of senseless psychopath? But I mustn't think those dark thoughts, those noisome squatters that occupy my mind.

'*Brona's* cat? Why did you say *Brona's* cat?'

He blinks. Again, he considers putting on his earphones. Again, he decides against it. 'Does a teenage dirtbag not have ears? Can a teenage dirtbag not hear you shouting over the hedge about what the cat looked like? Could this teenage dirtbag not help but listen to that wanker say that it was a white cat? And does this teenage dirtbag have a brain to calculate that his suspicious auntie would associate white with Brona's white cat? Simple, yeah?'

I picture him as a baby, and me opening and closing the poppers of his nappy – was it too tight? While Emer recovered after a difficult birth, I visited twice a day and kept examining every inch of Finbarr, convinced that I was going to find something wrong with him. But I never did. He was perfect. His skull perfectly formed, his fontanelle so soft and vulnerable. His long eyelashes. His mouth a rosebud.

Maybe Finbarr didn't do it. Or maybe it was a misunderstanding. Maybe he was just trying to put the cat over the wall, *not* feed it to the dog. But if he did do it – intentionally – then it's the type of thing that only a mother could forgive a son for. *Get well soon, Emer.*

'Aunt Mary?'

'Yes, Finn?'

'What are you going to do about the man next door?'

'There's nothing to be done. It's over now.'

'You believe that?'

'Of course.'

'The same way you believe that I didn't do that to Brona's cat?'

'Of course. Why would you do such a terrible thing to a defenceless animal?'

'I would assume that if I'd done it, I would've done it because of my mother, because of where my mother is, because of who put her there. *You*. And because they won't let her out so I can go home and not have to be stranded here in this area that is just a giant posh old folks' home. I would assume that I would've done it specifically to Brona's cat because of Brona's role in making this even more of a pain in the arse than it has to be. I would assume that I would've done it to make her hurt… just a little. Acting out, as Mam's jailers say. So – just as well I didn't do it, right? Any more questions, Aunt Mary?'

'No.' My tone is neutral, even tired. I'm used to his resentful, clever soliloquies. Sometimes, when he's picking me apart, I just fold my arms and admire the sharpness of his thoughts, their viciousness. If only his intellect could be garnered and trained for some good in the world. But he's young. His life is before him. If his life began as a tragedy, surely it should conclude in triumph? Surely that's only fair?

All afternoon, I'm in and out from the decking, listening for any sound of my new neighbour during the breaks in Finbarr's bouncing and singing on the trampoline, and his walloping the ball against the wall separating the top of Connor's garden from ours. Looking down the garden to Brona's, I wish for another cigarette and scold myself for having broken my rule.

Finally, it's time to get Finbarr his dinner. The microwave dings, and after peeling off the translucent wrapper of his favourite TV dinner he insists on having about five times a week, I begin scooping the yellow strings into his red plastic bowl. He's suddenly beside me, nudging my elbow a little, trying to make the spaghetti fall into his bowl faster. When the steaming mass finally plonks into the bowl he just snaps it up without even a grunt or a side glance and strolls bare-chested, barefoot and extremely handsome, onto the decking. He begins eating by just leaning his face into the bowl and slurping up the strings.

'Finn, look at me.' Holding up the red plastic spoon, I wave it at him. 'You know you have to use this? Google the instructions.'

For a moment, he stands on the decking staring: blond, gorgeous and dead-eyed. Then he marches back in and there's a little warning flash in his eyes, the one he gets right before he tries to stab you with something. My stomach hits the floor. *Oh God. Not again.* It seems as if he's going to put me through the wall but instead he gently takes the spoon and softly pats my shoulder. Finbarr then makes parallel digs through his spaghetti and mutters, 'Basically, I don't understand your loyalty and affection for crumbs like me and Mam.'

'What? How can you say—'

'Basically, Mam hates you. You know this. I've told you over and over what she's said about you over the years. I don't know why, though. That's the one thing she never reveals. The big, fat, sloppy, gooey "why". And you won't either.'

'There is no "why". Your mother is just not well.'

'Let's not do this again. All I was saying is… she hates you. And the fact that I'm here, being looked after by you, will make her hate you more. She'd never have wanted that. And ironically, that'll make her recovery slower, probably, and therefore I'll be stuck here in this hell for an even longer time. And I'm not easy to live with. I get that. I do. Really. My boo-boo. So… thanks. That's all. I hate it here. You hate having me here. But I have no choice because without you I'd be homeless or whatever. But you do. You have a choice. So, like I said… thanks.'

And that's all I need to… Is 'love' too strong a word? But it's all I need to really care for him, properly, until his mother returns.

He goes over to the sofa, sits down, picks up his set of cards and shuffles the deck, his riffles as smooth and quick as brand new stainless-steel machinery. He halves the deck and raps their sides on each other, zipping them together like closing a slick new coat.

At last a text arrives from Brona. I turn away from Finbarr and, without my attention, he returns to the garden. He's spending extra time today on the trampoline because he's interested in our new neighbour. Finbarr doesn't only use the trampoline for burning energy and killing time – he uses it to look over hedges and to see beyond walls. Finbarr likes to know exactly what's going on.

Alone, I hold the phone up to my face.

Kitty-Kat's missing. Must have been her the dog attacked. Haven't seen her all day. Keep an eye out. Shit!

Oh no. So Connor was telling the truth. What to do now? Anything? I suppose I should call in to the Kellys' and tell Bairbre what had happened with their dog. Maybe they'll be relieved that we're not putting it down. That might be the outcome. Or more likely, they'll be disturbed, bewildered and anxious that Finbarr tried to feed their Alsatian a live cat.

The security system beeps and down the hall, the front door unlocks – just a click and a whisper of air. Andrew is back. Right on time. Quickly I fire up the range. The frying pan sears our steaks. Andrew likes it bloody, very bloody; cut off its horns, rip off its face and put the rest on his plate, rare.

The kitchen door opens. Andrew presses one big hand against the wall and glares about as if expecting burglars. I know his mood instantly. He's in 'man-of-the-house' mode. The way he gets when something needs to be fixed and he reckons he can do it without calling in a professional and I have to act impressed or else he sulks like a child. Andrew has always been like that – someone who is very easy to offend. It's endearing.

'What the hell's going on?'

I can't help smiling. 'It's over. It's fine.' I take the pan off the flame. 'Tell me what happened when you went in next door?'

'Hold on. Elena called earlier. Left a message. She was in a state, said there was an emergency with Finn. I couldn't get you. And missed Elena. But she then left another message that it was all fine. Mary… are you OK?' He takes a step towards me but maybe I flinch because he stops himself before his fingers touch the bare skin of my arms.

He looks at me questioningly. He tries again and this time his hands succeed in landing on my arms. Once I'm not surprised, I don't mind *his* touch. My body makes sense of it. He's blushing beneath all that black stubble. His eyes wander around the room. He needs to move the conversation on. We both need to.

Andrew says, 'I was at work. I get these messages. No one calls me back. Now – what the hell happened? What's going on?'

So, I tell him. I only get to the part where Finbarr is trying to feed Brona's cat to the Kellys' Alsatian when Andrew interjects.

'I don't believe that. Elena saw this happen?'

'I'm not finished yet.'

'Did *you* see it happen?'

'I said, I'm not finished yet. But it happened, OK? Are you really surprised?'

Andrew playfully shoves me aside from the cooker with a mere swing of his hips. His height and width I've always liked. He's never used them to intimidate me and he rarely uses them to press home a point by towering over me. Andrew likes his size too. It's better to be a big man than a small man. No one ever wanted to be a small man.

Andrew takes hold of the frying pan handle, shakes the steaks, sniffs them and then puts it back into the fire. He turns the gas up and, grabbing a carving knife, quickly halves each one.

He says, 'Finn has his own ways of doing things.'

Andrew scans the herb shelf, grabs Italian seasoning and coriander and sprinkles them over the meat. There's a bowl on the counter with onion and mushroom I'd chopped earlier. He upends it into the frying pan and continues cooking. He cooks in a very masculine way – the way he does everything – mixing the food with a flip of the heavy pan, tossing in more ingredients without measuring, without a cookbook in sight, all above a roaring gas flame.

Finbarr marches back into the kitchen, my dad's cap on, earphones on, music blaring into his skull, humming loudly but nothing melodic. His humming is just a continuous noise, trying to be annoying, the notes randomly going up and down, guttural and then high-pitched. His black T-shirt hangs off him. He's so skinny and slight he appears to be no match for ex-first lieutenant Andrew. But then something happens – the internet connection drops or he reads something online that he doesn't like or a dark mood simply descends that makes every other person in the world extremely irritating to him – and then every molecule of him turns into a raging furnace of devastating force. I've seen Andrew pin him to the floor and Finbarr still raise my husband's bulk feet into the air with just his thrashing arms and legs.

Andrew raises his right hand and smiles broadly. Finbarr stares at him and although he doesn't smile, his eyes widen, making them a deep blue as if he'd caught the sky in them. Then he slips off the earphones and also raises his hand and high-fives Andrew as he passes by on his way to the hallway.

'That's my buddy,' Andrew says, and means it. He would've been a great father if we'd decided on kids.

'You're the man, Uncle Andy. They tried to turn you into corporate rock but you are *still* punk rock. *Always.*'

Andrew swallows uneasily, but persists with a chirpy enquiry. 'Did you watch that *King Kong* movie I told you about? The original? Black and white classic.'

'Uncle Andy, when a guy turns a conversation too quickly to movies, it's a sign of weakness. Movies are for when you've nothing else to talk about. Movies are for the end of the night. And guys like you and me – well, we have *sooo* much to talk about.'

Andrew laughs as if he's sharing the joke rather than being the brunt of it.

'Enough, Finn,' I snap to my nephew's back as he disappears into the front bedroom. Then I say to Andrew, 'Now, tell me. What happened when you called in next door?'

Andrew passes me by to the decking. Outside, above the tall hedge and Zachery and Brona's balcony, the late dusk is still pale and shot through with rose. Andrew scans his land, first looking towards the wall that barricades in the Alsatian. He says, 'Hold on. If you didn't see the cat and Elena didn't see the cat, then who did? The Kellys?'

I try to tell him the rest of the story but at the earliest mention of Connor, a glare of disdain exerts gravity on his features. Men – so territorial all the time. It doesn't matter that Finbarr might have been trying to kill a cat. It doesn't matter that Finbarr could've been hurt by a stranger. But what *did* matter was that another man had come into Andrew's territory, uninvited, and sprayed his scent all over it.

Right now, Andrew's eyes are so dark I can hardly see his pupils. Despite myself I find there's something attractively primeval about that type of masculinity.

He stares at the hedge surrounding Connor's small garden, trying to figure out where the chink in the armour is that allowed him to get through it so easily. Then he speaks. 'No one saw the cat. This guy who sent us a hate letter – a cowardly anonymous note – and then barges through my hedge to attack a… a… child and then—'

'He didn't exactly attack—'

'He held him in a full nelson?'

'That's what you would call it, yes. But Finn was upset and needed calming.'

'Finn is seventeen. He's still a child. And Finn looks what? Fifteen? He's not exactly a rugby player. If another child – a normal child – was chasing a cat or whatever, do you think a neighbour would've invaded our private property and assaulted that child? Huh? Of course not. And to do so when I'm not here? After I *warned him* to stay away? And you know what? He knew there was only the wife here. Nothing against you, Mary – but you know what I mean. Do you think he would've barged through the hedge if he'd seen me out with Finn beforehand? Huh? No way.'

'Well, it's over now.'

'Over? No, it's not. When he talks to me and apologises… When he realises that there are ways of doing things around here… *that's* when it's over.'

'What are you going to do?'

'I'm going back into him. Finish this for good. What has happened is unacceptable. Mary, I *warned* him.'

Following Andrew inside, there's a strange excitement buzzing in my head; me and Connor are not yet done with our affairs.

My husband fastens his jacket, intimating that he means business.

'I don't think you should do that,' I say, because I should.

'Keep my fucking steak warm.' When Andrew is in ex-army man-of-the-house mode, he has the unfortunate habit of interjecting expletives into sentences that would've been more powerful without them.

For the more rational man, waiting until tomorrow would be the smarter thing to do – to give himself time to formulate his complaint and the point of the visit. But Andrew can't do that because when he feels this confident about himself, he knows that the feeling will only last hours. It will certainly be gone by the morning. Andrew worries about sunrise. Daylight would mean that he might lose heart, that he might come to an unfortunate conclusion about his true worth. Yes – Andrew needs to do it now. He needs to commit.

As I hear him struggle back into his shoes, open the front door and then slam it shut behind him I feel a shiver of excitement. Things are going to get very interesting. I rush into the front room – Andrew's study – and watch out the window. He stops at his Land Rover and opens the boot. What's he looking for?

Oh my God. Not again.

The last time he lost his temper was a year ago at the golf club Christmas dinner. He had stormed out, opened the hatchback and taken out the eight inches of stainless steel that is his army knife. Andrew will now do anything to make Connor hate him as much as he hates Connor.

As he slams the Land Rover boot shut, colour creeps up his face. It's hot pink. I've never seen such a high colour like it. It's as if an IV bag is transfusing blood into him. I retreat back to the kitchen, out to the patio and face the bungalow, waiting to hear the war.

CHAPTER FOURTEEN

CONNOR

The doorbell sounded over the shrieking noise of the boy next door.

'Great,' Connor muttered, while staring out the kitchen window watching Finbarr's head appear and reappear over the top of the hedge as he bounced on the trampoline, one finger raised and directed up to Connor's kitchen. It was hardly someone welcome at the door. It was hardly good news. *The noise. That kid. Jesus, what am I going to do?* The week ahead was a wound he had not yet been able to steel himself to look at. However, he felt it bleed.

The front bedroom could be an office. A small office. *A too-small-an-office.* If he put in a desk and two chairs it would be too tiny for his executives to even take off their coats. Anyway, he could hardly move the bed into the kitchen/living area. *What am I going to do?* His deposit was gone. He was stuck here.

The doorbell sounded a second time. It was probably someone from one of the electricity companies wanting to know if he was happy with his current supplier. He thought of Mary next door. *She has it rough. She has problems. And that boy has real problems.* But the fact was, Mary's problem had become his problem and her problem was now blowing his life to pieces.

The doorbell sounded a third time. 'Jesus. Fine. I'm coming.' Connor opened the front door.

'Hi. I'm Brona.'

I know who you are.

'I live nearby.'

Connor nodded. *I know exactly where you live.* Brona's voice had a smooth melodic velvet tone. Up close she didn't disappoint: smooth skin; shoulder-length brown hair; wide, intelligent, hazel eyes; slim. She was wearing a two-piece black suit and a white shirt with a wide navy tie that was knotted too far down to be accidental. Slick red trainers made the outfit entirely cool.

'Brona,' Connor said, wonderingly, not acknowledging that he knew who she was. She wasn't wearing any earrings. The top two buttons of her shirt were undone revealing a bare neck. He looked at her fingers – no rings. Connor had always found that no jewels were more stylish than everyday jewels.

'I'm told that you're my hero.'

Was she joking? A man who tackles a skinny teenager into a full nelson is many things, but not a hero.

'My cat,' Brona elucidated. Her smile revealed white teeth that on most people would be too Hollywood-perfect to be their own. 'You saved Kitty-Kat from that awful dog.' She vaguely nodded in the direction of the Kellys', two doors up.

'Well, it was actually…' He stopped himself from blaming Finbarr. 'Sure. No problem.'

'The thing is, Kitty-Kat is missing and—'

'I have her. It's OK. I was going to bring her to the vet and hopefully she would be chipped.' Connor had found the cat in his own garden. She'd squeezed herself beneath a bush to groom her wounds. Connor knew nothing about cats but guessed that it would like milk and cold meat. He'd guessed right.

'Oh, brilliant!' Brona clapped and looked to the sky with a huge smile, and Connor imagined how rich a man's life would be if rewarded with that sight once a day. Did Zachery deserve that?

'Come on in. She's in shock, I think.'

Connor stepped to the side but Brona was looking over at Andrew standing in his driveway. She called out, 'Hey, Andy, everything OK? Want me for something?'

He waved a short quick salutation solely at Brona, shook his head, popped the boot of the Land Rover and lowered his head into it.

As she stepped through the door, Brona said, 'That's Andrew. Mary's husband. But you know that, right?'

'Yup,' Connor said, already forgetting about him, not aware of anyone else in the world besides Brona. She was following, three feet behind, towards the opened door to the decking, from where the thumping sound of Finbarr's ball slamming repeatedly against the decking wall pounded into the kitchen. Out in the small garden, beneath the hedge bordering Mary's, was the white cat, hedgehogged into a shivering ball. It wasn't clear if her trembling was because of her wounds or the noise. Little remained of the luxuriant cat it had once been. With much of its white fur hacked away, it was only a skinny, shivering, semi-rat-like thing peering up at them. One of her eyes had mooned.

'Oh. My. God.' Brona descended the steps, crossed the ten feet of lawn and crouched down.

'I'll just... leave you to it,' he said, uselessly, while leaning forward on the rail and folding his arms. So, this was Brona; the woman that, before wanting to kill her, Zachery had once described as being like a tailored suit.

Connor glanced over to Mary's to reassure himself that Finbarr wasn't trying to get through the hedge. But he was busy simply kicking the ball from toe to head, over and over. Connor then looked across Mary's garden to where Zachery's balcony was large and empty. *Has she any idea who I am? Can life be that coincidental?*

The wings of a magpie chopped the air as it fled through the leaves of a distant oak, crying harshly. The cat was back on its feet and Brona was on her knees before it. Gently they knocked foreheads before Brona stood. 'Just seems to be scrapes, believe it or not. Chunks of fur plucked out but no real wounds. The dog must've grabbed her by the coat rather than her flesh. That's why she's half-naked. Poor thing is mortified.'

Brona continued talking about the cat and from the balcony Connor nodded and made the right noises as he soaked her up. He was doing that thing he did when the waitress recited the specials – trying too hard to pay attention so that he was paying attention to paying attention. *Focus, man! Focus*.

Brona returned to the decking, her trainers padding the ground. 'You should've killed it.'

'Huh?'

'The dog.'

She is *joking?* 'I couldn't do that. I'm not a killer.'

'Well, I am.' She stares back down to her cat. 'Well, I am if something like a big crazed Alsatian attacks a lovely little ball of fur-love that belongs to me.' Brona shook her head as if she still couldn't believe what she was looking at. 'Kitty-Kat is a very sheltered puddy. If someone hisses at her she needs to lie down for a week. So right now, I'd say her mind is totally blown. I'll take her to the vet later and have her checked out.'

'Cool. How'd you find out anyway? Mary your friend?'

'She's my sister.'

'Your *sister?*'

She seemed surprised at his surprise. 'My big sister. Well, one of them. Mary texted me. Haven't got into it yet with her. She doesn't even know I'm here – yet. Poor Mary… on top of everything that's going on in there…' Brona's sentence trailed off like a song fading out before a sudden unexpected crescendo arrived with, 'But she's probably lying.'

'Huh?'

'Just Mary's situation. It's terrible.'

'Yeah – it must be so hard with Finbarr.' The ball started thumping against the wall from next door.

Brona's eyes swept back to him. 'Finn?' she said, as if Finbarr was the last thing on her mind. 'Oh yeah.' Again she lost focus and her gaze drifted over the hedge towards the back of Mary's house. She muttered, 'I just wish she didn't know.'

'Know what?'

Brona sucked in her lower lip as she chewed over a decision. Then, as if having determined that this wasn't the time for *that* story, said, 'No. Forget it. Just thinking aloud about the dog and the hassle. Nothing.' Quickly she seemed to relax into the relief that her life was hers and not Mary's.

Standing by Connor on the decking, Brona folded her arms on the railing in such a perfect postural echo that for a moment Connor wondered if she was mocking him. But there was a peaceful vibe to her expression as he gazed on her profile. Brona was very attractive but she also had a natural shine that came from an innate vibrancy and enthusiasm that most people don't have, the kind of shine that people always like to dampen. But she was also about thirty and so, against the odds, that hadn't happened so far. Therefore, she was probably very resilient.

'Hey, do you see over there…' She pointed to the back of her house. 'That's where I live.'

No kidding. 'Ah. Right.'

'But you knew that. And you know exactly who I am.'

Uh-oh. 'I do?'

'Really? Are we going to play that game? 'Cos that would be pretty disappointing… unless you're the type of clever man that only acts this dumb so as to lure people into lowering their expectations and then quickly, you pleasantly surprise them.'

'I don't know what you're talking about.'

'*Bzzzz*! And that's the incorrect answer. Thank you for playing. Now, I'm gonna grab my cat and go. Ha! *Cat* and go. Not coat.'

'No. Wait. I'm sorry. Let's talk. I'm just… well, you know?'

Brona's smirk seemed to say that it had been too easy. Connor tried not to show his relief at the fact that she was only aware that he was Zachery's therapist and not that he had been spying on her from this exact spot.

Brona said, 'And now I understand why you thought we couldn't see you when you were watching us. You must feel almost totally camouflaged behind these hanging plants.'

Damn! He rubbed his forehead. *Deny it.* But that would just make it worse. He closed his eyes. *Make up an excuse.* He opened his eyes. *There is no excuse.*

Brona continued. 'From our height over there, your reflection on the glass slider behind you is crystal clear. So, we can see you in the glass, arms raised, the side of your hand tight against your eyebrows. You kind of looked like a desert general... you know that pose? Legs parted, as if you were glassing the battlefield, about to give the command. Rommel! *That's* who I'm thinking of. Anyway, I thought it was funny. And creepy. But not any more. You're just nosy. And you did save Kitty-Kat.'

'Look, you do realise that your boyfriend manipulated me into moving here. The minute the kid started shouting, he texted me and... wait. Are *you* in on this?' Next door, Finbarr emitted a loud roar for the first time in a while – some type of strangled lyric.

'Sorry, *what* now?'

'Are you *in* on this? Has Zachery sent you round? Is this why you're here?'

Brona's face screwed up into the expression of a fantastic *Huh?* that usually only North Americans did very well. 'What are you on about? I'm here for my cat. Just look at the poor thing.'

Kitty-Kat gazed up sphinx-like at her mistress. Outside of missing tufts of fur and a few bloody scrapes, she had miraculously recovered.

'But you know what's after happening, right? You know what he's doing, yeah?'

'Well, you're Zach's coach, as he calls it.'

'Was.'

She reddened. 'Yes. He said it's ended.'

Connor turned from the railing and faced her full on. 'That's all he said?'

The colour remained in her cheeks. She was either guiltily betraying Zachery's confidence or was a terrible liar and was about to hold important information back. 'Zach didn't go into it. He just... yesterday, on our balcony, after he got back from work, he told me that you had cut him adrift. He was *very* pissed off about it.'

'It's for his own good. Think I like throwing clients away?'

'I don't know anything about it or your clients. He just pointed you out to me from our balcony and said you were living over there now. Oh, and he said that you were a prick.'

Connor looked at his feet. 'I didn't know where you two lived until I'd moved in. That and the kid next door and my savings flushed away into a deposit and a year's rent in advance... well, Zachery's play was all just slowly becoming apparent.'

'Becoming apparent?'

'What Zachery had done.'

'It's still becoming apparent,' Brona muttered.

'What do you mean?'

She sighed, not at him, but rather at some private thought in her head. 'Nothing. Just Zachery, ya know?' She looked back over to her house, the windows on the empty balcony reflecting the neighbourhood like one-way glass. Then she abruptly looked away from it.

'You see, I didn't know I'd gotten this place because of Zachery. I just didn't think of him as the same type of extremely wealthy businessman I usually deal with. Like, he seems to actually realise that we're here on earth to have amazing experiences, learn stuff and perhaps make ourselves and the planet better – that we're not just here to leave school, grab a business degree and then join a solid company at twenty-five years of age because it has a great pension scheme. He was always something different, something more creative, more like the musician he is. Or used to be. You understand what I'm saying? Of course you do – you work for him. You understand his life arc even better than I do.'

He paused for her reply but she remained peculiarly quiet.

'It didn't register in a real sense that he's a big deal property dealer. That he owned or controlled or bought and sold or whatever he does with all those properties, including this one. I forgot, or didn't take into account that this type of business – property – makes him a very powerful and wealthy man who could effortlessly bully someone like me out of existence.'

Why is she staring at me like I'm the only one who didn't get the memo?

'What's wrong?'

'Nothing,' Brona answered, editing her expression like a poker player.

'Buzz – incorrect answer. Did I say that right? And I assumed the gist behind your "bon mot" was that we weren't going to lie to each other?'

'I'm not a liar. I'm a diplomat. I want to know all sides to the story before I condemn my boyfriend. 'Cos that's what you want me to do, right?'

'Zachery – your boyfriend – is just a little boy who has been allowed to barge his way through life, who isn't used to not getting what he wants when he wants it and how he wants it. He's a spoilt prick.'

She looked at Connor blankly but still had an aura about her. She seemed to only belong in five-star hotels, on cruise liners, red carpets, behind the high walls of Hollywood mansions or French chateaux. It was in her melodic delivery of every word and the brightness of her eyes that, taken together, hinted at the type of great intelligence that would make her higher functions just wither up and die whenever she was around ordinary people for any length of time.

As Finbarr began to bounce on the trampoline again, her expression softened and she nodded slightly to herself. 'So, you dumped him from your therapy and—'

'I had no choice. I'm a professional. I had his best interests at heart. That's my job. That's what he was paying me for. He needed... He *needs* to move on to another therapist.'

'Yeah, well much more important than your feelings of professionalism, or your principles, is knowing when you're fucking with someone.'

'If I'd kept him it would've been akin to bullying. The worst type of bullying. Like work bullying. You know? Beating someone up – but not too badly – because you want him on his feet again tomorrow so he can come back in and you can do it again.'

'The problem, Connor, is that there's some other truths out there, such as, you hurt him and now he's hurting you. You dump him and *then* decide to use the connection he'd given you when you were still his therapist. What the hell?'

Connor looked away. Out of context, Brona had a point. There was also the fact that he was beginning to recognise within himself a certain attraction towards her that made him almost admire the way in which she refused to apologise for her boyfriend's behaviour. She was beginning to captivate him – as there must be something interesting about such a content woman being happily in a relationship with such a complete bastard.

'I was desperate, and what difference would it have made to him?'

In the last few minutes he felt the vibration of a few texts arriving on his phone.

Brona said, 'So, you use his connection for personal gain and do you think he stops it? 'Cos that's what I'd do. No, he doesn't.

He lets it go ahead. He doesn't stop you moving into a neighbour-hood in which the only social disorder in its microhabitat is the inequity between the rich and the disgustingly, moltenly, liquid. To put it bluntly, Zach lets you take possession of a prime piece of real estate that's part of a one-hundred-million-euro property bond.'

One hundred million. The figure hung in the air for a few moments, the way figures like that often do.

'Hey, can we go back inside?' Brona quickly wiped her nose with the back of her hand. 'Kitty-Kat will be fine down there for a bit longer – won't you, angel?'

'Summer cold?' Connor asked, though he suspected that the random punctuations of noise from next door was getting to her.

'No – my blood sugar levels always go up after an abortion.'

Connor halted mid-step. He knew how gormless he looked but couldn't help it.

'Hay fever,' she said, drolly, while passing him with an elbow nudge. 'Thought I'd address what Zach has no doubt been going on about in therapy. You know? Me not wanting kids with him, blah, blah, de-blah? So, after everything you've heard about me, I hope I live up to your expectations rather than down to them.'

Connor followed Brona inside to the kitchen with its counter tops, stools, booze and ice machine. It was a more private setting – one in which he had total control. But Brona was confusing him. Why was she still here? Her cat was outside, ready to be taken home. Her partner was two gardens away hating him and being responsible for taking his grand vision of the future and shattering it on the ground – something which Brona didn't seem to particularly care about.

As he sat on a stool by the counter, his phone buzzed again in his jacket. At the same time, he realised that Brona was no longer behind him. Instead she'd walked up to the wall mirror. 'So... Zach told you I work with him... well, for him?'

'Yeah.'

'What else did he tell you?'

'That's about it.' Realising how that sounded, he quickly added, 'And you're very good at that too. Even if you're no longer totally satisfied by it.'

Regarding herself in the glass with a meaty pause, as if totally unaware that Connor was also in the room, she said, 'This place is bigger than it looks from our place.' Brona fixed her tie, moving the knot even further down the V of her shirt. It seemed as if she was performing herself to herself. Brona's head moved about, using the glass reflection to look around the kitchen and sunken living room behind her. 'I have to pop into my sister now.'

'OK.' Inside Connor's jacket, his phone was buzzing every few seconds now. *What the hell is going on?*

He was about to take it out when Brona said, 'Can I leave Kitty-Kat here? Like, outside? And I'll pick her up after? Finn doesn't play well with others.'

You don't say. 'Sure.'

Closing the front door, he locked himself inside and Brona out. Again, his phone vibrated. Retrieving it from inside his jacket, he flicked it off 'silent' and immediately it began to bleat with an unknown number.

As if about to swim through an undersea tunnel, Connor held his breath and answered.

'What've ya done, Connor?' Zachery's smooth, calm voice demanded.

'Huh?'

'I suppose you could change your name? That's what I'd do if I were you.'

Connor anxiously scratched his hand back and forth through his hair. 'I really don't know what you're on about.'

'It's like fuck'n anal leakage or something. Now who's going to help *you*? And believe me, you now need help. Thing about you, Connor, is that you always want someone to *need* you. Jesus, there's something deferential about the way you insist on helping people – as if you somehow owe it to them. But all you do is top-end social work. Yeah, you're just a glorified social worker – a perfect thing for a loser to do, look after other fucking losers.'

'Come on, Zachery – isn't this venting all a bit beneath you? And putting me here, with the kid next door, trying to destroy my livelihood? Why would you do that? I've done nothing against you. Look, call round and we'll talk about it. Sort it out. What do you think?'

Connor held his breath. Could it be that easy?

'Fuck you,' Zachery said.

Connor took the phone away from his head and stared into the screen as if staring into his client's eyes. He said, 'We can sort this out, Zachery.'

'You don't know, do you?' It was more a statement of incredulity than a question. 'It's all over the net. Everyone who knows you will soon know.'

'What are you talking about?'

The silence on the line lasted so long that Connor checked the screen to see if they were still connected. Five full bars were lined up. He put it back to his ear.

Zachery said, 'I sent you the link.'

'I haven't checked my texts.'

'You need to look at it, Connor. Your world has changed forever.'

'I don't understand.'

'You will now be screwed beyond what you really understand.' Zachery hung up.

Connor took the phone away from his ear and stared down on it. There were many texts waiting for him. The first was from Zachery. He clicked the highlighted link and within seconds of it opening, Connor knew what it was.

The footage, obviously shot from Brona's balcony on a phone, showed Connor swinging the slight-framed Finbarr around, before ensnaring him into a full nelson hold. The boy kicked out and tried to wrestle free while tears streamed down his red face. There was no sound. Instead there was music – the theme to *Jaws*. Then the screen went dead.

CHAPTER FIFTEEN

MARY

Where's my husband? How long ago did he leave? Was that five minutes ago or just two? My wrist twitches but I refuse to check my watch and be dismayed at knowing precisely the inevitable drag of time. Finbarr is jumping on the trampoline again and my foot taps to each shriek and thump of the canvas.

I lean against the rail in the corner of the raised decking. Connor's little bungalow is on the same level as our ground floor. So in effect I get to look down on his flat roof, the frosted side window of the bathroom as it lights up and darkens any time he enters, and the dusky zinc of the patio lip. The fact that I know he's just a floor below, five feet away behind the hedge, excites me. Just after Andrew left to call in to him, I could hear Connor's footsteps on his decking. It made me feel like a child creeping out of bed to listen to what it is forbidden to hear – the mysteries of the adult world as seen through the banisters. I love it. It could be a fact that Connor's presence next door will enrich my patio life substantially.

I don't want to like him and it's stupid that I do – especially since he's writing me hate mail. Is that why I've sent Andrew in to him? To ensure that there will be a safe distance between us? To kill those thoughts before they go any further? I don't want to think of Connor that way. Just look at how he dresses. Vain single men have a habit of posing around like they're in a boy band. It's not a look that sits well when they're in their thirties. I wonder what demons there are inside him. I wonder why someone whose job it is to listen and analyse is so rubbish at talking about himself.

I picture myself twenty years ago with him. Would I have liked him? Maybe it's not the young things he chases. Maybe it's the married kind – the kind married for so long that they can hardly remember the brief period of their lives when their husband had faced the future with ambition, confidence, hardness.

What *the hell* am I thinking? Swallowing, my throat feels as if it's closed in on itself. I need to clear my mind but I can't stop thinking about him. I don't want to stop thinking about him. A man like Connor – a bachelor in a neighbourhood like this – he would tempt any housewife. Especially if the wife was a gentle, selfless, virginal angel before she'd gotten married. And that's what I was. No. Wait. Yes. *Forget the laneway.* It's as they say – there's no better wife than a ruined good girl. And a ruined good girl makes men live longer. Because without sex, their prostates begin to calcify. *Damn the laneway.* Because I'm not going to make Andrew, or any man, live longer. The laneway ruined me, but not in the way any man would like.

Of course, if I'd married a different man to Andrew – a more experienced man, a man who recognised a repressed Catholic girl as a prime candidate for corruption – then it all would've worked out splendidly. I often wonder what that version of me would've been like – that rewired, updated model.

There's that bloody voice again. The man on the lane. He hadn't just jumped on his bike and cycled off without saying anything. He'd been laughing. And just before he'd thrown his leg over the crossbar, sat astride the saddle and left me behind forever, he'd pecked me on the cheek and spoken one final time.

We shouldn't have done that.

What he did is still inside me and therefore can never be washed away. If I think about it for too long it makes me want to vomit – but vomiting has never dispelled it. It's the thought of my body's integrity being breached – it just never becomes normal. I can never get used to it. And because it has happened, there's just no taking it back. So, you just put that mess in a box. Lock it. Bury it deep. Throw away the key. What's done is done. Mother taught me that.

Leaving the patio, I walk through the hall, into Finbarr's bedroom and look out the window. Andrew's Land Rover is gone. Has he already spoken to Connor and waved the knife at him? A pang of disappointment jolts me. But what had I been expecting? Explosions and gunshots and the clash of steel from next door's patio? Or maybe Andrew to return with Connor's bloodied head on a platter? I don't know what's wrong with me. Well, I do. It's guilt. Guilt towards my debauched, illicit thoughts.

Back in the kitchen, I once again consider what a rewired, remodelled version of me would've been like and I realise I can't do it any more. Because I'd always have Emer and Brona as my sisters. And the person I am is because of them. So, I could only be a different person if neither of them had ever existed. Emer in particular.

Even though Emer was eight years younger than I, and we'd never shared a room, we had once been *very* close. Before the laneway at the back of the church, we'd both absolutely believed that there was no believing or disbelieving in God – you either knew Him or you didn't.

But after the laneway, I lost my faith. It was inflicted with a fatal wound by the man on the bike. My parents had no idea anything had changed except for my tastes in music and literature. When I finished school, my parents wanted me to go to America and do a business master's at an ultra-modern Christian business school in Maine. But I was adamant that I would do English in a big old European university full of robes, cricket fields and societies. I just *had* to do literature. Novels had the answers – not the Good Book.

After that, so much happened really quickly. First my father disowned me. That still hurts so much. We had always been close. When I was a teenager he could talk to me like an adult and sometimes told me things that he knew he shouldn't. I was too young to hear about his problems. But I listened. I was always such a considerate girl. But it was our registry office wedding that finally did it. Mother came but Father didn't; instead he sent a note describing his disappointment, his sense of (unexplained) betrayal, and his absolute certainty that I'd committed the biggest mistake of my life by not only marrying a Protestant who was seven years older than me but a Protestant who didn't even believe in his faith.

I couldn't handle my father. There's a simple rule you must obey when dealing with very religious people – you don't. People who think they've heard the voice of God cannot be reasoned with. And so I waited and waited for him to cool down. I missed Dad, and each day that passed was a day that I knew was going to bring me closer to finally mending ways with him. I knew that soon he would be there for me once again and ready to get to know Andrew for the great lovely man he is.

But Dad never got the chance because shortly after I married, Emer broke his heart and he died. Within five years, Mother was dead too. Emer killed our parents, one after the other – with shame and disappointment.

But over the last seventeen years Emer's personal sense of self-loathing has manifested itself into an intimate hatred of me. The few times I've seen her since our father died – at funerals and weddings – the abhorrence would be blazing in her eyes. That's the thing about every family unit. Each member gets to invent a history and soak in their personal version of all the injustices.

The core of all families is an ugly thing – rotten with the disappointments, the disgust.

The doorbell chimes. It's not Andrew – he has his own key. I open the door to Brona.

'Wasn't expecting you until tomorrow,' I say.

'Well, I'm picking up poor Kitty-Kat next door, so thought I'd pop in. See how things are. Maybe throw a Molotov from your patio over the wall at that bloody dog. Let's see how he likes chewing on that.'

Well, at least she isn't blaming Finbarr. Wait – *she* was next door?

'You were *next door*? With *Connor*?'

'Yes. And yes, I owe you an explanation. A big one. C'mon. Bring me in.' She pushes open the door even though I was leaning against it and marches through into the kitchen. I follow her as if it's me who's just called in.

Finbarr is taking a break from the garden and is sitting on the sofa on the other side of the kitchen, his legs tented and the laptop across his narrow thighs.

Brona places her elbows on the island counter and, resting her chin in the palms of her hands, says to me, 'Is *that* Dad's cap?'

'Yes.'

'Right. And why is he wearing Dad's cap?'

'It suits him.'

She curtains her face with her hands and whispers, 'Jesus.'

I sigh and look away. Brona needs to be more supportive of Finbarr. She needs to accept him as one of us. Brona can be so self-centred, so selfish, so spoilt.

Finbarr is looking at her with his wide blue gaze. Already you can see the man he's growing into. His face shows the last flushes of that changing teenage seismic shift.

'Good to see ya, Auntie Brona. Real good. Real… real… *goood*. Just want you to know I respect your lifestyle choices. The vaping and the booze. There's nothing worse than seeing yoga chicks obsessed with showing off their perfect yoga bodies on social media. It's so pointless, yeah? I mean, you can keep your perfect body if you're not going to abuse it. And I like the way you abuse *your* perfect yoga body, Auntie Brona.'

Brona and I both ignore him. He's always trying to instigate embarrassment. It's like he owns a mortification laser ray. But we're used to it, and one day he'll have gone away and life will be back to its normal station. Until then, we just have to be aware of his terrible background, the failure of parenthood, the absence of any normal childhood – and, of course, it's also an adolescent thing. His hormones are bouncing around inside him. And yes – it *is* embarrassing. But the fact is, my baby sister is very attractive. It doesn't matter that she's ten years younger than me; I've *never* looked like a Brona. And that had never bothered me until she moved to the neighbourhood – to the bottom of my garden, to be precise.

Finbarr keeps talking, the way he usually does when he's being ignored. 'Aunt Brona, it's cool the way you keep yourself so hard and trim without giving up living. You know, health freaks and gym bunnies – they're so boring, they don't even get the odd routine from a stand-up. But in boxset land and console games – where it *matters* – the alcoholic is romanticised. Films, games and TV shows get made about people like you and Aunt Mary and Uncle Andy. The best actors play them, even novels and plays are written about them – or so the characters say on the games and boxsets a halfwit, troubled, almost-orphan like me, watches. Anyway, Aunt Brona – keep drinking and vaping and working out and looking like that and soon, like Mary and Andy, you'll be so very fucking now.'

'Language,' I say. 'And be quiet.'

Brona asks, 'Finn, maybe you should try *disconnecting* when indoors. Like, read something. Don't you have a favourite writer?'

Finbarr isn't finished with me. 'Or what, Aunt Mary? You'll have me locked away, like my mother?'

Brona persists, 'I said—'

'I heard you, but I thought you were kidding.'

Brona smiles. 'By just sitting on the sofa, watching, smiling, you're like a fish in an aquarium. Is that what you want to be?'

'Yeah,' he answers with exaggerated boredom. 'I'm a *fish*. A big *fish*. It's what I've always wanted to be. Obviously. When I grow up big and strong I want to go to the university of *fish* and study *fish* and then teach *fish*.'

'You're a shark,' Brona muttered.

I stare at my little sister. There was no need for that. But I can't help myself and immediately think of Finbarr's shark-like smile when he's destroying another Wikipedia page. I think of Finbarr's shark-like smile moments after punching the wall non-stop for five minutes. I think of his shark-like smile when a bowl of boiled spaghetti with no sauce, or a plate with chips with no ketchup, or burgers with no dressing, is placed before him because he hates anything with flavour. I think of his shark-like smile when he was inside his mother killing his twin.

Brona looks at me and I subtly shake my head – *stop*. She reddens slightly; her apology and regret are communicated by her sucking in her lower lip.

But, alas, Finbarr heard her and says, 'Nothing wrong with sharks.'

Brona's remorse instantly vanishes and she says, 'Unless you're attacked by them… incessantly.'

'Know what a shark is that doesn't attack, Auntie Brona?'

'What?'

'A shark that doesn't attack is a dolphin. And you know what a dolphin is?'

'Yes, Finn, I do know what a dol—'

'It's delicious. That's what a dolphin is.'

For a second too long Brona stares at him. But then she catches herself and does what she's really excellent at – dismissing him. She scoots about the kitchen like it's hers and grabs two wine glasses. Though, of course, Finbarr doesn't mind – it means he can watch her twist and turn and bend without interruption. If used properly, beauty is a type of international passport into anywhere. And Brona uses her beauty properly. Sometimes I wish she wasn't my sister. Then I could decide that she was an idiot, the way some people like to decide that the very beautiful *are* idiots: bereft of depth or darkness, no interior life whatsoever. And just like that, I hate myself with every fibre of my being. I never wanted to be this kind of person; the kind that holds another woman's beauty against her.

Thankfully Finbarr has lost interest and is once again staring into the blue light of the laptop – as usual, he's sought out the only company that will have him. He's wearing his gaming headset beneath his cap as he always does when online. Not that he talks to anyone – the microphone part just hangs there like a big black fly hovering before his mouth. But he likes to sample the white noise sound files that he has a habit of infecting random Wikipedia pages with. He presses a button and music starts blasting through the headphones, forming a wall of powerful noise to keep the world at bay.

'Love the hair, Mary-Contrary,' Brona says, hands inches above her hips, fingers resting over the corrugations of her ribcage. 'It gives you an even more… *distinctive* look.' Her sugary tone bores into my ears.

'You think so?' I ask, but not really asking, just fishing for another compliment because that's less irritating compared to the alternative of not being able to take one.

'Uh-huh.'

Nodding down at her red sneakers, I say, 'They're nice.' They are not nice. I get out a bowl and fill it with crisps. She never eats them but I live in hope. Brona has always had a city body. Clearly junk food will never be her consoler in the early hours of the morning.

'So,' she says while demonstrating her well-practised routine of taking down a bottle of wine – this time a Salice Salintino. 'What were you up to before I rudely interrupted?'

'Nothing much. Just cooking. Keeping the steaks in the oven for when Andrew gets back. He likes them rare… but too late now.' I lean on the island counter opposite her, both of us ignoring the background noise emanating from Finbarr's makeshift electronic headquarters on the sofa. Holding my wine glass in such a way as to make sure the fingers of my left hand are facing her, I blast Brona with the sight of my wedding and engagement rings. It's as if I'm trying to dazzle a teacher by reflecting the sun with a glass ruler.

Brona's finger lacks a wedding band, and even though she has never bemoaned the fact that she is not married, it feels like a harsh and unavoidable judgement about her; a judgement that evens things up between us. *I have ended up with a husband and you haven't. I did things the correct way. And you – despite all your fun and freedom and money and travel and business success – you have failed at such a simple task.*

'Brona, when I was texting you about the cat, I told you that there's someone living next door to me. I thought—'

'Yeah, I know. Only found out yesterday.'

'Yesterday?'

'Uh-huh. It's… it's awkward.'

I touch my ring again and allow myself to embrace totally, without guilt, the unaccountable suspicion that I can't trust her. And that suspicion always comes down to a litany of superficial things; she's younger than me, successful, happy and very pretty. In other words, the problem is and always will be that Brona is the type of woman who has the power to lie all the time simply because people will believe her.

I say, 'Start at the beginning.'

'OK, well—'

'No. Wait. You were just next door with him. Connor. What's he like? Fill me in.'

'You've talked to him. You already know what he's like.'

'We only had a brief conversation. Just told him about Finn. A neighbourly thing, really. Tried to put all that messy stuff with the dog and Finn behind us. He's… totally harmless.'

'Harmless,' Brona repeats as if it's the most offensive thing one could say about anyone.

'Well, what's he like?'

'What do you mean?' Brona won't look at me. She swirls her wine about as if she's wondering how to change the subject. It's unusual behaviour for her – there's generally nothing she won't talk about. She's a forward woman.

'What's. He. Like?' She's annoying me now. Who cares if she wants to flirt with Connor? She wouldn't have to try hard. Brona is a woman who is always noticed when she enters a room. 'What is it? Feel guilty that you like him after what he did to Finn? That you don't really want to… you know? Say nice things.' I laugh awkwardly, making light of it. 'I mean, I know he's funny. Like any cool villain, he has his good side.'

Brona doesn't reciprocate my laughter. Instead her eyebrows raise as she says, 'I don't feel any of that. It's something else. About Zach. I'll get to it. But Connor… I just met him. He's OK. No. He's nice. Interesting, I suppose. He's some type of therapist. Did you know that?'

'Yes, he told me. Therapy, though – doesn't really fix people, does it? It's not really a cure, yes? Psychotherapy just makes you take an obvious truth about yourself and consider it a deeply felt intellectual revelation. Like… my parents messed me up. Wow – stop the press. But don't get me wrong – I don't think it should be banned or anything. If certain people want their therapy and crystals and angel healers and what have you, then what is science to tell them what to do with their health? Let them have it. It's the medicine they deserve.'

'Oooh, cold, Mary. But I think you're wrong with therapy. It is sciency. Like acupuncture and herbal medicine.'

'Nonsense. It's more like a religion. Maybe Buddhism? You know, like, it has excellent answers to stupid questions.'

'You. Are. On. Fire. But do you think it's that easy – that if you want to change yourself then all you have to do is shout orders loudly down your brainstem? Therapy helps people. I know lots of people in it. I know lots of people who *should* be in it.'

She matches my gaze for a moment too long.

I say, 'I've met lots of psychologists of one kind or another. And I still don't rate it. Connor probably became one because he feels insecure or worthless and so wants to be around fuck-ups who make him feel competent and normal.'

Brona is shocked. I rarely curse. I've blown my cover. It means I'm annoyed. But before she can say anything, Andrew walks in. Brona thins her lips and flattens the collar of her white shirt, narrowing the exposure of flesh in the V beneath her neck. I've seen her around other men and she certainly doesn't act like that. It's just my husband. Her self-obsession is embarrassing – as if Andrew would actually be trying to see down her deeply décolleté suit from way over there.

'Would you like me to top that up?' I ask Brona in my changing-the-subject voice.

She covers the top of her glass with a palm and shakes her head.

Andrew reaches out for an apple but changes his mind and washes his hands first, which he wouldn't have done if Brona wasn't here. *Men.*

'So how's Zach?' Andrew asks, like a shy schoolboy, the whiskey capillary bloom across his nose reddening further.

'Zach is Zach.'

'He's at home now… all alone?'

'Suppose.' Then summoning some gusto, Brona enquires, 'So what's the story, Andy? How's things?'

'Same-same,' my husband replies, and Brona ignores the sadness in his voice, the downward gravity pull of everything contained in that remark. Each time I witness Andrew's silly crush in action, it surprises me. Fine, even if marriage isn't a magical ceremony that has the power, overnight, to make a husband not want other women, I still wish he wouldn't let me down like this.

'I got my big sis' to raid your stash,' she says, holding up the glass by the stem.

'Ah, Salice Salintino – good choice, pet,' he says to me. 'Brona, remember when you saw my collection downstairs for the first time? What did you say?' He pauses as if waiting for an answer but is actually summoning a moment of great personal triumph. '"Your personal stock makes the Roman Empire look like a midlands backwater". That was it, wasn't it?' He then chuckles, basking once again in the memory of all that attention and praise.

Andrew places a netted bag of mandarin oranges on the counter and says, 'Oh, I picked these up for you.' I hadn't asked him to get them but they're my favourite snack. He must have discovered that Brona was next door and went to the shops instead and saw the oranges and thought of me and bought them. Just a simple thing. It emphasises the meanness of my thoughts. Back in the early days of our marriage he used to buy me fussy jewellery – the type a man would buy his mother – and then sulk when I didn't wear it. I'd liked him moping more than the fact he'd bought me jewellery. It meant he cared emotionally. It meant he'd invested himself, rather than just money, in the gift.

'Mary, I'll get my dinner later. Just leave it in the oven. Right, ladies, time for me to leave you to your gossiping. I'm sticking on earphones downstairs, so if you need me, don't roar. You'll have to descend to my lair.' Andrew then takes a bow and exits to the hall and the stairs down to Hades – that cave where Andrew finds the space and time to think about things that he would presumably never talk to me about – or maybe he just stares out the window through his telescope to the sky and whatever, letting the view suck his mind clear. Who knows? I rarely go down there, and when I do, I make it quick. Each time it's like surprising someone in prayer. Like, I want to apologise and swiftly close the door. He's never said it, but we both know I don't belong in the basement.

'And there he goes,' Finbarr suddenly exclaims too loudly from beneath his raging earphones and without even looking up. 'Down, down, down, to his garden shed that he cleverly built underground. Mum goes on about Granddad's shed. He used to fix bikes in it, right? You married your da, Auntie Mary. When's he gonna move his bed down there? That's what he wants to do, ya know. He'd love that. Just him, his precious weird telescope, his bed, his bar. Pretty lit, man. Pretty lit.'

Finbarr's right. Andrew should have built himself a shed. A shed with insulation and electricity and anything else he needs. A shed at the end of the garden where it should be – rather than down there, too bloody close, always beneath my feet.

Brona says, 'C'mon, let's get some air,' and without waiting for permission, takes her wine and strolls out onto the balcony. Finbarr, too, gets up and leaves the kitchen, heading back to his bedroom. With no choice, I follow Brona outside.

Looking down the garden and over the hedge to the back of her own house, my sister balances her wine glass on the rail and takes out her vaporiser. She sucks on it. Then – so much steam.

'You're like an old train engine,' I mutter.

'You not going to light up?'

I have a good poker face because usually nothing fazes me. This time I'm fazed.

Brona laughs. 'I won't tell. Promise. Hubby is downstairs playing air guitar or whatever.'

'I… I don't smoke.'

'We see you. Just like we can see Connor next door. In the reflection of the glass behind you. And the smoke drifts out above the hanging plants like they're chimneys. And at night the tip glows – you know? Like, that's what fire does, yeah?'

Smiling, as if I think she's really funny, I sip the wine. Why does she think she's earned the right to talk down to me: *me*, her big sister. Everything was just laid out before her. Unlike Emer and I, Brona's upbringing didn't try to ensure a sinkhole of a life. But luck only lasts a lifetime if you die young. She'll get hers yet.

Brona says, 'Actually, I've been meaning to ask – why don't you vape?'

'Because fake cigarettes can't kill you.' I'm staring at her with undisguised hostility which Brona either chooses to ignore or does not see. It was supposed to have been *me* on this balcony spying up at *her*. And I had often felt guilty about it. But now I see that all along it had been Brona who was the sick voyeur.

'This has been the strangest day, Mary. I mean, you wouldn't believe what's happened.'

'Our father always said that "anything can happen in twenty-four hours. After all, the world was made in six days". You wouldn't remember that.'

She blinks for a second longer than normal. 'Two days ago, I was someone else totally. I don't even recognise myself now.' Her eyes well up. Is she about to cry? Her usually crystal-clear eyes are suddenly smeared with rosy slicks.

'I said it already but nice new red sneakers,' I say, thinking, *they bring out your bloodshot eyes.*

'What? Oh. Thanks. Again. Anyway, there's lots of explaining, and it also includes why there's a tenant next to you that I never told you about. You must've thought that had been bloody weird.'

Bloody right I did. 'Not at all – it's your business. You don't owe me any explanations. Ever.'

'Look, it's a long story but… as I was telling you, I only found out yesterday that the bungalow was rented… Well, I'll get to that but the fact is, I'm kind of in shock. Because Zach and me are done.'

I squeeze the stem of my wine glass to make sure it doesn't drop. 'But you and Zach. You're so happy. You two… you have it sussed. What's happened? What's changed?'

'It's like, I have only one chance left. Only one chance, and if I don't take it then I'll have nothing left – no future tense.'

'But you two: so young, so together. God, you were born to nestle into each other like spoons in a drawer.'

'It's biology. Our genes aren't meant to mix.'

'Hardly fair to Zachery. He is who he is and that was good enough for you the last three years.'

'Come on, Mary – you're my big sister. Stop automatically laying on the sympathy for "the other". Zach's "I-had-an-unconventional-upbringing" story is the one area in which he has traction in the sympathy market. Fine, an allowance must be made for him, the poor unloved child that he was. But that's then. This is now. The fact is, I haven't changed. And he hasn't changed. And *that's* the problem.'

'Are you sure you haven't changed? Because something has, and if it isn't Zachery, then—'

'I *haven't* changed,' my little sister states again, coldly, like I'm an employee challenging her. 'Zach, from the beginning, pushed and prodded me to transform into the woman he wants me to be. That was fun. A power struggle within a relationship keeps things ticking along nicely.' She puts on a sleazy Transylvanian accent and says, 'A master–master relationship, ha-ha-haaa.'

When she sees that I'm not even smiling, she continues. 'But then that's meant to end. You know, at some stage you accept the other for who they are. But it hasn't ended. It's got more intense – the prodding and pushing. And I don't like it any more. I haven't liked it for a while.'

'He wants children, right? And you're open to them. You've said that before. Just not now.' I don't know why Brona doesn't have the child that she's keeping on the long finger. One day, sooner rather than later, even a woman like Brona will have no eggs left. What is she scared of? 'That's all very... well, blah, in terms of relationship quarrels. I mean, it's not like he's having an affair or is a secret gambler or something. This is something that most couples can sort out with a plan. You can't just walk away like that. It's so... so catastrophic in outlook.'

'Nah,' Brona says, as if I've just offered her a packet of peanuts. She slips her vaporiser inside her suit jacket and retreats back inside to the kitchen. 'The kid thing is just a symptom – a token to what he really wants.'

'And what's that?' I ask, once again forced to follow behind.

'What most men want from their partner or wife. They want us to be some type of shiny surface to reflect back the self he wants to see. And I'm done with saying "no". And he'll never be done with asking.'

'You're very sure of yourself.'

'Uh-huh.' She places her glass on the island and folds her arms across the marble. 'I've made a mess of things. Zach has made a mess of things. You wouldn't believe what he's gone and done. You wouldn't believe what he's been spending his time doing. It's so depressing. I mean, we're relatively smart people, me and him. How didn't we see it from the start? How come it took three years? The fact is, our relationship proved to have the emotional shelf life of radioactive waste: lasting for three years instead of ending when it should have – after about six weeks.'

She's probably right about everything she's saying. But it's disturbing how she came up with all of it so suddenly. When people realise they're in a bad relationship they still usually suffer on through months, *years* of it, before getting the confidence and courage to walk away. But not my little sister. She knows herself.

She knows exactly what she wants. She knows how to get it. That refusal to suffer like the rest of us… it makes her seem so bloody spoilt. It's like dealing with an automaton programmed for perfection, a person that simply cannot make a mistake. It's not normal. Talking to her can be soul-destroying.

'Mary, I know what I'm doing. I've thought about it a lot.'

She doesn't even want my opinion. Why does she tell me things? She already knows precisely what she's going to do and she has no doubt. Doubt: that spark that gives us all our humanity. Brona seems to imitate emotions rather than feel them. It suits her preference to err either on the side of wild enthusiasm or disinterest.

'Zach and me are finished. I'm ending it. It's the best thing for us. For me.'

Brona succeeds at everything she tries. Even the failure of her love story with Zach has been turned into a textbook example of how to conclude a relationship with clear thinking and the minimum of fuss and drama. But underneath it all, it's just self-obsession. Because if we all did that – acted like and thought like Brona – then how many marriages would survive a year? It's not normal to win at whatever life throws at you. She must be cheating at it. She *has* to be. That must be how she hides the fact that she's a hysterical neurotic like the rest of us.

'Well, Mary? You're very quiet. Don't you want to know why? Don't you want to know what I've just found—'

'Sometimes your very existence gnaws at me.' I hear the sentence, hardly believing that it's my voice that just said it.

She squints, as if I'm suddenly in the distance and she's not sure it's me. Wrinkles appear like withered petals around her eyes. She'll be a pretty older woman.

'Who do you think you are, Brona? The king and queen of absolutely everything and everyone that you survey?'

'Where did *that* come from? Whatever I've done to—'

'Oh, just stop it, Brona,' I snap, feeling my heart pounding, each pulse sounding the arrival of another stainless-steel thought. 'Pleading the fifth about everything is pathetic.'

'Oh my God.'

'You're too shiny, Brona. Something so bloody flawless is… can be… by its very essence, nothing but a huge bloody irritating flaw. It's like by being superhuman, you're not human.' Anger has always given me the clarity to examine my feelings in a new light; to look at things from a new, hyperaware perspective. 'And since you want to be a flawless person, you fail at that spectacularly by not being a *fucking* person. If only everyone else could see you as I do.'

'I can't believe you're saying this to me.'

'Yes, I'm saying this to you. But are you listening? Are you taking it in? The essence of what I'm saying? I don't think so. I'm not sure it can make it past the firewall that blocks everything in the world that you don't want to hear.'

A cable seems to snap in the structure of Brona's composure. Then a second one. Suddenly the entire bridge tumbles over the edge. She sweeps the drinks onto the floor – a gesture of pure cinema. The two wine glasses shatter and the liquid splatters everywhere, burgundying further the burgundy rug. The immediate impulse is to grab a cloth and start minimising the damage. But it's superseded by the instinct to be calm and unperturbed so I can finally end this.

Finbarr strolls back into the kitchen and takes off his earphones. He stares at the mess on the floor and says, 'I just love these family get-togethers. So much shared history. So many happy memories. You're all such open books. No resentments. No secrets. All light and day. I love you both. I love being here. I can't for the life of me think why Mum hates you, Aunt Mary. And it seems Brona does, too. Silly Brona – doesn't she know how to play this game?' Then he walks by as if we're not there, his bare feet padding on the kitchen floor, smiling and whistling as he strolls outside to the garden.

Brona stares at me for a moment. Then she snorts and says, 'Just listen to yourself. The viciousness. It's incredible. And from nowhere.'

'Oh, come on, Brona, is that the best you can do? Christ, your entire essence is just an act. It's charm. That's all. And what's charm? It's just a trick. It's easy really. Just behave unto others as if they're about to become rich and famous.'

'Wow. Just wow.'

'You probably thought you were being charitable coming here every second day with the gift of your presence. My set-up here with Finn and everything else, it just makes you feel good about yourself in so many ways. But you're just a bloody sadist.'

'Excuse me?'

'Coming here, soaking up my life and inside, behind those eyes, alone in the chill of your mind, you can sit back and watch the show, thankful that none of this is yours. That none of this can touch you. That your life is simple and glorious and not mine. And you enjoy being here the way Andrew and Zach enjoy some sick HBO show.'

'I *enjoy* being here? Like, the way you enjoy Emer being locked up? Like the way you enjoy denying the past? The way it's *your* fault that she's locked up? That you... you didn't just let it happen, you *made* it happen, you *ensured* it would happen? You basically killed her, Mary. And not six months ago when you just got rid of the body by putting it into a mental hospital. But eighteen years ago. That's when you killed her. Oh yeah, the only thing I learned off you is that you can kill a person and yet leave them alive. I know everything, Mary. Everything. You have no secrets left. Got that? No. *Fucking*. Secrets.'

Ignore. My arms have folded. I don't know when.

Brona rambles on, her face petulantly childlike. 'You actually think I have to come here to think of you, to see you, to ponder over everything you've done – or what you didn't do? The fact is,

I hear it from my house every day. You have aimed it all at me with Finbarr in the garden screaming and singing and bouncing and kicking that bloody ball. I have to put my hands over my ears about ten times before noon. I've been hiding beneath the blankets in broad daylight trying to blot him out. How do you do it?'

'I do it because *somebody* has to. We're not all focused on just our own needs. We're not all able to use our career as excuses not to be around to help.'

'You do it because underneath it all you know it's your fault. Finbarr is a mistake. He shouldn't exist. But he does. And he's Emer's. And there were *so* many things that could've been done with Finn but weren't. You only decided to help when it was too late. You could've done earlier – when it would've mattered. Instead you wait and wait and *then* decide to bring him here. But, of course, like I said, something within you enjoys having that shark swimming about inside your house.'

'Stop calling him a shark.'

'You said that Kitty-Kat jumped from Finn's arms over the wall…? Oh my God, he tried to kill my cat.'

'We don't know that. Is that what *he's* still saying, next door?'

'He never said anything.'

'Liar.'

'Psychopathy isn't a sickness. It can't be cured. Psychopathy is a defect. A design fault. People like that need to be taken off the shelf. A factory recall.'

'Brona! Oh my God!'

'That's *not* what I mean. You *know* what I mean. Jesus!'

'No, I don't. Brona, you really hate him, don't you?'

'Of course I don't. That's not what I'm saying. I mean, I thought I had it bad living all my adolescent years *alone* at home with no one but a depressed widow as a mother – so after what he's been through, it's a miracle he's turned out so well. Look, Mary, did you know that certain sharks are so vicious their embryos eat each other in the womb? They develop teeth and cannibalise the weakest until only the biggest is left. The strongest, the hungriest – that's the one that gets born. Finbarr. Gangly, slight, bony Finbarr with a temper that can frighten even your big sergeant major downstairs.'

'Andrew is excellent with him.'

'Stop lying to yourself, Mary. How do you live like that? How can you take it? When you know… when you know that it's—'

'This would be the dullest conversation I've ever had, but a conversation only happens when two people speak.'

'Speak then. Speak!'

'Oh yes. I've plenty to say. We're two smart women, Brona. Let's not pretend that we both didn't realise the pathetic nature of this ridiculous relationship. You know the truth. I know the truth. And that truth is the exact reason why we can never be real sisters. We can never be there for each other. You should never have come back. Back here. To Dublin. To St Catherine's Hill. To my bloody back garden. You should've stayed away. You weren't wanted. You *aren't* wanted. Why are you looking at me like that? Oh my God, don't tell me I've actually overestimated your intelligence? Tell me that all along, you *knew* this? Well? Did you know?'

She crosses the kitchen, being considerate enough not to walk across the wet patch of wine and fastens her suit jacket. 'Did know. Couldn't give a shit.'

Brona then marches into the hall and just before exiting, turns and says, 'You should never have brought Finbarr here. It was the worst thing you could've done. The very worst thing.' And then she's gone. And I'm surprised – almost impressed – that she didn't slam the door.

Quickly I rush through the hall where I can hear the tinny sound of Bruce Springsteen and the E Street Band blaring through earphones in the basement and then I enter Finbarr's bedroom.

There she goes, down the driveway. But she stops, sits up on the wall and swings her legs over to Connor's side like she's ten years old. Bitch.

So that's it. She's gone from my life. Why have I done this? I'm the one with so much to gain from our relationship. She actually takes time out from the multicoloured adventure of her everyday existence to sympathise with the grey mayhem of my house. And I just let her go. There's an overwhelming urge to call out to her. Our parents hated us sisters fighting. Not Brona and I – Emer had killed Dad before Brona was old enough to be interesting. But they hated Emer and me fighting, and as long as Mother was alive we tried not to. Mother had never responded well to emotion. Mother had never really done confrontation. Mother knew what control was.

I remember her sitting opposite me in my bedroom, asking, 'What's wrong, Mary-Contrary?'

And it came out, everything I'd been storing inside. Pouring and pouring forth. It didn't emerge in words. But in tears and gulps, gasping breaths to feed yet more tears as hysteria tried to communicate my abhorrence of my own body, a repugnance of the flesh, a dread of physical proximity, a suspicion of the opposite sex.

And Mother moved to sit beside me on the edge of the bed and she hugged me, she squeezed me, and she said, 'There, there, let it all out, hold nothing back. Better out than in.' Soon I'd calmed and she asked, 'Are you ready yet? Can you tell me what happened?'

I just covered my face with my hands, elbows on my knees. I couldn't. I wouldn't dare.

But she said, 'Are you being bullied?' Silence. 'Mary-Contrary, is it a boy? Did a boy break your heart?'

And then I saw it again – the blood, the moisture, the infection – everything that was now broken, and I started crying again but this time I *could* speak and with my face still covered by my hands and Mother's arm tight around my shoulder, I told her what had happened in the laneway behind the church. I left nothing out. How it hurt. The liquids. The internal cuts. The discharge. The books I'd looked up in the library to get rid of bacterial infections. And when I'd finished, I waited.

Mother sat there for what must have been a full minute with her arm around me. Then she removed it. She rose from the side of the bed and once again sat down on the chair on the far side of the room. She waited until my hands lowered and revealed my sodden, snotty, destroyed face. Her expression was calm. Her eyes soft. They understood.

And then she said, 'Mary, why should the world be a better place for you than it was for me?' I remember not breathing. I remember the sound of my beating heart just stopping. But that didn't happen. It had just felt that way, because I was deafened by the sudden silence of the bedroom. Then Mother stood and opened the door to the outside landing where Father was passing on his way to the bathroom. She looked back at me and smiled. 'Come on, Mary, you'll put this behind you. And we'll never talk of it again. So is everything fine now? Is everything better?'

'Yes, Mum.'

'Well done,' my mother had said, as if I'd passed my driving test.

And I never spoke of it again and everything became fine. So, I'll let Brona go from my life and I'll box away those feelings that are here now: the fear, guilt and sadness. Because they're nothing much. Or they *will be* nothing much soon. I'll miss her and then, after some time, I won't miss her. That's the way it goes. Life is too busy for silly dramas and little spoilt sisters like Brona who can be such a drain. A favour has to be answered by another favour and the courtesies become a chain that imprisons us both. Well, I've broken that now. I've freed us. One day she'll look back at this and be grateful.

From the window I watch her as she disappears into the little bungalow. I picture her next door, face-to-face with Connor. Yes – she's sexually forward but willing to be dominated by the right man. I mean, Brona was never a good girl, was she? She was always a little 'out there'. Always a little wild. Now – her and Connor; God, I can see it.

She's probably stepped into his hallway, like a call girl who reckons that she has the best job in the world. What are they talking about? Me? She's obviously interested in him outside of simply appreciating a single young-ish man's attentions. She probably thinks he's interested in her mind, in her life. And in turn, Brona already feels a connection; she feels that he knows something about her that others don't. She sees his psychology skills the way a seventeenth-century African girl views a witch doctor. And that's disappointing. But the chemistry between them probably embraces the entire periodic table. Brona would know very well that casual disdain works perfectly on men like Connor. Plus eyeliner. And cleavage. And, like most men, Connor will somehow still actually think that he is in charge of it. He genuinely will have no idea that Brona steered him all the way, dropping hints that even he could pick up, letting him get her alone over the damaged cat, over the loud, crazy boy next door who happens to be her nephew, over being new to the neighbourhood. She's a snake, hypnotising him with her big hazel eyes and that smooth voice of hers. She doesn't have memories of church laneways to hold her back. She doesn't have a long-term marriage to be responsible for. She can just look at a man like Connor – who would have no idea what he's dealing with – and decide to have him, the way she would a coat in a shop window. Brona's life has been such a cakewalk she's likely always dressed for fun things like seduction. Underneath her suit she's probably wearing a black bra, panties and red-nylon-lace-trimmed stockings – the white sugar of raunchiness. And they won't be itchy or scratch her thighs because she's so used to them being itchy and scratching her thighs. And they'll make her feel sexy because she always feels sexy. And it's *not fair* on Zachery, who is a nice man. He could be told in a letter. An anonymous letter. They work. Wait – *what* am I thinking?

Turning my wedding band, I imagine rubbing Brona out like a mistake on a drawing. Time to get on with my day. Entering the kitchen, I have every intention of cleaning up the mess on the floor – the broken glass, the pooling wine, the destroyed rug. But I keep walking and, unlike Brona, my slippers glide right through the mess and I continue on outside to the balcony.

In the garden Finn is at the bottom of the steps, eating another plate of cold pasta. Sitting cross-legged on the grass he shovels the food into his mouth with the wooden spoon, demonstrating that he is totally beyond conventional manners. He's like a food mixer churning hungrily. He swallows without chewing – like the shark that Brona says he is. Beside him, a red Coke can is on its side, foaming.

'Auntie Mary, that was something else inside.'

'You ignore it. It's nothing.'

Putting on a Deep South accent, he says, 'Well, I'm just a dizzy blond, so I believe you. But don't go saying that to any brunettes.'

'It was nothing,' I repeat.

'I remember one priest telling Mam that she was to forget about you, to not let her memories of you keep interfering with her sleep, her daydreams, her life, and that you probably meant nothing bad by always towering over her. The priest said, "Older sisters always condescend to their little sisters – it's a sign of affection." But now that I've seen you in action… man, you really are a fucking bitch.'

'Language.'

'Jesus. Respect. No wonder they both hate you. I hope their spite nourishes you. 'Cos if it doesn't, it must be tearing you apart.'

Staring down at the hedge hiding Connor's bungalow patio from being overlooked by our great cruise liner of a house, I whisper, 'Some see what is and ask why? But others see things that aren't and ask why not?' Kennedy paraphrasing George Bernard Shaw. My degree was not wasted.

Finbarr flings aside his bowl of pasta and turns his attention to the can of Coke still resting on its side. Wasps hover over the opening. Finbarr watches as one of them lands and, curious, crawls inside. Staring coldly at me, he picks the can up, covers the opening and shakes. Still staring at me, he drinks from it. Then he says, 'A guy like him next door – he wouldn't do you for practice.'

I want Finbarr back on his feet. I want him bouncing, bouncing, bouncing and singing and kicking his ball. I want to shout, 'Louder, Finn. Louder.' I want to show the new man next door that nothing about his life is acceptable. *Nothing*. If he's so eager to write anonymous letters, to seduce my little sister, to bully my nephew; if he's so keen to get involved in my life, to examine it, to interfere in it, then I'll make damn sure that he'll fall into all our dramas like Narcissus into his own image.

CHAPTER SIXTEEN

CONNOR

The doorbell sounded and he opened it to Brona. Her cheeks were coloured and she was breathing deeply, almost irregularly.

Holding the drink he'd just poured himself, Connor asked, 'Everything OK?'

'Of course not. I was in my mother's womb the last time everything was OK.'

He knew what she meant. 'What's wrong?'

'It's just so stressful in there. I know it's not Finn's fault. His life… Jesus. But still…'

'I'm sure it's tough on everyone.'

'Finn is very special. We all know that. Like, at least Mary, Emer and I do.'

'Yeah.' Connor felt he should add his name to that list but all he could think about was the noise, his reputation, his career and most imperatively – what was unfolding right now on the internet.

'But he also has a shark's way of doing things. He's our blond, blue-eyed, handsome shark. He's a machine that eats and cruises around, his brain and guile urging him from A to B.'

Connor's eyes widened. 'Well, as you said, he's had a different type of life. A difficult upbringing. He's learned to act in certain ways to survive.'

'Survive? He lives here, in St Catherine's Hill. Not in a cave in the mountains of Afghanistan. Not that he'd notice as long as he has meat and spaghetti delivered three times a day and Wi-Fi. And his ball. And his MP3 player.'

'Well…'

'Yeah, fine. I know, I know. Just because he's not autistic or whatever doesn't mean he's not wired differently to us. And he certainly has a different type of intelligence.'

'Exactly. And if he has a different type of intelligence then he needs to feed that intelligence.' Connor had surprised himself. He was sticking up for the young man even though his last sighting of Finbarr was of his raised finger gesturing at him over the hedge just a minute ago. 'After the type of upbringing he's had, we can't possibly comprehend what goes through his mind.'

'Connor, we can't possibly understand what goes through a shark's mind. Except that the end result of its thought process is usually danger for anything in its vicinity.' She sighed with resignation. 'Oh look, I'm waffling. Spending so much time with Mary… Seeing her these past six months has been like watching a vase fall off the shelf. Don't mind me. It's just sibling stuff. And I'm stressed… Have to go to the vet. Lack of time. Other things to do. You know the drill.'

Connor wished he had other things to do. Things like that. Ordinary, dull things. Instead he had nothing to do but to wait and see if the link Zachery had sent him was going to extinguish his future.

Connor led the way into the kitchen but as he approached the sliding door leading to Kitty-Kat, he realised that Brona was no longer behind him. Instead Brona had veered off and was now stepping down into the sunken study. Slowly she walked around his desk, rubbing her hand over the printer, paper ream and opened laptop, like it was all something in a showroom.

'This is where you do your analysing?'

'It's where I'm *meant* to do my sessions. Like, before I realised your boyfriend had ruined my life.' He took a long sip of his drink.

She stared expressionless across the room at Connor and Connor couldn't tell if she was refusing to acknowledge criticism of her partner or whether it simply meant nothing to her. He was beginning to feel like an exhibit. Was that why she was here? To witness Zachery's prey flop about before being pummelled out of its misery? *But remember what Zachery had been saying in session – their relationship was strained. Zachery thought she was losing interest in him. He thought she didn't appreciate him. He feared he loved her more than she did him.*

Connor said, 'What are you going to do about it? Are you going to help me?'

Brona took a step back. 'I'll have to find out what's happening first.'

'I told you what's happening.'

'There's two sides to every story. Three sides to the best ones.'

'Just help me sort it.' Connor didn't appreciate the sudden callousness of her comments – their speedy, careless, go-fuck-yourself spatters. 'Look at the page opened on my laptop.'

'Why?'

'Just do it. Your boyfriend called me. He's very annoyed. And he sent me a link.'

Brona bent over the desk, positioning her face before the screen and read. It was that afternoon's headline on a blog called TheCityJournal.

YOUNG BOY ATTACKED BY NEIGHBOUR FROM HELL

Check this out, folks. A posh resident of fancy St Catherine's Hill is really a bullying asshole who seems to have taken exception to this young child's trampolining on a hot summer's afternoon in his private back garden while his parents were out. See what the asshole does with your own eyes. An innocent bystander saw him barge into this private garden, shout at the child to be quiet before grabbing the poor kid like a rag doll. We're surprised the police haven't arrested the psycho-nut – but then, the police don't like to bother posh bullies like him who need peace and quiet for sipping sherry while 'perusing' the *Financial Times*. VIEWER DISCRETION ADVISED!!!!!!!!!!!!

Brona pressed play on the video and muttered, 'Oh. My. God,' as its contents began to stream to the theme of *Jaws*.

When the footage finished, it looped back to replay and Connor shut the screen over. He said, 'I had just rescued your cat because that prick had tried to feed it to the cuddly Alsatian next door. After nearly been eaten alive, I climbed out of the coliseum just for Finn to punch me in the face. So, I grabbed him. That's where Zachery started filming. Or rather, that's where he *chose* to begin his edit from.'

A fatigue had fallen on Connor, draining him of vitality. His bones felt heavier, his thought processes now seemed too slow, his eyes felt drier, less focused. For the first time in his life he felt every day of his thirty-six years. He'd believed that ageing was a slow and gradual process. But now he realised that it really happens in a sudden rush.

Finally, Brona said, 'Are you sure it's—'

'You do recognise the view from your own balcony, right? I mean, I'm here one day and I can tell—'

Brona's raised finger silenced him. In her other hand was her phone. She held it to her head. 'Zach… call me when you get this. Actually, *don't* call me. Just take down that video. Immediately. Tell TheCityJournal that a mistake was made. Whatever it takes – just get that video down. Now!'

She hung up and looked out the window towards the back of her own house.

Connor said, 'Something like that can kill a person's career. It can ruin a life.'

'That's not going to happen. It's going to be removed. It'll be like it never happened.'

'We'll see. Your boyfriend is out of control. Brona, I need you to help me.' His anxiety was suddenly in the air like a rainforest mist. 'And I don't like to need.'

'There's stuff about Zachery you don't know. You don't understand.'

'Oh yeah? Like what? Like… now you're sounding like maybe you *are* keeping things from me.'

'I've absolutely nothing to hide,' she said, pulling up her shirt to hide the top of her cleavage. A thin, hot line of anger split her smooth brow.

'I'm sorry. I apologise.'

'It's just a social occasion. I'll recover.'

'But you'll help me?'

'You heard me on the phone. Of course I will… Look, Connor, it's just some online blog. I never even heard of it. Have you?'

'No.'

'Well then, don't worry about it. Zach is probably having it taken down now. He's just making a point. A stupid point. He didn't think it through. It's over now.'

Connor put the glass to his lips and sipped and sipped some more and kept sipping, because sometimes when he did that the world would become soft and warm instead of sharp and cold. It was as if he was trying to rinse the contents of the link Zachery had sent him from his mind, his body, his soul. *What. Am I. Going. To do?* Maybe the Health Board wouldn't find out. Maybe the world would move on. He looked around the kitchen. It was full of breakable things and yet not a single item was out of place. It was *he* who felt out of place.

Brona was examining the two seats on either side of the desk. She chose the one facing the garden and sat in it. Connor bristled. That was his seat. As she gently spun to the left and then to the right, he asked, 'Drink?'

'I really shouldn't.'

'That's the point of it. Drink?'

She stopped spinning. 'OK. Whatever you're having.'

'A Harvey Wallbanger.'

'Harvey Wallbanger? They still exist? Awesome. Bring it, fella.'

Connor took down two tall glasses and filled them with ice. Quickly he blasted in two generous doses of vodka and topped them up with orange juice. He stirred the drinks, the silver spoon clanging against the insides of the glasses. Glancing back over, he watched Brona relax into his office chair, twisting it gently from side to side, looking out the window to his small garden and Mary's much larger one. Even in such a mundane setting she was spectacular. Gently, carefully, he poured the vanilla shots over the screwdrivers. In the background was the pounding of Finbarr's football. But it didn't intrude as much as before. Perhaps Connor was getting used to it.

Brona said, 'Let's talk about something else. Let's try and forget about it all. Not because I don't care. I do. But because it's probably a good idea. Think we can do that?'

'We can try.'

'How'd you get into this therapy stuff?'

'By accident. I studied psychoanalysis because I thought it would help explain certain things.'

'What things?'

'Just things.' It was strange having someone ask *him* so many questions for a change. However, there were areas he didn't even like to go to in private reveries. 'I got a first from UCL in Lacanian Philosophy and Practice and they wanted me to set up there in London. But the psychoanalytic community are far too uptight for my liking. I mean, when one of them asks, "How are you doing?" it isn't a polite aside, it's an existential question. And so, wanting a discipline rather than a religion, I switched to psychology, specialising in couples therapy. My girlfriend – *ex*-girlfriend – opened doors to some heavy business people. She was with a Singaporean bank and said I should get a USP of helping with executive stress and simplifying their lives. So that's how I ended up working with the rich and "wonderful" – like your boyfriend.'

'How was your childhood? You had it bad?'

'No worse or better than most people.'

She waited for more and Connor searched his brain for an appropriate memory. But the essence of his childhood escaped him. *Loss* was the only feeling that came to him. 'The worst thing is that I had a bad speech impediment when I was a kid. My mother worked with me and worked with me and worked with me and I'd got rid of it by the time I was ten.'

'A speech impediment at that age must've been frustrating.'

Connor felt a beating in his chest like a panicked bird's wing. But his face showed nothing. 'Nah. Mam took care of it – doing speech exercises. Slowing things down. No need for the mouth to be up to speed with the brain. It was possible to do two things at once. You know – say something and be thinking something else entirely? Useful skill to have. But Mam died just before I'd got it under control. And, yeah, I regret that.'

Crossing the room, Connor stepped down into the sunken area and placed Brona's cocktail on the table.

'What are you? Leo? Virgo?' she asked.

'I'm pissed off, actually. Maybe even emotional. The way people generally get emotional when they could lose their livelihood.'

'Pissed off but contained: a Virgo. Now sit. Over there. Enter my office.'

'I'll stand.'

'Connor, sit down. I mean, you can have your chair back if that's what it takes?'

'Keep it, if you like.'

'I like.'

He rounded the desk, turning his back on the garden, and pulled out the patient's chair. Then he sat straight in it, like an exclamation point.

'Drink,' she ordered.

He drank.

Then Brona sipped. 'It's awfully strong,' she said, as if a Wallbanger could be weak.

'You're welcome.' He took a deep swallow and immediately felt his insides warm. Alcohol was perfect for today – anaesthetic and stimulating at the same time.

Brona took a large gulp from her glass and asked, 'Do you not find it incredible how people with so much make such a cock of their lives?'

'Not really. The source of their unhappiness is usually all their money. It gives them too many tricky options.'

'As in, money is the source of all evil?'

'Nope. Money's just a tool – it's neither good nor bad. Unlike the people who use it.'

'Well, I think money really *is* the root of all evil.' Brona paused for a sip and then continued, her voice smooth caramel. 'Not because of what a person does with it. But because a person who has money is envied and when people are envied, they have enemies. Like Zach. He has money. You don't. You envy him. You're his enemy.'

Connor felt the sting but it passed. Calmly he drained the entire cocktail dry and admired how her spiky thoughts were thrown out into the world with a nice smile and serene delivery. He knew that Brona was simply trying to get a reaction because reactions open people up. Connor rattled about the ice in his empty glass. 'I've never envied Zachery or wished him ill – *ever*. I care for all my clients. I worry about them. And I want them to be happy. So, you need to calm down, Judge Judy.'

'OK. I'll calm down and let you carry on. And while you're doing that, I'm just going to sit here and be right.'

'Jealousy is little boys' work, Brona. You know it. That's what little boys do when they see others with something they can't have. And I'm not a little boy.'

A silence began to stretch. Brona was gazing at him, her mouth somewhat ajar, eyes wide.

'Don't you think I'm smart enough not to waste my life doing something that I don't want to do? I like my clients and my job and I categorically don't care about money.'

She smiled knowingly. 'People who have no money always say that they don't care about money.'

'I hope this isn't an earth-shattering revelation, Brona, but I've no interest in five-star hotels or Kobe steak dinners, and it's not like I want my own Wikipedia page either. And just so I'm clear – is this the way it's going? Like, you're just going to keep jabbing at the buttons until you hit the right one and get the reaction you're looking for?'

Brona's eyes narrowed and that pleased him. Not just because he'd scored a point but because he needed space to get his thoughts in order; because part of him, paradoxically, knew that she was somewhat right. The fact was, he would love to be opposite her in a dark Michelin-starred restaurant. He'd love to be sliding his card into the lock of a luxury hotel suite with Brona waiting over his shoulder. He'd love to impress her with the tasteful ornaments and artworks he'd decorated his architecturally designed home with.

Brona said, 'You got me. Damn, you weren't meant to notice. Normally I can depend on people *not* noticing.' Her accent was becoming more North American shopping mall-ish the more she drank – almost like she was a typical middle-class Dublin teenager rather than thirty years old.

Connor said, 'Anyway, my therapy is just a vessel to get me close to realising my long-term goal. And I've finally done it. It's *this* close to fruition.' He lifted his hands until their fingers were just centimetres apart.

Brona stretched across the table and took his hands in each of her own. Their eyes met. Connor felt himself begin to redden but Brona didn't. Brona released his hands and once again he was adrift. She asked, '*This* close to what?'

Connor breathed in – enjoying the space his chest made for all that extra air. 'I'm helping to set up the Committee of Mental Health and Noise Pollution. It's going to have legal powers and will work in tandem with the Minister of Housing and Dublin City Council.'

'The what?'

'Basically, what we're aiming for – what *will* be done eventually – is stuff like schools starting later. Like companies rewarding—'

'Wait. What?'

'Schools in countries that have later starts correlate with improved IQs,' Connor quickly explained before getting back into his stride. 'Companies should reward sleep because those that do – in America – have seen productivity rise, and motivation levels *and* honesty levels. You know, some companies already give time off if their employees use sleep trackers and record enough of it. It's the future, Brona. And I've started to bring it to Ireland.'

'So, you're influencing policy on education, health and—'

'Uh-huh. The Department of Environmental and Mental Health Epidemiology at Trinity College are also working with me. And I have representatives of the Finnish Government about to come over on an advisory level because they've already implemented their own quality of urban living dictates and they reported on how production was up and people are happier. The Finnish tourist slogan is "Silence, please". Did you know that?'

'Like, duh. Of course not.'

'So I just need to stay afloat with my current business until the green light is given. Which will be in a couple of months, as long as I don't have my current business ruined by, say, a video of me beating up a screaming kid outside my therapy window… or if that doesn't happen, they find out I'm broke and lose all confidence in me.' Connor was finding it hard to suppress the intense dread of what would happen if Zachery didn't take the video down and it went viral.

'You're really doing all that? But why? I mean, I know *why*. But why *you*?' She was looking at him like she was suddenly observing him through distorting glass. Her lips were dry and she quickly licked them smooth again.

Connor stared down into his drained glass, watching the melting ice cubes lose traction and softly clink together as they sank further into the drink. Her gaze – so clear and bright – intimidated him. It was as if he was afraid that she could read his mind and decode his shameful thoughts.

'This is boring. There's nothing more depressing then having a chat where the conversation is all shop.'

She put on a cute British accent and said, 'Oh, do be amusing. I can't bear it when people aren't amusing.'

Connor leaned back in the chair, his arms still folded. 'I hate my family. There. That's the first time I ever mouthed that.'

'Yes – that's good. That's amusing.' Brona looked pleased with herself. It was as if this was all a game and she'd just put him into check – with checkmate imminent. 'Why? Tell me. You know I can keep it on the DL.'

Connor crunched an ice cube. Was it time for another drink? Already? He needed to slow down. He was talking too much. He was too relaxed. He was enjoying being open. That was dangerous and stupid. He wondered if the drink was hitting him. But it couldn't be. He'd only had two and usually needed two just to unwind. *It's the stress. Lack of sleep catching up with me. The ongoing shitstorm of my life. The disaster that's unfolding out there in the world that I should be dealing with right now – but instead I'm talking to her because… because…* Outside, there was no sound of Finbarr. He must've gone back inside. Maybe he was done for the day.

Connor quickly told her his family story – his stammer, his mother dying, his father drinking, his brother Frank becoming feral. 'He was given free rein and that meant the drums. Pounding, pounding the bloody drums all day. And his mates were always around. Blasting music. Shouting. Laughing. Jesus, I had to study, you know? My father had a shop. I didn't want to go into the family business. I wanted to get out. To get away. And I needed results – really good academic results.'

He'd never wanted to speak about his family before. The drink, the wrong side of the desk, her attractiveness, her intelligence, his own financial obliteration in return for disastrous living arrangements, Zachery – gardens away and maybe looking on, the stress of having talked to him on the phone and the ramifications from seeing the link he'd forwarded – it was all making Connor want to treat himself with a little truth, with a little soul-searching.

'How are they now? Your dad and brother.'

Connor's stomach cramped suddenly, at the truth of what happened to them. He smiled to hide his discomfort.

'Well, my father's dead.' Any time he spoke those words aloud, he felt a twinge of guilt. There was a regret there – a regret that he still cared deeply and that he shouldn't. His father had stopped caring when Connor's mother died. 'Over twenty years ago.'

'Sorry,' she said, almost as if she could possibly mean it. 'How did he die?'

'Heart attack.'

'And what about your brother?'

'Frank got the house and threw me out. So I had to work just to eat and pay the rent on a dingy bedsit for three years. The only thing it had going for it was that it was quieter than home. And you know what? That made it a palace.' It felt good to be talking like this – spitting out his words like bullets.

Connor believed that you only got to truly know about a person when you knew about their kin. *So why do I want Brona to really know me?* He felt a tightness in his chest. It was as if words were solid things and they were getting caught in his windpipe. Or maybe he was too full of words that he had to get some of them out.

A silence grew in the room. Brona seemed to be considering everything Connor had just told her. But Connor was looking at his phone, trying to keep away the sense of foreboding that was growing every time they stopped speaking. It was beginning to fizz and ferment inside his head until he couldn't take it any more and reached out to lift up his phone.

Brona said, 'I'd love another. Up for it?'

Connor lowered the phone. 'I'm up for anything.'

She banged her empty glass down beside his and as she crossed the room to the counter, said, 'Let me make the next ones. This time just screwdrivers. OK? Don't act all like you're too good for 'em. OK to open a new bottle?'

'By any means necessary.'

Brona flicked on the stereo and started bobbing her head to the beats that began emanating from the hidden speakers. She called over, 'Connor, does your field make you see the world differently?'

'Yes.'

'Really?' Brona stood still, holding the bottle of vodka a few degrees away from a pour, as if posing for an advertisement. 'When I saw Zachery for the first time ever, I bet I saw the same thing you did the first time he walked into your office.'

'No, you didn't. You saw a very important, self-contained, very busy, toned hunk. I saw a panic attack.'

Her smooth forehead became a Sahara of rolling dunes. 'Hey, you're good.'

'Good? I'm super-great. I don't deliver on my promises. I *over*-deliver on them.'

Brona stirred the ice around in the drinks. 'If I came to you about my boyfriend and after one session you knew my relationship was doomed, over, kaput, how would you tell me to end it?'

Connor smiled. Were they going to talk about Brona and Zachery? Now that would be interesting. 'I'd steer you to it. All my clients have to figure it out for themselves. If I tell them how to do it, they'd just resist it. They'd convince themselves that I didn't know what I was talking about because that would mean they could do what they *want* to do rather than what they *should* do.'

As Brona sipped her way back over to the sunken study, she asked, 'So, I'm in therapy with you – how do you make me realise?'

'First by making you realise where it all went wrong.'

She placed the fresh cocktail before him and Connor could hear the ice rattle. He raised his cocktail in salute. 'In vino veritas.'

The two full glasses touching in mid-air made a deep sound like the chime of a grandfather clock. He sipped and felt its burn.

Brona asked, 'And where would it have all gone wrong?'

'I would assume that it's not a case of the relationship having "gone" wrong. But that it was "wrong" from the very beginning. Some people – a lot of people – choose relationships that are doomed to fail. Look, a bad relationship is kind of like a nasty habit – like chain-smoking. It has its dark, wounding, ongoing pleasures that if removed would just leave a vacuum.'

As Connor drained half his drink, Brona seemed stunted. Then, she seemed abruptly sad. Finally, she leaned back in Connor's chair and muttered, 'Interesting take. So, you'd tell me I'm addicted to my relationship?'

And suddenly Connor felt bad. He didn't want to hurt her. He sighed, more loudly than intended. 'I'd tell you that sometimes pain is the only acknowledgement of life.'

She stared at him as if he'd suddenly found her long-lost ring and then exclaimed, '*Shhhhit*,' her consonants sodden with vodka.

Connor said, 'I'd also tell you that there is, after all, a perverse satisfaction to picking at a scab – the long-haul married do it all the time.'

'Jesus, do your clients kill themselves, like, regularly?'

Connor placed his glass on the table. 'Brona, the fact is most of my clients who have relationship difficulties *never* leave their partner. In fact, when my clients finally figure out that they're better off divorced, separated, alone, they will still choose to remain wounded. So, if you were my client and you came to me about your shitty relationship, I think you'd quickly realise that the reason an intelligent woman like you *thinks* they need someone like me to point out the blatantly obvious things you already know, is because sometimes unhappiness is the only reminder of being alive. Especially when you have everything that people think they need. So, you'll stick with Zachery – no matter what your therapist says.'

Connor watched for her reaction. She didn't even twitch.

'What's the point of therapy with you if you're not going to fix things?'

Connor shrugged.

'Bullshit. You know but you're not going to tell me. Not yet.' She necked the cocktail like it was a pint until it was half-drained. 'So, should we be talking like this?'

'No.'

'Ah, so that's why it's so interesting.'

Connor knew what she was thinking and he wasn't interested in changing her mind. He could tell that Brona considered the room a friendly place. The music was easy-listening pop. Anyone would have to admit that, *Yeah, it's pretty cool here*. She was getting drunk. They were both getting drunk. This was what happened when people got drunk. It was good. It was sensual. But not quite hot enough to sweeten the sour knowledge that this wasn't just about Brona, who was now unconsciously curling her finger through her hair. It was also about Zachery. And it was about those messages waiting on his phone and what was now happening out in the real world. It was all about keeping that stuff OUT.

She withdrew a vaporiser from her suit jacket. Sucking on it, the tip glowed luminous green and the air filled with a cloud of steam.

'I used to puff away like there's no such thing as people in their eighties. Now I vape. Offended?' She took another inhalation and, while holding the device to her lips, Connor noticed a small scar stencilling the back of her left hand.

'Nah.'

'C'mon, let's go outside.'

Connor followed her to the decking. Behind them, through the opened slider, music seeped from the maw of the kitchen. Above, moths stumbled drunkenly around the spotlights. On the right-hand side, many gardens away, the setting sun's rays pierced the fortification of leaves like bullet holes in camouflage. A few houses away a lawn sprinkler hissed – *fist fist fist*. They both folded their arms and slouched forward onto the rail.

Connor said, 'With you living over there, always in my sights… a man might get a little obsessed with you.'

'Only a little?'

'Obsessions are never healthy.'

'Don't you want to get obsessed by me?'

He held up the remainder of his screwdriver, admiring it, and thought about fucking Brona. He sipped the drink and tried on the thought. He imagined himself pressing up against Brona, caging her between his chest and the banisters of the decking.

His fingers twitched as he pictured his hand glide between the split of her skirt. She wasn't wearing underwear.

Wait, she's wearing trousers.

He said, 'People can see us out here. Drinking. Having a good time. That's not allowed. People will talk.'

'Let their imaginations run wild.'

Her could-not-give-a-fuck attitude was infectious. Was this the way to live a life? Was that the key to contentment? Her attitude didn't have to mean unfettered mayhem. It simply meant having the confidence to recognise what things are worth caring about and what things aren't. He soaked Brona up like she was an abstract painting that had suddenly revealed itself to him; that captured the composure of a person who was absolutely sure of how to live life at the right temperature – not too hot, not too cold. And she wanted him too. Of that he was certain. It was obvious by the way they comfortably lounged next to each other on the deck, the way their gazes kept locking, the way they inched closer at every opportunity, that they were both very aware of what fun they could have fucking.

Connor said, 'But there's a specific somebody out there…' He nodded towards her house two gardens away.

'You can say the word "boyfriend". I won't spontaneously combust.' She sighed and looked to the ground.

'Then why look so guilty?'

'The nuns were very thorough.' She turned away from the falling night and leaned her back against the rail. Keeping her eyes on his she undid the single button of her suit jacket. He noticed how low her loose-fitting trousers were worn, just below her hips, making her so accessible. The white shirt stretched against her breasts and she smiled a little. *Don't do it.*

'I like you, Connor.'

'I like you, Brona.'

'Good. But *I* might not be telling the truth.'

'You might not. But are you?'

'It doesn't really matter what I say now, does it? I mean, I'm a world-class liar so if I was you I wouldn't believe me either.'

'I don't have to believe you to like you.'

'If we were in a club right now – a dark club – would you kiss me?'

'I'd try to.'

'You wouldn't have to try hard.' She laid out the words, one by one, like cards onto a table.

'Should you be flirting with me, Brona?'

'That isn't flirting. If I flirt with you, you'll know it.'

Connor watched her lips and wanted to be there, up close, because the inside of Brona's mouth was velvet ropes, leather sofas, chandeliers and champagne – Members Only. Surfing the perfect alcohol buzz – enough to diminish his inhibitions without making him stupid – he was suddenly better than cool. He was a wounded god.

'That's cool. I like easy women.'

'Bad men like easy women. And a therapist who hits on his client's girlfriend… that's a *very* bad man. I think I like bad men. I'll need therapy for that. Months of it.'

'Years. And he's no longer my client.'

Connor saw himself fucking her, fucking her like he could somehow correct her preference for Zachery. He placed his hands on her hips. They were pronounced beneath the trousers' light material. She leaned her head back and looked up to the sky.

'I don't know what I want,' she whispered.

'Yes you do.'

'Should I be ashamed?'

'Of course not.'

'You're the therapist. So since you know everything… what are you going to do?'

For once he had no rejoinder to the insistent static that pleasantly hummed between them. As the alcohol coursed through the engine of his brain, he rapidly saw Zachery's life implode in a beautiful supernova that served as a backdrop to him taking Brona against this very rail on this very decking.

But Connor's life was already too complicated, and all he was doing about it was trying to screw his enemy's girlfriend. He knew that he had to fight against the primitive instinct insinuating that the occult power of sex would have the energy to make everything better again. The fact was, he should be cancelling his clients' appointments for the rest of the week. He should be searching his contacts for a short-term loan to rent new premises. He should be on the phone, on the computer, trying to find a quick fix for that other disaster sitting in his inbox. He *shouldn't* be drinking and flirting and soaking up every word that comes off this woman who happens to be Zachery's girlfriend.

'I can't... we shouldn't do this.'

'You decided this now?'

'He's over there. We're here. It's wrong. For both of us. He's your boyfriend. He's my ex-client. Anyway, I have to focus on what's happening to me now, online, out there in the world.'

Brona inhaled slowly and exhaled quickly, simultaneously pushing his hands away from her waist, as if picking a scab clean from a healed wound. She had decided that the evening was over. He could see it clearly.

'I understand completely.' Brona wore an expression of magnanimity – as if she knew something about Connor, some damaging truth, but had the good grace not to have brought it up that afternoon. 'It was nice to take that holiday in an alternative universe with you where everything was as it should be – even if it was just for what? Twenty minutes?'

'No. Wait.'

'Goodbye, Connor.' And suddenly it was obvious that her mind was elsewhere. She'd tired of the conversation. It was as if she'd suddenly just closed a book. Brona descended the few wooden steps to the lawn, fastening her jacket as she went. Gently, she scooped up the calm cat, which curled up like a furry comma in her arms, and she pushed herself through the hole in the hedge.

The chilled night air pushed in – starry cool. Standing on a flowerpot, he carefully balanced himself so that he had a clear view of Brona and her cat walking down Mary's lawn, until she disappeared through another narrow opening in the hedge at the end of the garden.

Gradually Connor turned away from the view. *Another drink?* He retreated indoors and reluctantly took out his phone.

'Jesus Christ.'

Two thousand people had already seen it.

Finding it difficult to breathe, he scrolled down through the first few dozen of over two hundred comments. Most of them were from men threatening him with violence or, bizarrely, deportation. Most of the comments from women wanted him arrested or were of the over-empathetic #IAmThePlayingChild variety. But scattered amongst all this rage and affront were a few comments that consisted solely of his name or worse – his business email address.

There was a list of other missed calls from one number – Derek at the Health Board. *Oh, Jesus.* He checked his texts and there they were – a flurry of his messages. Connor opened the last one.

What have you done? This changes everything. My reputation is attached to yours. I put forward your scheme. I vouched for you. WHAT HAVE YOU DONE? I've been taking calls for the last hour. The press could get this and make a connection. 'Irish Calm and Quiet Pioneer Launches Nuclear Attack On A Playing Child'. How will the department look? How will the Minister look? All support is gone. I can't believe you've done this – to both of us. You had the bursary in your hand.

We were both going to get an award. How dare you. How VERY dare you. Do not call me. Call Johana.

Johana was Derek's assistant's secretary, clarifying, should there be any doubt, Connor's new meagre status in the health department. It wasn't fair. Even though it was filmed – even though there was nothing cut from the thirty seconds on show – it DID NOT happen like that. With social media, they could reach into your life as a child reaches into his world of toys. They could rewrite your life. Play with you. Punish you. Crumple you like a discarded wrapper.

He looked out the kitchen glass and felt that there were eyes behind every window of every house that faced him across the gardens. His life was on the internet. Strangers knew personal details and events that he had intended to tell no one about. It was as if, unbeknownst to him, his home had been opened up to the public and anyone could come inside and root through his drawers, his files, even his hard drive. No – it was worse. It was as if everyone in the world had the power to see into his mind and read his thoughts.

Where's my right to privacy? But he felt like a moron for even bothering to think such a thought as he knew full well that these days you may as well argue for your right to own a horse and cart. It was just not part of this world any more. Secrets plus technology equalled no secrets. It was that simple. Everyone insisted on more and more rights, convinced that rights make the world a better place. But they didn't. They just gave people like Zachery the means to exhibit, unchallenged, their own particular brand of unpleasantness.

And suddenly there was something else. An alarm. A car alarm. *His* car alarm.

Connor grabbed his keys, marched through the hall and opened the front door. The yellow warning lights of his Saab were flashing on and off in jerky rhythm to the screeching alarm. Pointing the dongle, he silenced the blaring racket. And then he saw it.

Connor slowly rounded the car, looking down the driveway as if expecting to glimpse someone running away. A golf club rested across the Saab's roof while its back window was mostly shattered. Though part of it was still in place as the defrosting wires had formed a scaffolding support to the glass.

Connor picked up the club and rested his hand on the base of the head as if to absorb the weight of its power. He looked over the wall into Mary's and the house next door to that. Blank windows stared back. He dropped the golf club and it went *crack* against the stone drive. Connor leaned against the car, his feet on glass diamonds, waiting for reality to return – as if that would be a good thing. *This is what it's like to have your life battered. This is what you get when the powerful want to crush you.*

He retreated indoors, his shoulders a little hunched, like a beaten player leaving the pitch. Connor looked out to the gardens again. He *was* being watched. Andrew was standing next to the trampoline. He regarded Connor coldly, as if he was blatantly daring his neighbour to object to being stared at. And then there was someone on Brona's balcony. He squinted. Zachery. His hands were on the railings. Staring. And suddenly Finbarr's head appeared and reappeared over the top of the hedge as he jumped and jumped on the trampoline, growling out the words to a heavy metal song that played through his earphones, this time both hands raising a middle finger towards the bungalow.

Connor felt as if he was watching St Catherine's Hill from the end of an extraordinarily long, dark tunnel. Then he stared down at his phone's screen. The power warning light was flashing and any moment the screen would go black.

CHAPTER SEVENTEEN

THE DAY OF

MARY

As I turn the ignition, my heart is pumping, not in the usual anxious way but with excitement. Ten minutes ago, Bairbre from next door sent me a link to the TheCityJournal which is running a story about Connor assaulting an hysterical Finbarr in my back garden. It looks like Zachery filmed it and put it up. Or could it be Brona? If it was my little sister it would mean she'd seen everything and had just pretended she hadn't when she'd called in to me. I wouldn't put it past her. But thankfully the report and video don't mention Finbarr or us by name.

However, Connor hasn't been so lucky. TheCityJournal have exposed him as not just a psychotherapist but as a governmental candidate for a new post concerning city living and noise pollution. There's an online meltdown. Already someone in the Department of Health is claiming that the government were only vaguely associated with him – and that they were never seriously considering working with Connor or setting up the Committee of Mental Health and Noise Pollution. It would all be hilarious if it wasn't for the fact that he lived next door to me and was sending me threatening notes – another of which had been deposited through the letterbox overnight and was waiting in the hallway for my breakfast reading pleasure.

Finbarr's in the back seat of the SUV staring into the glow of his new tablet. I drive extra carefully because he refuses to wear his safety belt.

'Is that the new tablet you asked Andrew to get you?'

An infinitesimal nod.

'You seem happy with it.'

No response at all.

'Is it cool?'

A sigh. Then, 'You know, I thought about getting a cool one but then decided that I'd prefer a really shit one.' Finbarr then nods to himself, pleased that he's managed to once again demonstrate his sharpness of thought.

'Language. Just to be clear – you're being ironic and you actually like it?'

'Yes, well done. You catch on slow.'

Jesus. At the lights, a plain teenage girl on the passenger side of the car next to us registers Finbarr's blue eyes, smooth skin and thick blond hair. She smiles coquettishly and as Finbarr stares blankly back, she interprets his disinterest as a hard-to-impress coolness. Blushing, she smiles and wrinkles her nose. Finbarr finally deigns to respond by jabbing the inside of his cheek with his tongue and gesturing with his fist to his mouth in the universal mime of oral sex. The lights turn green, I pretend I don't see and we zoom off.

Finbarr and I are risking another trip to the park; partly because I need to get out, partly because Finbarr *should* need to get out and partly because I feel guilty over the way I treated Elena yesterday. So, I've left her in the house with the task of trying to clean the rug Brona had attempted to destroy. Whenever she's finished, she can leave early.

In general, I can only have the house properly cleaned when Finbarr is out for the day. He hates the hoover, the taps pumping hot water into a basin, the sound of a saturated cloth being wrung.

His finger starts tapping and he gets angsty, pacing around, sighing loudly, almost hyperventilating and begins shouting, 'Leave it. Leave it. Just fucking leave it.' Busy housework is clearly one of his triggers – just what that boy's home life must have been like… But last weekend was a momentous time. Andrew took Finbarr out hiking to Wicklow and did not return until 6 p.m. Apparently, they hardly talked but I'd felt like it was the happiest time of my life. The quiet then, in each room, was the prettiest song I'd ever heard. The house became a therapeutic space. Because that's all therapeutic space is – silence.

The last time I took Finbarr walking in the park he broke off, put on his earphones and ran around scaring old people while screaming heavy metal lyrics about suicide and self-harm. That awful out-of-tune whining that the doctors advised Emer to let him emit because it's venting and he needs to vent. But it isn't simply the sound of some type of prehistoric beast. It's the sound of a broken one. I'm used to it at home because there's no escape from it. I can't even turn the TV up to drown it out because when I compete with his noise, his finger will start tapping and just like that, the rapid countdown will have begun. But he's been calmer recently. Quieter. He actually briefly hugged me the other day when I gave him his dinner. That's why I'm risking the park again – I believe life is settling for Finbarr.

After sending Andrew the TheCityJournal link, Finbarr and I walk side by side through the park's central avenue. Finbarr is moaning, low, under his earphones. It's a drone but not too irritating. Otherwise, it's peaceful – we look like any mother and her teenage son to passing strangers.

Two women from St Catherine's Hill jog by. They're like Olympians, waiting for their turn to break the next record. Women from St Catherine's Hill jog, cycle and wall-climb. Anything but walk. Walking is cerebral. Walking sharpens the thoughts and processes the emotions. Of course they don't walk.

They wave at me and smile kindly at Finbarr who openly leers at them and says loudly, 'So *very* don't-touch-that *hot.*'

I wave back and call out a jolly, 'Karen! Julie!' Thankfully they don't stop. 'How are you?' It's the first thing people ask. I dread the question. Then, 'How is Finn doing?' Another question I hate. Since Finbarr arrived, I find people apologise to me constantly – or are waiting for me to apologise.

I'd like a cigarette but that would be breaking the second rule of my secret habit – the one concerning it being a secret. The first rule is that it was supposed to have been just a single fag at night. But I've tossed that decree aside. However, this second one I'll keep. It doesn't matter that Brona knows. She's nothing to me now.

So instead of taking out a cigarette, I take out the latest anonymous letter. Again, it has no stamp and on the front a black biro has scribbled – *FAO Mary Boyd #13 St Catherine's Hill.* Carefully I unfold the A4 page and read it once more.

YOU SELFISH BITCH
HOW DO YOU LIVE WITH YOURSELF? HOW DO YOU LOOK AT YOURSELF IN THE MIRROR? WHAT TYPE OF PERSON DOES WHAT YOU DO? YOUR GARDEN IS NOT THE GROUNDS OF <u>ANOTHER</u> MENTAL INSTITUTION. STOP INFLICTING YOUR PROBLEMS ON THE NEIGHBOURHOOD. WE ARE ALL WATCHING. WE ARE ALL LISTENING. WE ARE ALL BEING DRIVEN DEMENTED. EVERYONE IS TALKING ABOUT IT. ABOUT YOU. DO SOMETHING ABOUT IT! EVEN IF YOU HAVE TO DO WHAT NATURE SHOULD'VE DONE.
THE NEIGHBOURHOOD

A thought occurs – could it actually be Brona? That's something I've never contemplated until being exposed to her real personality, her real feelings, her *honesty*. Maybe. But then, why would she have waited for so long? Finbarr has been doing what he does for months. No, it has to be Connor. The timing is too obvious and it's not as if his personality doesn't fit. I saw him attack Finbarr with my own eyes and now the whole of the internet has seen him for the sociopath he is. Occam's razor. It's he who has so much at stake – his work, his privacy. Well, if he thinks the internet can be cruel, wait till he faces my husband again.

Finbarr takes out his earphones and without looking at me or breaking stride says, 'So before we left St Catherine's Hill, you'd said that you had something exciting to show me in the park. But since then, you haven't expanded on the oxymoron.'

'This is it, Finn. I'm showing you it. The central avenue of the park. Space, trees and peace. Can you handle such a drastic prospect?'

'I'm working on it. So is this "quality" time?'

'Yes.'

'Between you and me?'

'Yes.'

'So after you die, I'll look back on this day, tearfully?'

'Of course. Unless you die first. Then *I'll* look back on it… with regret.'

'OK, let's talk.'

'Great. How about—'

'Who was my dad? Mam won't tell me.'

'That was all just a silly mistake so—'

'Poor little me, the silly mistake. But who was he?'

'Not you, of course. You're not a mistake. But… the event. A silly mistake. In other words, she doesn't know. No one does.'

Finbarr's gaze is fixed ahead but his eyes are making a decision – he's clearly wondering whether to ask me something inappropriate. Finally he speaks, 'Why does she hate him then?'

I stop walking and glare at Finbarr. 'Is that what she says?'

'No. But I can sense it. She tenses up. Am I a rape kid?'

'No! Absolutely not. Oh my God, Finn. Never, *ever* think that. You're a great creation that resulted from a... a... a silly mistake Emer made when she was *very* young. You are the living, breathing silver lining!'

'Jesus, you sound like a fucking Disney movie.'

'Language.' Finbarr's apparently super-smart but sometimes it seems that without the F-word he would be lost. He uses it as a verb, a noun, as an interjection, as an adverb. We continue with our stroll. 'No one knows your father because it happened at a party or something, with someone she didn't know and never saw again. No wonder Emer tenses up. If your father knew you existed he would've helped you both through all these years. If you sense hatred towards him from your mother then it's because Emer hates herself. That's why she is where she is right now.'

I sound as if I'm reluctantly saying these things about Finbarr's mother but it actually feels good vomiting a rush of Emer-bile out of my system. It's good for my mental health. I know it's not fair – but poor Finbarr is the only person in the world I've spoken to about such things. And I'm enjoying this walk with my nephew – he's behaving. He's in control. We're talking; actually having a meaningful conversation. Sometimes he *does* get along OK with me – as well as possible with someone he hates.

I smile at him. 'You look so like your grandfather. I wish you'd known him.'

'So Mam's been telling me recently before you had her locked away.'

'He'd have been so proud of you.'

'Auntie Mary, you sound faker than the porn sites telling me that there's girls near me that want to fuck.'

'Language. Jesus. Finn.'

'Auntie Mary, I am seriously running out of nice juice to spray. Are you ever going to tell me why you got Mam put away?'

'I didn't. You know that. Emer surrendered herself to the clinic.'

'I recall that *first* she asked for your help.'

'True.'

'And you finally said you would help us if—'

'False.'

'False?'

'False. I didn't *finally* agree to help you, because I'd never been asked before.'

'Why not? We needed help and you have all this.' He gestures to the park as if it's mine. I assume he associates it with freedom, space, manoeuvrability, solid life choices.

'I had my life. Emer had hers. And she'd always insisted on living her own way and doing her own thing. So, I let her do that – not that I, or anyone, had a choice. Now if your mother wanted to bring you up by homeschooling assisted by teachers from her religious sect, then there's nothing I could do about that. And if she doesn't save or get a real job and instead moves from some rubbish neighbourhood to another with you – and later sends you to rubbish schools – then there's also nothing I can do about that. I was kept out of your life. You were hers. Not mine.'

'I'm still hers,' he mutters.

'Yes. Of course. Anyway, Emer was not talking to me. I didn't know you. I hadn't had access to you since you were one year old. One! And even if she'd asked me for money, I wouldn't have given it to her. I don't mind telling you that. She would've just given it to some pig-ignorant, God-fearing and God-awful religious sect. You're old enough by now to understand, surely?'

'So, when Mam had no money and was losing our home and she finally asked you for help, you—'

'I said I'd help but not until she spent some time in a care home, for a rest. And while there, I'd take you in. I'm the one who spoke to her on the phone. I'm the one who heard her talk. The state she was in. Her mind… her paranoia…'

'You left her with no choice but to go inside. That's what Mam told me.'

'Emer was always a liar,' I state factually. One can only imagine the sort of stories she's told Finbarr over the years. It's for his own good that he begins to realise that he can't trust everything his mother tells him. 'We all have choices.'

'She didn't think she'd be in there for more than a week or two.'

'None of us did. She had a complete breakdown after a few days. Lost her marbles.' I bite my lip. Too much? Is he shocked? 'Look, Finn, I'm paying for both of you. *Not* the state. *Not* Brona.' That blood-drinking empress who believes deep down that she's probably a god. 'But me. I'm the cash cow. You need to respect that and maybe, one day, show appreciation – because I know your mother never will. Even when she's better and gets out.'

He grunts. He's not shocked. He says, 'Here's the headline… Fine she would've given away any money you gave her to the God-gang… *But*, you could've just paid our bills directly. And it's not like you don't have it to have bankrolled us. Ten thousand is in the margin of a rounding error for you and Uncle Andy.'

'That was money she just needed to get by for a month or two. What happens after that? You're apparently a smart boy, Finn. When dealing with the future one needs a plan. You *know* this. You might have been homeschooled but admittedly they did a very good job of it.'

'Yeah. Fuck you too, Auntie Mary.'

'Language. Your mother thought and still thinks that she has the superpower to pray everything better but—'

'Yeah, I know. "This isn't going to work unless we all believe". That's why she got angry with me. Because she slowly realised that I don't believe in that bullshit. I never really did but she didn't sense it because the fact was I cared so little for God that I couldn't even be bothered to deny His existence. With the internet and when she finally let me out there to go to school with real people, it became very clear that the single fact that the priests can't grasp is that any average teenage boy will eagerly swap an eternity of God's love for one good blowjob.'

'Not appropriate. For God's sake, Finn.'

'I just watched and listened to all the God stuff and waited for it to end. And finally over the last few years when they were beating me half to death in those first few schools she sent me to, she couldn't understand why I wouldn't pray it all away. She couldn't understand why I decided to fight back instead. To throw the first digs. Not to wait for it. But to go to it. And to keep getting up. And getting up. And getting up. And finally she realised that no school would take me because – according to her – I'm not holy. And then Mam got angry.'

'She didn't just get angry. She wanted to hurt you. She tried to hurt you. She threw a bottle at you. She took a swipe at you with broken glass, for God's sake. And remember, Finn, you were frightened. And you – the big man – were crying.'

'Jesus. Fuck you.'

'Language. If you want to talk about things, then grow up and talk about them properly. If you think you're mature enough to ask adult questions, then be adult enough to accept the answers.'

He glares at me with bright, blue, cold eyes. I let him and feel a little ashamed because I've enjoyed putting him in his place. I picture his fist indentations in the walls, the bruises on my arms and legs, the meteorite-collision-shaped hollow from his forehead in the bathroom door. Well, scream here if you want. Run and punch a bloody tree. No one cares. Well, I don't. Not right now. I've other problems besides Finbarr and he'd better get used to that.

With lowered voice, he says, 'I'm not exactly easy, Auntie Mary. I know I'm not normal. I know I don't act the same as others. Maybe if I'd been a better son, then—'

'No. There is *nothing* wrong with you.' I catch my breath. Try again. 'I know there is *something* different about you. But you have had a different life. And one day that difference will be the making of you. It is the making of many great and successful people.' The most difficult thing about Finbarr is that he insists on being loved when there often appears to be no love within him.

'But if I'd been a better and proper son, then—'

'No, Finn. This is all on your mother. What kind of mother tries to smash her son over the head with a bottle? Twice! And on the second time picks up a shard and continues attacking him? It's not because you didn't "pray" hard enough or because you were expelled or because schools wouldn't take you. It's because your mother is no longer well and now she's somewhere safe that will make her better. It's that simple, Finn. You *have to* and *you will* understand this.'

'I'll try.'

'Don't try. Do! Triers are criers.'

'I just wish… I just wish I was a better…' He wants to say 'man' but can't. So instead he says 'boy', and it rips something out of him. And away he goes.

'Oh my God!'

He's no longer beside me. I should be crunching up the letter, jamming it into my pocket and calling out for him. But I can't. However, I do fold it faster than usual – but carefully – and return it to my bag. Then I scout about. There's the sound of children nearby. Lots of children. A playground. I'm making my way there through the trees, off the pathway, my heels making hard work of the grass and I know I shouldn't have worn them, but we were supposed to just stick to the central avenue.

The playground is packed. It's designed like an old cowboy fort with Wild West log fencing and even pretend guard turrets at the boundary corners. Inside is a selection of swings, slides and climbing structures, also made from logs and chunky ropes. Amongst the children are the local mothers, all glowing with the energy of their bright futures. But it's not just that they're younger than me. It's as if they've evolved into a different species. They seem taller than my generation and most are clearly worked-out, like they're a generation of professional dancers. But when summer ends, autumn will finally power-wash them out of the park.

And there is Finbarr – thank God – in the corner of the playground, after running through the sandpit, his back to everyone. Most of the mothers have clocked him already. He's the only adolescent-looking male in the vicinity and he's gorgeous and he's strange and he's getting onto a children's swing, standing on the seat, putting the earphones back onto his head.

I march through the entrance of the fort, smiling at the faces as I pass by the mothers, trying not to break into a jog because I know that something terrible is about to happen. But I'm too late.

Finbarr is swinging too high and too rapidly. The little children are moving away from him and he's begun shouting, singing; some awful song with the lyrics, '*I gave my heart to a pretty little fuck pig!!*' Over and over.

Someone calls out, 'Hey you! What the—'

Another woman shouts, 'Oh my God, is he…?'

I spread my arms like the arriving messiah. 'It's fine. It's fine,' I announce, as if the fact that a seventeen-year-old boy who has commandeered one of the children's swings and is loudly singing disgusting songs, is the most everyday thing in the world.

The chorus of mothers continues:

'What on earth…?'

'Disgusting.'

'Call the police.'

'Oh. My. God.'

'What's that big boy saying, Mummy?'

One of the mothers has her phone out but she's not making a call. She's lining up a shot or about to record a video. I think of Connor.

'No!' I shout and raise my hand before the phone like the bodyguard of a royal. I feel like I'm fourteen again – down that laneway – that awful laneway – a paralysation of white fear, a dread of offering any resistance because defiance would certainly result in an escalation of that tormenting blitzkrieg that results in my every fibre exposed, revealed, splayed out for the whole filthy world to examine, to interfere with.

At that moment Finbarr stops singing, jumps down off the swing and strolls across the sandpit back towards the entrance, ignoring the fact that everyone in the playground is staring at him, aghast.

'He's mine. He's with me. I'm sorry. I'm so sorry.' I desperately search for an excuse. A reason. Anything. 'He's severely autistic.'

There's a few silently mouthed 'ooohhhs' and the woman with the phone is already half-smiling sympathetically.

I'm still thinking of possible lawsuits, so I quickly correct myself with, 'He's got a mental disorder. He's with me. I'm so sorry. He's lovely. He really is. He doesn't know what he's doing.'

Even as all the mothers quickly understand the situation and remarkably demonstrate a communal consideration, I'm wondering if there's a possibility that he'll be labelled by the police as a sex offender. Because there's nothing worse than sex offenders.

One of the mothers is already holding forth on how everyone should just get back to normal, that there is nothing to see here, that it was all a misunderstanding. From beneath her grim manageable hairstyle, she glows at me with condescension and I *have* to glow back with gratitude. She's not a St Catherine's Hill housewife. None of them are. I don't recognise a single one.

'My son is also autistic,' she says and quickly gets on a roll now, talking about the difficulties that people don't understand and the 'gifts' that people don't appreciate. I'm using the space of her soliloquy to compose myself, normalise my pulse until I feel the right face smoothing itself across my features.

'I live in St Catherine's Hill. Have I seen you around?' I ask with a smile, though I may as well have roared, *I'm NOT like you!*

'Erm… no. I'm not from—'

'Oh. Anyway, I've got to get Finbarr back. He's just my nephew.'

Kicking off my heels – because three inches are hard work when you've gone wildly off course from the main avenue – I walk back through the playground. Finbarr's waiting at the entrance. Trying to ignore the sponginess of a blister beneath my tights, I keep an eye on his hands, checking for the telltale tapping fingers. But everything is fine. Everything is OK. I don't think anyone videoed him. I don't think anyone phoned the police. It's tough to breathe just thinking about it. Murderers are released from prison to blend anonymously right back into the neighbourhood. But sex criminals are branded for life. Sometimes the sex offender's address is announced on the internet. And that would be *my* address. They have to report their whereabouts. There's 'No Go' orders around playgrounds and schools. These 'No Go' orders are widened each year. I know. I check up on them.

I wanted to be your first time.

Christ, *he's* there again, in my brain, somewhere in a mental laneway. Until yesterday he was absent for decades. But now he's back, striding out every few hours, reminding me that he's really gone nowhere. That he's been here all along. Why is that? There's no longer anything about him that could interest me. He isn't even a fragment of the past. Instead he's like a stain; a smear on the wall from a dirty hand left years ago. Grimy fingers. Paw marks.

'Come on, move it,' I snap at Finbarr as I march by. 'I'm *so* disappointed. That disgusting song. In front of *children*. You're deranged. You're… you're *the* animal.'

We're walking in silence. A minute passes – one glorious minute where I'm outdoors and pretending that he isn't there beside me and that the world is normal. And then he suddenly shouts, 'Tell me why she hates you!'

'Don't start.'

Finbarr is determined not to get off the subject. 'You know why Mam hates you. She knows why. And neither of you will tell me! Jesus fucking Christ.'

'Language!'

'No wonder my *fucking* head feels like it's going to explode every single minute of every *fucking* day I spend in your company! You labour under the impression that I'm a *fucking* moron who will swallow whatever *shit* you tell me. And that means that *you're* even more stupid than the idiot that you think I am. Just once I wish—'

I stop walking and grab him by the shoulder. 'Go on. Explode. Do it again. This time I won't come after you. This time I'll let them take you away. This time they – the police, the state, the whatevers – can bloody well have you. And then you'll see how sympathetic to your tantrums they'll be. You'll see how much patience they'll have for your sob stories. And when you're alone in a police station about to fall down a flight of stairs ten times in a row, you'll then perhaps finally understand what the real world thinks of stupid, horrible, seventeen-year-old delinquents who go berserk in a children's playground, frightening infants.' I twist his collar tighter. 'Am I, *for once*, making myself clear?'

He's actually paled. 'Crystal.'

I release him and begin walking. He keeps pace beside me.

'Auntie Mary.'

'What?'

'Why does she hate you?'

'Jesus Christ!'

'Is it because you allowed me to be born? Or is it the opposite – you wanted to have an abortionist scrape me out of her but my religious nut of a mother wouldn't be having that, even at fifteen.'

I twist round, lashing out – but gain control of myself at the last split second – so that my fist thumps his shoulder and not his cheek. 'Don't you *ever* say something like that again. It's stupid. It's self-centred. It's the result of self-obsession. You're not the only child ever born out of wedlock, you know? Half that bloody playground probably is.'

'Wow – that's interesting. It's almost as if three feet north of your tits there's a brain. Now tell me. Fucking tell me!'

Once again I grab him by the top of his shirt and I yank him into me until his face is centimetres from mine, and I now know how it feels to be a thug, a gangster, violent. Through gritted teeth I begin to ramble, 'Your mother simply has problems. She resented me. That's all. I married. I had a normal life. I made the correct life choices. She didn't. That's it. It's not Shakespearean. It's just another typical Irish family story that's not like any other typical Irish family story because every typical Irish family story is bloody well different in a secretive way to all the other typical Irish family stories. Now shut up and walk, or I swear…'

He shuts up. We walk.

Driving home, Finbarr sits in the back seat, working away at swiping his screen as if it were a rosary. I pretend I'm coming from what used to be my weekly visit to the spa. I hear the masseuse's parting shots as I'd wave my farewell: 'Don't live too hard.' 'There's nothing there in the hard living.' 'You can't get water from the sun.'

Back in the house, I carefully reseal the hate letter and place it on the floor beneath the letterbox. My plan for Connor isn't cancelled – it's just delayed. I picture Andrew finding it when he's back from work and immediately I'm reminded of what I love most about him – he's big, strong and aggressive; the type of lonesome man whose only friends are enemies he has yet to defeat – and yet so kind and considerate to me – always. Before Andrew came into my life, my now manicured nails had been chewed down to the quick. But I've never bitten my nails since knowing him.

Elena is gone and remarkably, she's managed to get the stain from the rug. It's like the last of Brona has finally left the house. Finbarr is already in the garden, grunting loudly as he takes up his practised southpaw stance, learned from his favourite Mixed Martial Arts website. Then he begins to go through his 'home-made' Muay Thai workout – kicking and punching in slow motion, each new stance greeted with a roar, as if he's just chopped a brick in half with his hand. I take my place on the patio and light up a much-needed cigarette. Finbarr glances up but doesn't comment. I don't care who sees me smoking. Whether it's the hate notes, that final confrontation with Brona or suddenly thinking so much about that bloody laneway – but something has changed within me. I don't know what. And I'm not sure it's a change for the better.

I don't even glance towards Brona and Zachery's. I don't care whether she's in or out. Instead I'm looking down on the zinc patio lip of Connor's bungalow. I pull on the cigarette deeply, enjoying the tug on my lungs, appreciating the jolt of life each inhalation gives. But my eyes keep slanting towards the hedge and what lies on the other side. What's *he* doing now? I haven't noticed any clients calling this morning. Is he drinking himself out of reality? Is he rerunning his viral video? Maybe he's planning to go out and forget about it all. I mean, why would he stay in when the only thing to stay in for is to watch his life self-destruct live on social media? And if he turns off the phone and computer, he'll just be alone in a bungalow: a failed bachelor, waiting for middle age to settle around him like an autumnal chill.

No – he'll visit some pricey, elegant, private members' club – the kind of place that has slutty strippers to make its clients feel that they're designed to rule the world. I can see him with younger women. I can see him with older women. I can see him pondering which model to screw tonight in his St Catherine's Hill bungalow. He probably has so many girlfriends that he's able to coordinate them with his ties.

My parents' generation had tried to ruin sex for mine and mostly succeeded. Well, they'd certainly ruined it for me. From the age of twelve I'd seen sex as the 'shame of arousal'. Meanwhile, at the convent, the nuns told us that exploration of our own bodies would lead to the sin that causes Our Lady to weep. And then, of course, the laneway happened. But what would've happened after that if I'd met Connor at fifteen, sixteen or seventeen years of age? Would he have saved me from the greyness of asexuality and fear that has stayed with me since then? Would he have shaken me out of it and made me explode onto the scene with no boundaries, no limits, turning me into the type of livewire girl that always offers people too much information about herself and whose favourite word is 'yes'?

I'm embarrassed by these thoughts. It's as if the anonymous letters and the return of that laneway voice is trying to break something within me and I'm protecting myself by focusing my mental energies on something novel and stupid – a younger man. It's so easy. Because if I'd met a man like Connor after the laneway, my life *would* have been so different. I could've been like Brona. He'd certainly have given me a huge interest in sexuality. So, by the age of sixteen the only time I wouldn't have been thinking about sex was when I was telling myself to stop thinking about sex. I would intimidate the local boys and the girls would try to slut-shame me. But I wouldn't mind. I'd also know that the loudest, bitchiest girls would be the ones eventually left behind in front of their TVs, sliding from channel to channel in their parents' house as their thirties approached. Because I would know that I was going to change the world or be a film star or property mogul or something. I'd know that I was getting out of there the minute I was done with school.

What would I be like at the club he's probably going to tonight? I can see it. Looking across the dance floor, he's surprised to find that he no longer has any interest in the younger women, the students, the bubblegum burlesques, most of whom have no frame of reference about anything and make him wince at all the things they don't know. It's because he's now approaching forty and all his experiences have transformed his brain into a muscle that has grown beyond such energetic diversions; because he has seen it all and now needs secret and very particular fetishes just to raise a lascivious drool. And when he sees me and I see him, I wonder what his very particular fetish is and how would it be revealed and would I be able to sate it, and he knows exactly what I'm thinking and he likes it.

Oh my God. What is wrong with me? What am I thinking? Why am I like this?

I stab out the cigarette and go inside, turn the kettle on and prepare a herbal tea. From when I was fourteen I despised my privates all the way through adolescence. Now, even though I've grown out of that, I still occasionally can't help considering the mere idea of female genitalia as a dangerous and repellent wound. And that's a handy psychological superpower to have, because usually it avoids having disturbing thoughts like those currently raining down on my brain.

When I read about the sex lives of women of my generation – usually famous actresses – I didn't envy them at all. All those partners and messy divorces. There's something wrong with that type of life. The kind of love that jumps from one person to another like a flea, can't be real love, can it? And Andrew had not been looking for that type of woman. Otherwise he wouldn't have pursued me all those years ago.

When I'd met Andrew, I was just twenty and he was twenty-seven. We married within the year and during that time quickly got to know each other's bodies. On some level it was simply getting to grips with something that needed to be done if only because we were married. It wasn't good. It wasn't intense. But despite that, for a brief while, it had been important to us – if only because it formed a unique bond between us that absolutely no one else could make. His constant blushing had flattered me but… I'd also have liked *not* to know what was going on in the man's head. It should've been a time full of wonder and experimentation, of lusts and ultimate satisfaction. Instead it had been incident after incident of mooring ourselves in the usual sexual paradox of the man wondering if he was only doing it for her benefit and the woman only letting him do it for his.

I rub the back of my neck. My rash has fired up again. Then I hear it – *clink*; glass against metal. I trace the sound to the hall and down the stairs to my husband's den.

Andrew must be home early. I could've been caught smoking; I must be more careful. He's having a glass of vino, which he does only after a difficult day at work; a shipment must've been late. Or maybe it's because of Connor next door. We'd never talked about his visit to Connor last night. In fact, we haven't seen each other since he'd delivered the oranges to the kitchen when Brona had been here. After she'd left, he'd stayed downstairs doing whatever he does and I'd chain-smoked for an hour before making sure Finbarr had gone to bed – which was difficult as you can't hurry him and yet you can't give him too much leeway; in other words, you have to take as much care as if handling an unexploded bomb. But last night Finbarr let me kiss him on the forehead. He looked beautiful when I'd left him, the sheet reaching his ribs and laying on him like moonlight. And then I'd gone to bed myself. I'd a headache. I'd needed darkness. I'd needed the bloody day to end.

From the hall, another *clink* rises sharply from the basement staircase. I've always been grateful that Andrew carefully monitors his intake. He certainly likes his drink, but alcohol doesn't suit him. When he's drunk, he wants to be sober. But the problem is, when he's sober there's something about him that wants to be drunk. Which is surprising because his father had been an alcoholic; that type that considered himself a beer drinker because he only drank whiskey in the mornings.

Andrew was the son of an army colonel and the result of a prematurely terminated orthodox education. While his father was off soldiering at the Curragh Barracks, his mother having left with another squaddie when he was five, he was eventually shifted off to boarding school to be another miserable soul amongst a hundred and eighty boys aged from twelve to eighteen.

When we got engaged he brought me there once on a bank holiday. It was as if he was trying to show me who he was; to demonstrate what type of man I was marrying so I could have no complaints later. It was the only time he ever really opened up about anything and he did so without words: show not tell.

The school was like a haunted house out of a Victorian novel. It was surrounded by woodland that kept out the sunshine and was only accessible by a long winding private drive off a minor road in a midlands county no one wanted to live in. Everything was brown and grey – the huge radiators, the stone floors, the chilly wall tiles. The dorms slept eight to a room on hard cold beds because they were 'character-forming'. The walls were thin and the boys would tap out Morse code messages from room to room in the middle of the night. I can still smell that strange, musky and acrid odour of so many adolescent boys.

The school uniform had never changed over the decades – grey jumper, grey shirt, grey trousers, brown tie. Because Andrew started in the school midway through term, they'd kept him back.

He'd just finished a miserable year and without explanation they made him do it all over again. It had made him feel that he would never get out of the place. It had made him feel like he was in one of those Russian Gulags where they lock you up without telling you the length of your sentence.

One thing I do remember very clearly about my visit to the boarding school was meeting the headmaster, who had been just a teacher in Andrew's day. He was the one who gave us permission to wander about the campus while it was closed for holidays. He was the one who recalled how that if a bigger, stronger and faster kid knocked Andrew down, he'd just keep coming back for more until finally he'd beat him. Then later, when Andrew went off by himself, the headmaster quietly said to me that for those who had known him, it was a very chilling thought that an already hostile man like Andrew had become a trained killer. I'd replied, 'It's OK, he's happy now.' But I didn't meet his eyes when I'd said that.

But at least boarding school wasn't quite as bad as being at home. Andrew's father was a physically powerful man and viciously sarcastic, which was bad news for Andrew, who apparently would never amount to anything. His father was someone who knew he was always right, especially on the rare occasions that he was wrong. Those times, his father's angry, fanatical eyes were powerful enough to change the laws of the world to suit his argument. But to give the man his due, it was only a few times a year that he beat Andrew till he bled.

I've frequently thought that an important distinction between the sexes is that often men desire weak women but women rarely desire a weak man. Andrew is many things but he is not weak. And yet he certainly never had a hankering for weak women. Andrew and I are one and the same. We are meant to be together – like a pair of drumsticks. We both had a difficult adolescence that we don't talk about – well, I know Andrew's, but he *does not* know about mine. We do have that in common, even if he'd escaped unmolested while being a scout, a swimmer and resident at an all-boys boarding school. So in effect our marriage mightn't have been arranged – but it had been arrived at.

From the kitchen door I can see that the latest 'anonymous' letter is still lying on the floor where I'd left it. Andrew had missed the envelope even though he'd taken his shoes off right next to it. Scooping up Connor's 'anonymous' epistle, I descend the steps to Andrew's lair which holds the same biscuity, hamsterish smell as his warehouses.

And there he is, bending forward, one eye shut tight, the other open and glued to his telescope. His white T-shirt is greying from having his blacks bleed into his whites from my successive poorly sorted washes. It's as if he's trying to perfect the look of a wife beater – the usual common or garden variety – the type that uses domestic violence to work through his anxieties concerning what a pathetic loser he is.

Without moving his face from the lens, his right hand reaches out and feels about until it finds the stem of his wine glass on the copper side table. He then takes a step back, straightens and sips. A ship's barometer hangs on the wall – it reads changeable. It *always* reads changeable.

Andrew's secret leering at Brona shouldn't be so hurtful. Surely he deserves that pleasure? It's hardly a judgement against me. Brona is beautiful. I'm a bit better than ordinary. And Andrew has never been unfaithful.

After another sip, he puts the glass back onto the table, slips the same hand down his trousers and peers back through the telescope. This is about the tenth time I've come across him spying on Brona and it's the first time I've seen him do this. Andrew had once told me, after we'd watched a documentary, that he'd never had any interest in pornography – that he'd never, *ever* even searched for it online. But now I know that he was lying. He watches porn through his telescope.

When I was thirty, I'd briefly investigated sex for the first time in my life. Pathetic but necessary. *Elle* magazine had done an article on the best porn sites for women and through them I discovered two things. First: that Burroughs was correct when he said that sex will invade new technology like a virus. And second: I'd discovered that older women could be in charge of non-threatening, polite younger men.

From those *Elle* links, I'd learned things they didn't teach you at the convent or that you don't pick up when you've only had sexual relations with one man – a man like my husband. But I didn't like the way those *Elle* internet links had made me feel. Because something in me was insisting that this is not what it looks like – it doesn't happen on a beautiful beach or in a six-star suite or on a private jet; it happens in a deserted laneway. And it doesn't occur with gorgeous tanned guys – it happens with the man in the laneway at the back of a church. And it doesn't make you moan and groan – it makes you cry.

I hate porn, because until it came along, I had done such a good job at not remembering all of that. And now, watching my husband watching his Brona porn, it's the same thing.

'Oh, for God's sake, Andrew,' I snap.

He lurches forward and for a moment I think he's impaled the telescope viewer through his eye socket.

'Ouch! Bloody… *feck*!'

'Look at the state of you.'

'What?' He's facing me now, one paw over his left eye and his cheeks are red, but that could be from pain rather than the mortification at being snared like a dumb animal.

'You really are a sad case.'

'I don't know what you're… What do you mean?'

'I want you to know something, Andrew. Since Finbarr has come here, things have been difficult. And things have changed. And some of them for the good. I'm suddenly content with who I am. I am content to do what I truly want to do.'

'Mary, are you mad? Are you—'

'After twenty years of marriage I'm done with being a forty-year-old tedious try-hard, pathetic husband-pleaser, the original bloody welcome mat.'

'What are you on about?'

'And I'm content with your disinterest. Now I refuse to take responsibility for your low-grade depression. Not any more. Maybe looking after Finbarr – seeing what it is to be truly needed – has allowed me to accept the fact that my bloody husband's happiness is no longer my responsibility. I've enough responsibilities – hear me? Including, and most especially, my sister being committed and everything that comes with it.'

'I didn't know you were unhappy. I'm *trying*, Mary. I'm always trying to be… trying to be the…' His words domino-topple to silence.

'Oh God, will you for once try and get over your ironclad policy *against* getting to the point? Just listen to yourself. Ignoring your behaviour. Ignoring what you've just been doing. I saw you. But guess what? It's *not* a surprise. You need to be like that because you've never dealt with your issues.'

'What issues?'

I actually laugh – genuinely. 'Andrew, don't you realise that you're the source of your own unhappiness? And that unhappiness is the source of your own unpleasantness. And it makes me so *fucking* angry.'

'My unhappiness makes *you* angry? Really? Fantastic. That's so reasonable.' Andrew's voice has risen to a shout, hoping to ram home his point. But my abrupt silence is louder, more powerful.

I should hate him. But I don't. Maybe it's because he still interests me. I do wish he'd talk about things. The problem with strong, silent men like Andrew is that under it all they're terribly sensitive but determined not to show it. Just like my father. When Emer broke his heart, I remember listening at his bedroom door, hearing him cry. Sometimes he bawled. Sometimes he sobbed quietly. But it wasn't until after marrying Andrew that I realised there were actually three ways for a man to cry: noisily, quietly or not at all.

'I'm looking at you, Andrew, and you know what I'm thinking? I'm thinking, "You're forty-seven, grow the hell up and get over it – whatever *it* is. If you need therapy, go to therapy. If you need to go into the forest and weep, then do that. But deal. With. It." *That's* what I'm thinking.'

A potential sentence drifts to silence on his lips. His hand lowers from his face and I'm relieved that his eye isn't damaged. It's not even red. But the irremovable commas of worry around his sockets remain. He doesn't know what to say. I've never spoken to him like that before. There's a syntax error occurring in his brain. He wants to tell me something important – something reassuring and thoughtful. But he can't. His brain is depleted of anything useful. Lack of communication in a marriage is meant to be a bad thing but it's probably what has kept us together the whole time – kept us so bloody happy for so long.

Still, my eyes laser blame towards him. I can't unsee his hand down his trousers. He disgusts me right now, with a day's growth of dark stubble on his face, his thick eyebrows that need to be trimmed, his bouncing Adam's apple and what look like two raccoons in his nostrils. I suddenly shout, 'And Christ Jesus, groom yourself, man. The state of you!'

He remains standing there, pale, a sheen of sweat on his forehead, an agitated glint in his eye like broken glass. Looking beyond me to the house above us, it's as if he's steeling himself to accompany me back up to that complete and utter cathedral of shit that our lives have become. Then he sighs, long, deep and sad. Andrew doesn't want me in his suffering and so he pushes me back into mine, as if I don't deserve to alleviate his pain.

I need to leave the basement. It's like being in the gut of something. But my phone's vibrating. Taking it out, I'm about to press 'decline' when I see that's it's Brona calling. She can't just leave things alone. She has to keep burrowing into things like a termite. I answer and my little sister's confident, could-not-care voice says, 'Mary, I'm willing to talk. Whenever. Just want you to know that.' I picture the bitch hooking her thumbs into the pockets of her suit trousers and raising a skinny eyebrow as she demonstrates her incredible talent at reducing pain down to bullet points.

I'm about to hang up when I hear a car horn and traffic in the background.

'Where are you?' I demand.

'At the supermarket. Why?'

'The car park?'

Exasperated, she replies, 'Yes!'

'Since when?'

'Jesus – since, I don't know, an hour ago. I'm just leaving now with my messages. Why?'

Messages – our mother's term for the weekly shop. I catch myself – *stay focused*. Hanging up, I stare at Andrew. He says nothing. I keep staring.

Finally I say, 'Who the hell are you looking at?'

Immediately he staggers backwards like I've slapped him. His elbow hits the telescope and that expensive piece of kit collapses to the ground like a malfunctioning three-legged robot, thus demonstrating what our neighbour has based his entire career on – that every unsuccessful act is a successful discourse. After vaguely attempting to grab at it, he instead veers to the right and plonks himself, exhausted, onto the wine-coloured leather sofa.

'I don't understand,' I say. 'If Brona's at the shops, then who—'

Suddenly, outside the basement's sliding door, Finbarr's voice shouts, 'What the actual fuck!' I approach the glass. Someone's moving through our garden. Someone's approaching the back of our house.

'Zachery?' I mutter.

Immediately Andrew is on his feet and takes up position beside me.

Zachery marches on, approaching, forty feet away, thirty-five, thirty. He passes the trampoline and Finbarr runs over to him but Zachery ignores him and keeps marching. He's carrying something. A stick. No. A baseball bat.

'What's going on?' I ask.

'I... I... I...'

Twenty-five feet away. Finbarr grabs Zachery's shoulder from behind but Zachery shrugs it off, pushes him and then trips him, sending my nephew sprawling onto his face. When Finbarr isn't in the throes of temper he's just a little boy all too easily knocked over.

'Oh my God, aren't you going to do something?'

Twenty feet away. Andrew has stopped breathing. If it weren't for his wide eyes and vibrating Adam's apple, his face could be a death mask.

Suddenly Zachery swerves to the right, straight through the breach in the hedge and disappears into Connor's. I look back to Andrew. Everything suddenly feels very off.

CHAPTER EIGHTEEN

CONNOR

He stood on the patio feeling the iced highball glass numb his hand.

That morning after a broken night's sleep, Connor had washed away the hangover in a steaming shower. But the relief had been temporary. The moment he'd stepped out of the shower, the mirror had showed him what he would look like at fifty. He appeared to have aged overnight.

Afterwards he'd checked the comments still coming in online across all his digital devices scattered about the kitchen, and ignored three messages from an *Irish Times* journalist who was covering his dramatic fall from grace in next Saturday's supplement.

Connor had called various people in the Health Board but he was toxic now and no one called him back. So he'd sent email after email to everyone who had been involved in the project, apologising for the disgrace he'd inflicted on everyone. Then he'd had another shower, dressed for the second time, poured himself a large vodka with a dash of orange and taken up position on the patio.

Connor sipped the drink, reflecting on how his life was now an endless nightmare that did not just reprise daily only upon waking, but repeated hourly every time he reloaded the comments section of TheCityJournal. He gazed out across the gardens to all that space and greenery and fresh air – it should have made him want to breathe deeply. Breathe forever. But now, as he looked out there, all he was aware of was this: that everything around him, all that natural cycle of birth, death, decay, sooner or later he would be a part of it.

Connor was now mindful of how hedges were poor boundaries. Despite the length of the surrounding gardens, he was still overlooked on all sides. And he also knew that beyond all doubt, he now hated this bungalow. It was not the luxurious and private home it had promised to be. Instead it felt remote, lonely and full of terrors. He scanned along the houses opposite. Every window was an open eye. His gaze drifted towards Brona's. All the while Finbarr was kicking a football against the boundary wall to the side of his decking. Connor placed his hands over his ears but it didn't stop the vibrating thumps.

Just three days ago, he'd had almost everything he'd ever wanted in the palm of his hand. He was the person who was about to change an entire country for the better. He was going to make people happier. And he had been free. Or he had thought he was free. But then he'd quickly learned that you're only free until someone comes along and reminds you that you're not.

On top of Finbarr's incessant noise, starlings began to aggravate each other in the branches of the tallest trees. And suddenly, twenty feet away, Zachery barged through the gap in the hedge. Connor blinked, not quite believing what he was seeing. But Zachery was still there, advancing, wearing a wine-coloured shirt, black jeans and snakeskin boots. He was holding a baseball bat.

So, things can actually get worse.

Zachery took two steps at a time up to the decking. Connor retreated backwards through the sliding doors and into the kitchen. As Zachery followed him inside, Connor raised his glass and drolly asked, 'How's it hanging, bud?'

'Right over your lips, bitch.' Zachery kept coming, the bat swinging more violently now.

He felt like daring Zachery to swing the bat. Is that where he wanted this to go? Did he want to feel the sting of a weapon smashing into his face? To feel something that would wake him up? Something that would make him feel alive rather than drifting, or worse, sinking?

Connor reached the range cooker, his hand tight on the highball tumbler, ready to fling it at him if he kept advancing. But Zachery stopped about eight feet away and tapped the tip of the bat three times against the floor.

'What are you on? Coke?' Connor asked, squinting at his eyes.

'Very good – the rich man's aspirin. I'm surprised you noticed, since coke makes me funny and good-looking but I'm already those things. So usually, I only really do a bump when a date starts to drag. And since I'm settled with Brona, I don't do any coke – hardly. Because it also makes me edgy and mean. Am I striking you as edgy and mean?'

Zachery vigorously rubbed the end of his nose. 'That fucking delinquent. Jesus Christ, does he ever give it a rest?' His tongue ran around his gums, freeing them from inside his cheeks. 'I thought it was bad from our place – but here! Wow, it's insane. Christ, when he sings he sounds like a piglet getting it up the ass from an angry stallion.'

'Leave the boy alone.'

Zachery's jawline tensed. He pointed the bat at Connor's head and shouted, '*You* caused this.'

'Get your shit together, man. Think about things. Look at this situation right now, right here, this minute. You've literally broken into my house and barged into my kitchen carrying a weapon.'

'This?' He held up the baseball bat. 'This isn't a weapon. Not yet. It's still just a gift I got back in the day from Bruce fucking Springsteen, I kid you not.'

'You're trying to destroy my future.'

'I didn't *try*. I *did*.'

'You haven't taken down the video.'

'Ask me. Ask me nicely. Fuck that – *beg*.'

'Get out of my house, Zachery.'

'You didn't come to confront me. So I've come to confront you. You should thank me – like, it must've been difficult to sleep knowing that you were reduced to going to a man's girlfriend and asking her to stop him from bullying you, you fucking bitch.'

'I don't care what you think – don't you realise that by now?'

'That's true. That's always been true. But you probably care what the fifty-thousand-plus who've viewed it think. Imagine, right now people are streaming it, wondering just what the government were thinking by spending even one nanosecond considering taking you on board for some vote-catching populist exercise in pure psychological bullshit. Man, I've been watching the comments pouring in. It's fantastic. It's like snuggling up in front of a fire on a winter night, staring into the warm flames, watching your life burn. No. It's better than that. It's such a colossal disaster for you – it's like… it's like I've nabbed a front row seat for the Hindenburg.'

Connor inhaled. His heart was banging again.

'But I suppose you've done some good. Entertaining the masses. I mean, when there's too much good news, people get bored. So well done – you've napalmed your entire career just to entertain the hive for about forty-eight hours.'

'Nothing I can't deal with. I'm on top of it,' he lied.

'Doubt that. Man, those keyboard warriors are relentless. But you can always depend on the simple-minded for encouragement in times of crisis.'

'You're better than this, Zachery. You manage a property fund worth millions and millions of euros. You can deal with stress. And you can work things out. So calm down and throw away this stupid idea of crisis management that involves running around shouting, "I'm fucked! I'm fucked!" before lashing out and destroying everything around you.'

'I trusted you.' Zachery swung the bat against the floor. It cracked a board. 'I depended on you.' He swung it a second time. The same board splintered. 'I needed you.' The third swing sent a chunk of wood cartwheeling off to the side of the kitchen. 'Why didn't you help *me*?'

Connor flashed an impatient smile, as if Zachery was too shallow to keep up. 'I *was* helping you. Jesus, it's as if you suffer from some sort of "TV resolution syndrome". It's like your neural pathways have warped and you can't help but expect simple solutions to your complex problems. You want your life sorted in fifty-five minutes, but it's not like that. We were getting somewhere, but then…' Connor caught himself and paused to gather his thoughts. *Stop trying to punish him. He's not your brother. He's a dangerous enemy that has the potential to make things better again.*

'You were meant to be my friend, man. My *fucking* friend. How did you become such a disappointment? And when exactly was it that you turned against me?'

'I was never meant to be your friend. That's the "transference" again, Zachery.'

'But you still accepted my gift. The brochure. Then you dumped me and still used it.'

'I had no choice.'

'There's always a choice. And you chose to take without giving. It was a test and you failed. And now you pay.'

'Zachery, it was just a brochure. I made a phone call. I didn't know you managed this place. Please understand that. I *did not know* you had anything to do with it.'

Connor waited for that final nugget of truth to finally hit Zachery like a cannonball and, then, in a perfect world, he could stop treating him like the enemy he never was and take down the video and replace it with an official announcement that it was all a misunderstanding; then Zachery could give him back his money and maybe even find him another place to live and work. Then the Health Board might reignite the big project. It was Zachery – and only Zachery – who had all that power to give everything back to him.

Zachery said, 'But I don't manage this place.'

'I told you, I didn't… hold on, *what*?'

'Never have. You're confusing me with someone else – someone else who is the entire work of my imagination.'

Connor stared at him, waiting for Zachery to make his sarcastic joke. Instead he pointed the bat at him and said, 'I fooled you. You weren't smart enough. Jesus, why did I feel so beholden to you?'

'Slow down and explain – you don't manage this bungalow?'

'Of course not. I'm not even sure exactly what a property bond is. *I'm* just a washed-up fucking guitarist.' He made to once again swing the bat against the floor but changed his mind. 'It's Brona who manages this place, and every other place. She's the big swinging dick. She made it from nothing. I'm just along for the ride.'

'Jesus…'

'Brona spent two years flipping houses in London areas where the Krays wouldn't have walked alone at night. Then later forms an Irish company to capitalise on how everyone's spending money they don't have on things they don't need to impress people they don't like and manages to make a real fortune.'

'*You* work for *her*?'

'Yeah. I played bass with some happening bands. I wrote some TV and radio jingles. That's all true. Then I met Brona in New York and we fell in love. Know why? Because before me, several guys had told Brona that they'd loved her. But it was desperation she'd wanted. And I gave her that. Me. My career wound down and she – the ball-breaking property tycoon – kept making money in real estate and, yeah, I work for her. I suppose I'm like her PA.

I make sure people are doing their jobs, like Tim and the management company that gave you this place under my instructions. That's the truth. The lie was better, right? Better for me, anyway.'

'No, not at all,' Connor said, sounding amazed and, despite himself, impressed with the width and length of Zachery's deception. He remembered Brona's strange reaction when he'd referred to Zachery as a property mogul and to her as his assistant. It was as if he'd thrown cold water in her face. Obviously Zachery had never intended for Connor and his girlfriend to spend time alone together in a room. But he'd still gotten away with it – just about.

'It's such a harmless lie – relatively.' Connor remembered how Zachery, at the first opportunity, would change the subject from property to reminiscence about his playing days, sometimes actually playing air guitar so he could demonstrate his fingers' intricate manoeuvres. 'You simply made yourself out to be a moderately successful businessman. Even as your alter ego, you didn't try and pass yourself off as a big cheese. You were never pretending to be the chairman of a FTSE 100. So why do it?'

'*Not* important.'

'You felt worthless next to Brona. You were never the alpha. And even though this meant nothing to Brona, your old-school ways mined deep down to a stratum of misogyny and chauvinism that demanded not only equal billing – but the flash-flash of the headline act. Jesus, Zachery, you're better than that.' *Capitalise on this. Do your job better and faster than you've ever done it before. Make him grateful. Make him your friend. Do it by giving him the impossible: happiness.*

Zachery withdrew a small cellophane bag from his trouser pocket, shook it to loosen the powder and then stuck his finger into it. Quickly he rubbed his gums and looked at Connor with those sad half-moons under his eyes. 'I never wanted to go to you. That wasn't my choice. That was Brona's. She sensed that I was… drifting in some private unhappiness. She thought that therapy was what I needed. Someone to point out all the great things in my life – the money, the travel, the lack of responsibilities, maybe get me playing bass again – you know, for something to do.'

'That all sounds like a good idea.'

'Jesus Christ, dude, I was unhappy because there was very little meaning in my life. And the one person who gave it meaning was palming me off to a therapist whom I was supposed to tell how useless and empty my life was. I know that already. I just ended up liking you and I wanted to impress you. And you threw the fake me, the built-up me, overboard. How did you think that would make me feel?'

He's trusting you. You're bonding again. 'Zachery, you need to stay in therapy.'

'With you?' Was there actual hope in his tone?

Connor wanted to say yes. He wanted to lie. *Your career, your money, your future depends on it. Say yes. Just say yes.* 'No.' Connor paused and took a breath. 'You need to get back to work with a new therapist. An excellent one. I know the right woman. She'll be great for you. You need to tell her everything that happened between us and what inspired you to invent a self that dwarfed your girlfriend. You can do this. And you'll genuinely find contentment. I promise, Zachery. The answers lie in your history. Your past. They always do. Respect the past, Zachery, because to be ignorant of it is to remain a child forever.'

'The only real truth I hit you with in our sessions was about Brona and me – and our *lack* of family. That's what I need. What *we* need. That would be something. A true anchor. Not just for me but for her.'

'There's no "we". There's no Zach and Brona. There's no future family. None of that is happening. You never stopped to think about what she wanted.'

'No, I have, man. And that's the problem. Brona has everything that she wants and therefore I can't give her anything.' He took the bag of coke out but changed his mind, shoving it away again. 'Children mightn't give her what she wants but they'd give her what she needs: a fucking reality check. No matter how good you are, no one stays champion forever.'

'You said you daydream about killing her. You don't fantasise about stabbing, shooting, strangling your girlfriend if you love her.'

Zachery gazed down. 'I think you made my cock twitch.' He laughed, childishly, almost a snigger. 'Nah, you weren't really listening to me. You weren't paying attention. You were just hearing what you wanted to hear. I did say I dreamed of killing her. Sure. But it wasn't "her". It was just killing. I daydreamed of *killing*. That's it. Brona's the only person of relevance in my life, so it's her that I painted into the scenes. But it could be anyone. It *would* be anyone. Maybe even you. Or that irritating prick in the garden. Do the neighbourhood – fuck that, *the world* – a service, you know?'

Connor glanced out the window to where Finbarr was back on his precious trampoline.

Zachery continued, 'Murder isn't the big deal people think it is – everybody dies. In a few years there will be all new people on the planet and everyone you know will be gone. Look at your neighbour, Mister Andy. I heard from guys over at the golf club that he killed at least one man in the Lebanon when he was out there with the UN. So last Christmas when we were around for drinks, I asked him about it and know what he said…? He said that he'd been up real close when some men *and* women left this earth. And I asked him, "What did this rare intimacy with death teach you, Andy?"'

'And what did he say?'

'Just this: "Death is something you should be *very* afraid of".'

Connor picked up his tumbler and took a sip.

'Nice guy when cutting the lawn, though. Real charmer when you pop round for Christmas. A lifesaver when some neighbour wants the kids picked up from school. But when he put a bullet in a man's head or bayoneted him or whatever he did over there – do you think his victim was aware of any of that? Or did he just see Andy for what he was? For who he really *is*? For what *we all* are? I don't know Andy that well, but I know him enough to realise that he feels just fine with what he's done. In fact, I bet he feels that he's the inheritor of a sacred knowledge that few of us will ever be partial to. And if you want to get philosophical about it, at the end of the day, murderers and their victims lie in the same fucking cemetery.'

Zachery tapped the bat against the floor a few times.

Then he continued. 'Now pay attention, because we're getting to the real interesting bit. The reason why I'm here. We went for a walk last night around St Catherine's Hill, Brona and me, and the only thing in the world she wanted was for that video to be taken down. Of course, I told her I would but I won't. All the time she was holding my hand like it was a fish she wanted to throw back. And where had she been before that? Huh? With you. Here. With *fucking* you, *fucking* here.' Zachery dropped the weighted end of the bat to the wooden floor like an industrial pounding hammer.

Connor winced as a second floorboard cracked.

Zachery continued. 'You were alone with Brona. You're smart. You're attractive. And so, like every smart, good-looking guy, you know that Brona is intelligent. Interesting. Creative. Strong and insightful. And you want to fuck her mouth.'

'Jesus, Zachery—'

'You fucked her, didn't you? Right here. Where? On that table?' The bat pointed to the sunken corner which had briefly been Connor's therapy space. 'Or did you bring her into your bedroom?'

'You're an idiot.'

Connor heard something in his own tone – a lack of commitment. Zachery was right about one thing – he *was* interested in her on some level. He saw himself kissing her and shifted awkwardly, searching for space to deal with the fantasy that was him and Brona while out there, looking in, would be Zachery.

Zachery raised the baseball bat above his head. Glaring into Connor's steady gaze, he inhaled deeply through his powder-coated nostrils. 'Yeah, just as I suspected – you reek of *eau-de-*Brona's-pussy.'

'I never touched her.' *This is not going the way I want it to go.*

'I put you here in St Catherine's Hill to punish you. To make you feel how I felt. Helpless. Powerless. But what I've really done was give you what you wanted – Brona.'

'I'd never even met her till yesterday.'

'Oh, but you've seen her from your old office in the Fitzgerald Building. You've heard me telling you everything there is to know about her. And she fascinates you. And the mad thing is, I've only copped on now. Talk about being dick-blind, cock-sucked and just plain fucking stupid.'

'Zachery, you need to come back down to earth. Have a tea. Drink water. You're wired and you're not thinking straight.' It was as if Zachery was holding a loaded gun and was about to pull the trigger and everything would be lost.

'Connor, you filled her head full of ideas. You pressed her buttons. You – what is it? – you *triggered* her. And now everything is gone to shit. And don't tell me that part of you didn't know what you were doing. You're too smart for that.'

'I didn't purposely try and hurt your relationship.'

Zachery's coked-up turbo-powered brain was now lengths ahead of what was coming out of his mouth. 'So – you're a bastard. And all this – the kid next door, you stuck here for a year, getting pumped and dumped by the money-monster, the shit-show online – you own it. Because it's yours. I've forced it all onto you. Play stupid games, win stupid prizes. When all this blows over, you'll be about as useful to the world as a one-inch cock.'

My chance – it's gone. Totally gone. Over. Zachery was just a meat grinder, mincing the exciting possibilities of the future into the failures of the past. Connor's hand once again felt out the glass tumbler on the cooker to his side. He wanted Zachery to swing. He had no doubt he'd manage to shatter the glass against his head before he got halfway through the motion. Plus, he'd just realised that if it was Brona who really controlled the money, then she could arrange for his deposit and rent to be returned, regardless of what Zachery wanted.

But Zachery didn't react the way he was supposed to. Instead he was smiling. Then he was laughing, a low, sly hiss chuckling up from the depths of his chest. A cold rage immobilised Connor's entire body. Zachery had destroyed absolutely everything.

'Yeah, that's right, Connor. I see it now, on your face, how it's all just sinking in. It must be strange suddenly having me being the centre of your existence. I don't just own you. I control you. From now on I'll be the core of every thought you have. I'm basically your life. And just like life, I've stopped you getting what you want. And just like life I'm going to finish you off in the end. And it isn't even over yet. I've more surprises to spring.'

Zachery mimed the unpinning of a grenade, rolled it across the kitchen and drily said, 'Goodbye, coach. Boom.' Then with a smile and a wink, he turned about and made his way back towards the decking.

Connor was behind him, turning Zachery about, grabbing him by the top of his shirt and getting his face in tight and close. *Hit him. Hit him. I can't hit him.* Not yet. Not until Zachery hit him first. Then he could. *Then I will.* Zachery raised the baseball bat, making a wide arc in the air, like a sigh of music. His grip tightened on the bat's handle and his raised arm jolted backwards, finally getting his chance to swing. *Bring it. And then I'm going to fucking kill you.*

A voice shouted, 'Enough!'

Connor and Zachery looked down the garden. Andrew was standing on the lawn having pushed his way through the break in the hedge. For a moment there was silence and then, as if having received a coded message, Connor released Zachery, who in turn slowly lowered the bat to his side. Then Zachery descended the steps to Andrew. Connor watched as their eyes met and in Andrew's expression there was something clear yet enigmatic – a stolen moment, something darker, more dangerous than the intimacy of friendship. Zachery just nodded and shoved his way back through the hedge.

And then there was just Andrew and Connor.

CHAPTER NINETEEN

MARY

Standing in the kitchen, I stare out the window and over the hedge to the bungalow. What's going on? What are the three of them doing in there?

The fact is, we're in trouble now – Andrew and I.

After almost two decades there had been still so much about my husband that I would seemingly never understand. And that was a good thing. Because the secret to the successfully long-term married is that the love between man and wife is two things: an enduring attraction and a constant state of curiosity. The reason Andrew and I did so well was because we had half of what is required – the curiosity.

But now that I know who – or what – Andrew really is, the mystery is gone. And it was that mystery that kept it interesting. Where the hell is he? On the kitchen table there's the *Irish Times*. I turn the page to the 'Death Notices' and skim the obituaries, though not because I'm curious to see if I come across anyone I know. I do it to reassure myself that I'm not the only one whose time is running out. A lot of people die young – more than you'd think. Elsewhere there's a piece on 'Discovering Your Potential'. I grab a pen and begin underlining certain words.

STRUCTURE FEAR OF CATASTROPHE
ADAPTING TO CHANGE DESTINY

And suddenly someone's moving in the garden. Zachery. He's returned from the other side and he's marching away down the lawn, the baseball bat swinging by his side. Finbarr, bouncing on the trampoline, this time ignores him. And then Zachery disappears between the bushes to his own turf and there's still no sign of my husband.

My body has gone into overdrive. It knows what it's doing without me having to direct it. I'm unscrewing the lid from a fresh bottle of Salice Salintino and splashing it into a big glass. I have to be careful about alcohol consumption. I like it too much. I used to just keep it to Brona's visits, but she's gone now. Dad never drank. He used to say, 'Alcohol is to clean wounds and get stains out of woodwork. External use only. Use it internally and you're pouring in pain and dulling the only weapon you have for the fight.' Draining the glass, I pour again. Does pain happen if we can't remember it?

And then I'm out on the patio, placing the glass on the banister and fumbling with the cigarette pack. I see Brona down there, over the trees, just for a split second passing by her lit-up kitchen. She makes me question myself; question the quality of goodness within me. And suddenly Brona is really on her balcony at the end of the garden and she holds a drink in her hand. No doubt it's her usual martini glass. It's so affected, as if the vessel is more important than what it contains. She's also smoking her weird glowing green metal stick. But at least she looks jaded and bored. Apparently being too satisfied and too wealthy is not a very nice sensation. It kills the drives. Desire for anything is energising. She turns away from me and re-enters the kitchen. What now? She'll put dinner on – something organic, nutritious and, no doubt, kind to the planet.

There's a slight chill in the air even though the darkened sky is clear and the horizon further along St Catherine's Hill is rosy with the promise of another bright day tomorrow. Damn the approaching winter. This new dread of meteorological conditions is a portent. When I was stronger, before all this recent drama with Emer and Finbarr, there was no such thing as 'bad' weather, there were only different kinds of useful conditions for my garden. With this long, warm, about-to-fade summer, I can pretend that the ageing process isn't happening even though my life is crumbling apart.

But Emer will have to be back by winter to take her son. Which is just as well. The idea of winter with Finbarr is unthinkable – soon it will be too cold and wet for him to be outside. However even with Finbarr gone, I will refuse to be trapped here with the force of nature that is my husband, grounding me down into some used-up husk for whom the tree for its coffin is already felled. I'm not going to watch myself live out my life here with Andrew, the two of us just existing, a kind of mutual parasitism. That is not what marriage is supposed to be.

Finbarr is gone from the garden. Where did he go? And then I hear my phone buzz. I pick it up and see that I've missed six calls, all from the same number, all in the last five minutes. The screen says:

St Joseph's – Emer's hospital.

'What the hell?'

There's four voicemails for me, all from St Joseph's. I'm about to play them when I notice five unread texts. The first line of the first text reads:

We have an emergency. Could you please call us back on…

The first line of the second text reads:

We are so sorry to have to inform you that…

And suddenly I know. It's happened. The worst possible thing.

Now it seems that it was always bound to happen. I'd hoped it wouldn't. I'd believed it wouldn't. Why? Because just like all those who want more than anything to go to heaven, none of them want to die. But Emer has. Emer finally did what she'd been threatening to do. And now… Finbarr. Oh God, Finbarr. Mustn't think about that. How could Emer have killed herself? It's a sin. The worst sin. The sin that sends you straight to hell, if you believe in that stuff. And Emer does believe that. She *did* believe that.

Emer, pregnant at fifteen. I was twenty-three and two years married. Brona was thirteen. I walked away from them all shortly after Finbarr was born. I couldn't take it after Dad died of shame, and later, Mother of a broken heart. It was Emer's fault. But how can I think that now? Back then, the religious fervour of her youth had solidified after her pregnancy. As I watched from a distance as she'd become an adult, I'd become saddened at the huge pointless decisions Emer was continuing to make; how misdirected she was, how wasted and silly her entire life was going to be.

She'd always been the passionate type, without having any talent whatsoever. So religion was where she'd channelled all that energy. It worried me to witness her going off to Christian cult meetings, Catholic Youth Defence rallies and getting arrested on her first trip to London outside an abortion clinic. I remember after Finbarr was born, when the initial nursing period was over, I'd have to remind her to pick him up. I'd have to force her to smile at him. Babies need smiley faces.

By the time she was twenty, Emer had become the type of tedious fanatic who wouldn't change her mind and couldn't change the subject – impossible to deal with. When she'd finished her finance degree, she'd wasted her sharp mind to work for free in an ultra-right-wing Christianity group. And all the while Finbarr was shunted from school to school and from one miserable small house to an even smaller one, and no matter how hard she prayed, things just didn't get better. And despite it all, she hadn't been a happy believer. She'd been a terrified one. Everything bad that happened was because of not giving God enough attention.

But in the end, has Emer managed to ultimately triumph over me and even God? Death is always just around the corner and not many people get to choose how. But Emer did. And she's left me to marvel at the ruins floating in her wake – Finbarr, Finbarr, Finbarr. Not too many people are capable of going to their deaths with dignity – and Emer, of all people, should've been no different.

There's movement in the kitchen window at the end of the garden. Brona again, clear as day beneath the rising moon, retreating backwards with her hands before her, pleading or wanting. And suddenly Zachery is in front of her, in her face, almost like – no, *just like* – me and Andrew a while ago. Zachery makes her look too little. Brona makes him look too big. They're not meant to be together. She was right. Of course she was right. He's shouting at her, his countenance dark and red. For the first time, am I about to witness them rowing? It's actually exciting until I remember Emer. And suddenly he's gripped Brona by the shoulders. He controls her like he's a great artist and she a life model. But he isn't a great artist. He's just another mediocre musician from a so-so family. And now he's holding her by the collar with one hand while the other hand is raised in a fist and there it remains in the air, threatening to pummel down, and Brona cowers.

Wait.

My little sister. In trouble. And I… and I what? It's as if I'm paralysed by my past – by the things I never did. The responsibilities I never accepted. The actions I never took. I look across the garden again. Zachery and Brona are gone. Gone from the kitchen. But my little sister is in there. And I should be doing something. Zachery could be beating her. No – of course he isn't. Zachery is not a violent man. I know him. I know my little sister. And yet, all these thoughts about Brona are now happening because I don't want to face the reality of what has just happened to Emer. She's dead. And Brona is being shouted at, being bullied. And it's like there's evil in the air, making all this come together at once. But of course, I don't believe that. How can I? I hear my father again – 'Coincidences only happen to atheists.' What's going on? How can my life implode like this – my husband, my little sister, my other sister? My future?

There's silence here in St Catherine's Hill. It's so still the leaves don't move. In the distance a child screams – joyous and shrill.

CHAPTER TWENTY

CONNOR

'You come to pay for my car?' Connor asked. Without waiting for an answer, he retreated into the kitchen where his drink was still on the range. He picked it up, took a sip and breathed deeply to regain control of his adrenalin.

Andrew stood at the opened door. 'Why were you fighting Zach?'

'It's complicated. But look, despite my car and what Finn obviously did to it, I appreciate you butting in.'

'Why? I did it for Zachery. I rescued him.'

'You *rescued* him? From *me*? He had a baseball bat.'

Andrew crossed the room with five or six broad strides until he was inches from Connor's face. The ex-army man was a different proposition to Zachery. He was big and strong, but there was also something about the retired male porn star about him: a little too old, a little too thin, a little too bony; skinny enough so that his shoulder joints bulged at the seams of his shirt. However, his knuckles stood out like knots.

Up close, Andrew's blank expression did not change. His tone did not rise. His eyes didn't widen. 'If you go near Zachery again, I'll stab you. Right through the gut. Six inches. You may live. But it'll hurt. And it will change your life forever. In a very bad way.'

Connor considered pushing him. But it just seemed so pointless, like throwing a stone at a tank. Instead he reached over the range to get his drink but accidentally tipped his glass over. It shattered on the ground, exploding orange juice and vodka in a flowering stain across the damaged boards. However he forced himself to put his game face on and keep his gaze locked to Andrew's. 'What the hell is the matter with you? Who do you think you are?'

A voice in Connor's head was demanding that he hit him, that he demonstrate he would not be threatened, intimidated or bullied in his own home. Connor crunched his fist tight. But he was also smart enough to realise that considering how badly his life was going, listening to his current instincts was like getting counsel from a general in the twilight of his life and who no longer feared death. And so, Connor discarded that voice in his head extolling the advantage of a pre-emptive nuclear strike.

'Seriously, Andrew – I'd seek psychiatric help. You can take that as my professional opinion. You're welcome.'

Andrew sighed and shook his head. He reached around the back of his jeans and withdrew a huge knife from the waistband. It was green with a camouflage pattern around its handle. Half the eight-inch blade was serrated like shark's teeth.

Connor said, 'You do know that I'm going to call the police? Right? Like, that computes?'

'Don't worry, I'll do it for you. I'll have to. You won't be able after I've gutted you in self-defence.'

'Self-defence?'

'Well, you are the guy who's been sending my wife anonymous hate mail.'

'No, I'm not.'

'Still denying it. Dearie, dearie me. You really are a weasel, aren't you?'

'I told your wife I knew nothing about any letters. She was fine with that.'

'Let me get this right – you send my wife hate mail, you attacked the disturbed child we're minding – my *nephew* – and now—'

'I didn't attack any—'

'Eyewitnesses aplenty. Mary. Elena. You're on the internet. It's the greatest show in town. Then, just two minutes ago, you were fighting with – *threatening* – my good friend and neighbour, Zachery. I saved him just in time because that's the kind of thing a decorated officer is trained to do.' Andrew looked at his watch. 'Now you're about to lunge at me in a fury – like the fury you showed a teenage boy who was just kicking a ball in his own back garden on a hot summer's day.'

'So... you're going to stab me?' Connor stared at the blade Andrew held by his side.

'Are you scared?'

Connor forced himself to say nothing but involuntarily his head minutely nodded.

'Yeah. That's probably the first honest thing you've communicated to me.' He held up the knife between their faces. 'I appreciate this blade, Connor. I know everything about it. It's curvature. It's temperature. Because unlike anyone else in this world, it will always do exactly what I command of it.'

Is he utterly mad?

'I never want you to step foot inside my property again.'

No problem.

'I want you to apologise to Mary for sending her hate mail.'

Never.

'And finally – and most importantly – I want you to tell me why you were fighting with Zachery.' He moved the blade a fraction closer to Connor's face.

'I'm Zachery's therapist.'

Andrew lowered the knife to chest level. 'You know everything there is to know about him? You've been in his head?'

'Professionally, I wouldn't put it like that. But after this afternoon I'd say so, yeah.'

'Why were you fighting?'

'He hates himself. He hates his life.'

'And Brona?'

'Brona?'

'Does. He. Hate. Brona?'

Just as Connor was about to answer, he noticed Finbarr beneath the border of the kitchen slider.

Finbarr smiled and said, 'Well done, Uncle Andy, once again you've lived all the way down to the world's expectation of you. Wow, I'm so lucky to have you as a role model. I'm so proud to be your nephew.'

Andrew's face reddened. Slowly he turned the blade left and right as if worrying over a decision. Taking a step back from Connor, he returned the knife to the back of his jeans. Walking away, he said to Finbarr, 'Come on, go. Home. Now.'

Slowly Connor moved towards the empty decking. It wasn't until he started to walk that he realised how shaken he was. He pressed his hand against the island counter as he crossed the kitchen. Once he got to the sliding door, he watched as Andrew leaned against the hedge, making the gap wider for Finbarr. But Finbarr ignored him and instead crouched down to the grass and overturned a rock. All kinds of bugs and insects swarmed out from underneath.

Finbarr looked up to Connor and said, 'Your car window – my bad. But look, man, if I'd known Uncle Andy hated you I wouldn't have done that, but, like, how was I to—'

Andrew suddenly shoved the boy, knocking him forward so that he sprawled face downward. But Finbarr didn't cry out. He just lay still and silent. Andrew stared down at him, shook his head and went alone into his own garden.

'Bastard,' Connor whispered. He watched as Andrew crossed his lawn. Mary was waiting for him at the bottom of the steps. When he reached her, she abruptly slapped him across the cheek. For a moment Connor assumed it was because Andrew had shoved Finbarr to the ground. But there was no way she could've seen that.

What's going on?

Mary had already disappeared into her house. Andrew remained staring into the space that, only moments before, his wife had occupied. His fists crunched into rocks and then loosened into ten loose digits, flickering as if discharging electricity to the earth. He crunched them into fists again and marched forward, following his wife to continue their crisis.

Finbarr was back on his feet. His head turned at an angle as if Connor was a wondrous, strange thing he had only now discovered existed.

'You OK?' Connor asked.

'Uh-huh. I feel for you, man. You're like me – you don't belong here. But that doesn't mean you and me belong in the same space. Me, I should be locked up, with my mum. But you – you belong in the ordinary world. Now your problem is that this place is your home – so you're lost.'

'Very philosophical and well thought out for a messed-up seventeen-year-old kid… as condescending as that sounds.'

'It's cool. I get it. See, I'm just biding my time, vegging out, till I'm eighteen.'

'And then what? You'll take Manhattan?'

'Huh?'

'Leonard Coh— It doesn't matter.'

'New York? Why would I go to… But since you asked – and you're the only one who has asked – I'm staying here. In Dublin. I'm going to code. For games. It's hard to get into, especially when they think you're a fuck-up and want you on meds. But I'll get it together. Of that there is no doubt, man. No doubt at all.'

'I'm sure you will.'

'Oh, I will. And ya know, one thing I've learned from gaming design is how reality-challenged people react in unpredictable situations.'

'And how do they react?'

'Unrealistically, dude. So you and me have no idea what's coming. We have no idea what these people will throw at us. We have no idea what's around the fucking corner.'

'Are you going to be OK in there? I don't like the way Andrew—'

'It's all cool.' And then he smiled – a bright beam full of red lips and white teeth. A moment later, he was back through the hedge, running after his guardians into the house, and Connor wanted to call after him, stop him, tell him that it probably wasn't a good idea. But like everything else in his life, it was now completely out of his control.

CHAPTER TWENTY-ONE

MARY

The heat on the palm of my hand feels like the warmth of a natural fire after a cold winter's walk. It feels like I've just done something good, right, useful. I cross the kitchen and hear Andrew's feet on the steps behind me, and beyond that I can hear Finbarr's panting as he fights to keep up. We are basically a nuclear family and anything nuclear will eventually explode. It will detonate.

'Why did you do that?' Andrew demands as he storms into the kitchen. 'You slapped me. From nowhere. What have I done?'

He actually wants to play that game of rebooting our relationship so that I can once again be the wife that I had been before he was caught. He wants me to act like it had never happened. He wants me to pretend that I don't know *who* and *what* he suddenly is. He wants me to pretend that he is still the man that he would like himself to be. But I'm willing to fight. I'm willing to battle all day. Anything to avoid thinking about my sisters. Anything to avoid focusing on what Emer *has* done and what *is* being done to Brona.

'Andrew, there are three periods to our marriage. There were the first ten years when I was the perfect wife. Then there were the next nine years when you grew disinterested and eventually didn't need me any more. And now the third phase, when we blow up.'

Andrew glares at me. When Andrew's angry, he grows quieter and quieter – the calm before the storm. Then he reaches behind him and withdraws that stupid bloody army knife that he carries around whenever he needs to be a real man. He holds it up and slams its tip into the nearest cupboard door, splitting the wood.

I remember the time just before we married when he'd brought me down the country to see his school. On the way home, he'd knocked down a sheep. Stopping the car, we got out and I started to cry because the poor creature was still alive but paralysed and bleeding. Andrew told me to get back in the car and I did, expecting him to make it all better. I remember his face, expressionless and dark, as he kicked and stomped and booted. After about thirty seconds he dragged the creature into the ditch and then we were on our way again. But he *had* made it all better.

The entire knife continues to vibrate as the handle sticks out into the room waiting for a fist to free it again. But none comes. Instead Andrew marches forward until only four feet separate us. Right now, his grubby silk shirt is the only soft thing about him. But his brutishness has never intimidated me. Nor has he ever intended it to; his violence against inanimate objects is just his version of cursed exclamations. But for just this moment, I wish he'd hit me. Punch me in the face. Knock my sisters from my head.

'Please stop acting like this, Mary.' His hands outstretch beseechingly.

'We never had a good sex life. But it's not as if it ever saddened you deeply. And I'd never needed physical contact to feel wanted. But you know what, Andrew? What does dismay me is the recent indifference in your eyes. It's like you've just gradually grown out of a habit that you'd indulged for a few years. The type of habit that you can't remember ever giving up, but one day you see someone sipping a particular drink – like Ritz – and you think, "I used to drink that. I drank it for years. But now I can't even remember what it tastes like".'

'No, Mary. It's not like that. I still want… I still see you as…'

'Oh my God, you can't even say it, never mind tell it as a half-meant lie. But I should've known. Maybe I did. Underneath it all. But I hid it from myself. I mean, we are who we really are in bed.'

'What?'

'We're in trouble, Andrew. There isn't a comeback from this. Don't you see that? Even though I'd always known that there was something wrong, something not quite right about you, it hadn't really mattered because there was still something I'd wanted from you. Some kind of comfort. Because marriage is such a strange arrangement.'

Yes – my sisters are beginning to matter less and less. Because this is the moment to deal with my marriage. This is the moment to finally put it to rights.

'Mary, what you saw… it wasn't like that. I was worried about Zachery. He's… he's fighting with Connor, next door. Connor is his therapist. And that's where he went. In to Connor, and I was watching through the telescope because… I knew he was going to do something stupid like that. Like attack Connor with a baseball bat and—'

'Will. You. *Please*. Stop. You're lying. Know how I know? Because your lips are moving.'

I try to imagine the alternate universe where Andrew and I have turned out like we thought we might. I know he sometimes does that too. Just last week he was down in his basement flicking through the 'family' album. He'd paused on pictures with just me in them – our one trip abroad – our honeymoon – in the blue ocean off Australia. Of course, I'd been pleased to see him spending his spare time with me. But there had been another feeling. An urge; something inside that had wanted to ask him to stop visiting that grave – because I'm not in it.

I ask, 'When you got the call from Elena yesterday in work, about the emergency, did you think something had happened to me?'

'What?'

'Would you have liked that?'

There's a hush that stretches. Between Andrew's world and mine there is a surging void of silence a billion light years wide through which no meaning can travel without being wrecked.

'Mary, what the hell—'

'Andrew – do you wish I was dead? Is it that bad?'

'Mary, I want you to know that I've never hated you.' He says it with such feeling and sincerity that it's almost believable. We stare at each other and the moment is loaded with the history of a couple that had once been marginal lovers, but were now convenient colleagues who had become very good at not crossing invisible lines.

'Andrew, you've never been openly attracted to any other woman before.'

'Of course I haven't. There's only been you.'

'During the first few years of our marriage, that trait itself surprised me. But your fidelity has never been a mark of dedication to me.'

'Of course it has.'

'The fact is, the only reason you didn't have eyes for other women is because you have never been very interested in them in the first place.'

'No. That's not true.'

'Your few friends are men. Your hobbies are extremely masculine. All your employees are men. And then, of course, there's the army background, your father – your father, always your bloody father. So finally, let all that go and just admit what you are.'

The army man with a cold gaze and hands so strong that they could, and would, kill for me, has diminished into something squalid, meek and pitiful. I'm tormenting him but he owes me the truth and I need this diversion. One thing I learned from Andrew's war stories is that torture works. Fear is the perfect truth serum.

'Please don't,' he says.

'Don't what? Don't look at you here, now, for what you really are? Don't refer to you as what you really are? Don't speak any more truth?' My right hand smothers my left. It wants to dig its nails in deep, to distract the pain inside my mind. 'We married when I was just twenty-one. I didn't know any better. But you did, Andrew. You were twenty-seven. Twenty bloody seven.' I close my eyes and refuse to cry. I will not be that woman. I open them and glare. 'Back then, I was so young, so ambitious, with life and life and more life ahead of me. But something inside warned that I had already lost myself on the map, that I had taken a wrong turn.'

'No. No. We were in love. We knew what we were doing. We always did. Our marriage – you and me – it was the right thing to do. We've always been the right thing to do.'

I took his surname. I'd always liked his surname. Becoming Mary Boyd had felt like a promotion. Maybe Dad had sensed that.

Looking up to the ceiling, I can barely believe my own ears when I hear myself moan the ramblings of one bitter with too much life: 'Dad, Dad, Dad – where are you? Can't you see me now? Can you, Dad? Can you see what's happening? What he's done? What Emer has done? What Brona is doing?'

'Mary – stop it.'

Slanting a glance at him, his wretchedness is extremely reassuring. 'I should've listened to Dad,' I shout. 'He always knew what was right and good and proper for me. Jesus Christ! It wasn't just your Protestant heritage and atheism that bothered Father. He'd also considered you a man beneath me – "He's a man with a limited menu", was how he'd put it. I'll never forget that. I wish I'd told you back then. Instead I hid the truth from you. And from that moment on, deception was our blueprint. Oh my God, is it my fault?'

Andrew's stare is beyond me, to nothing in particular. Maybe he's picturing his own original potential that is now nothing but a withered black pulp repressed deep in his core. But I don't care. He needs to direct his anger inwards. He needs to hate himself. Not for who he is, not for *what* he is, but for the creature he's pretended to be.

'You like men,' I say.

'No.' His eyes are wide. It's as if he wants to believe himself.

'You always have liked men.'

'I don't… I can't… I… I…'

'And you tried to hide it from yourself too – as well as from me and the world.'

He rushes forward, annihilating the four feet of space between us. *Hit me. Clear my head. Hit me. Make me focus. Hit me.*

His big hands land on my arms but his face radiates softness and desperation. He feels me tense up and immediately lets me go. For a moment he looks as if he's about to try and embrace me again but I lift my hand in a nonsensical inappropriate halfway gesture and move sideways along the counter to open up fresh distance from his compassion.

Andrew says, 'I'm not trying to hurt you. That's not what this is about.'

I nod. But secretly I know that it is. That's the thing. It's always been about hurting me. Because if you can summon the energy to lie to a person every day for over twenty years then it's not just deceit; it's manipulation on a grand scale. It's a subliminal assault. Turning away, I face the splash-screen of the cooker. 'Coward,' I whisper, just loud enough for him to hear.

I listen to my husband walk to the kitchen door. There's silence and I can feel his eyes still watching me. No one wants to be called a coward – least of all a coward. Finally, I hear him on the stairs as he descends to his crypt, his footsteps trailing off like an unfinished sentence.

And then I hear something else. Breathing. I glance over my shoulder. Finbarr has buzzed into the kitchen from the patio like the fly on the wall he's become. For a moment he stares at the knife protruding from the cupboard. Then he reaches out and with considerable strength, rips it out of the wood.

'No, Finn, put it down.'

Looking towards the hallway and the basement stairs, he says, 'I'll bring Uncle Andy's favourite toy back to him, will I?'

'Yes. Do that. Please. And thank you.'

Finbarr looks at the steel, turning it on its side, glinting the sun off its metal. Then he says, 'Get rid of him. It'll put you both out of your misery. And *you* deserve to be happy… for once.' With the knife by his side he crosses the kitchen, goes out into the hall and disappears down the stairs.

I rush to the sink and vomit, throwing up lunch – but it feels like I'm throwing up my marriage.

'Finbarr,' I mutter. 'Finbarr, Finbarr, Finbarr.' He's mine now. He's ours. This is my life. Emer is dead and Andrew is downstairs with his telescope looking at Brona. And… no. He's looking at a man. Zachery. And Brona's being beaten by that same man. And where's Finbarr? Finbarr is armed with a knife downstairs with my husband – my gay husband – my useless, lying, hopeless husband. I've got to get the hell out of here. I need space to think.

My secret place.

It's not too late. I can make it there in time. Through the hallway, shoes slipped on, out the door and into the SUV, I'm spinning the wheels on the gravel, pressing too hard on the accelerator, the gears slip and the sound of the engine revving is like a fistful of coins being thrown into a blender.

Glancing at Connor's bungalow, I recognise it for the repository of secrets that all therapy spaces are and I wonder what intimacies it holds today before suddenly St Catherine's Hill is blurring by and away into the past. More texts and calls are coming in. At first the drive feels like 'getting out', like being set free, as if by the time I return from my secret place, life will be guaranteed *to not* slot back into its discouraging station. But people aren't free. If they were free they'd be happy. Right now, every headlight rolling past seems to be pointed at me. And the phone keeps buzzing. I jam it into my trouser pocket. Drive. Don't think. Drive. Stop making plans. Drive. Ignore the future.

Parking near my secret place, I climb out of the SUV. The area hasn't changed. I grew up here and no one looks at me. Here on the street I'm not even a person. I'm just a peripheral blur in the early night as locals walk by to the newsagent, to the pub, to the Italian, past the travel agency I used to work in. All that matters is that I'm not in their way. Now that I'm invisible, I see it as a superpower. To look at me, you would have no idea about all the wrongness underneath. Above, a city train rolls by, its brakes squealing like fingernails running down a blackboard.

From the outside, my old parish church looks like what a church *should* look like, not like the newer ones that resemble American condominiums with bell towers. The eighteenth century delivered the arches. The nineteenth provided the magnificent wooden ceiling and altar. In the twentieth century some architectural vandalism filled in the vaulted side entrances. The twenty-first century has so far only provided a growing indifference from the once-devout parishioners.

I march up the central aisle of my secret place and stop just before the altar. It's breathtaking how even an ordinary parish church still holds the same power for me as St Peter's Basilica, Il Duomo di Firenze or the Santa Maria in Provenzano, Siena – all of which I've just examined in books and brochures because I have refused to travel. Staring at the golden door of the tabernacle, I'm always amazed at how the stained-glass windows refract light to make it glow technicolour. And with the surrounding hanging crosses with Jesus nailed to them and the white statues of Our Lady and all the lit candles, it's as if heaven and not a grubby, filthy laneway lie behind the altar.

Today I thanked God for you.

His voice again. A whisper close to my ear. Soft, yet desperate. His penis was bigger than Andrew's, darker, obscene with its greed against the pale white of my thighs. I'll ignore it. Put it out of my mind. Not here.

I remember my father's favourite saying any time someone dared question religious faith on TV or the radio: 'Just because you don't see any fairies out there dancing on the lawn, doesn't mean that they're not there, huh? Isn't that right, Mary-Contrary?' And I'd agree because he *had* to be right. What would the world be if a kind, gentle man like my father was wrong about such things?

Go home now. Fix things. Fix things for good.

Not yet. Here it's easy to ignore what I'm supposed to do. About five rows back from the altar I slip into a wooden pew. There's only one other worshipper here. She looks like my mother. With headscarf, heavy jacket and thick brown tights, she's the type of woman that I often forget exists any more. She shuffles by the pews in front of me, temporarily blocking the view of the altar before looking back at me with an understanding smile. It's as if we're both in on a big secret; as if this church is a hidden cave that only a few of us know about; as if we're in an exclusive clandestine sect in which only *we* are invited to escape the day's relentless bombardments.

You MUST go home. Deal with this now. Finish it.

The woman retreats from the altar and I slide out of the pew to take my turn at the candleholder. There are so many mothers out there, puzzling things out. I too am in danger of being a mother that puzzles. He may not be my son – but I am now his mother.

I remember kneeling before my bed after finishing homework, concentrating on each individual of the Holy Trinity, reminding myself that when praying, words are never just words. That if said in the right way, with the appropriate amount of absorption, then the simplest prayer can become a powerful spell. All it takes is faith to let the words of the Our Father sink into your intellectual and mystical psyche, and then like a dream decoded, the prayer's message would be revealed and the reciter would gain solace. One thing I know to be true of prayer, is that it opens up your thoughts so that you can get a good look at them.

Lighting a candle, I stare into the flame and wait for the flickering to clear my mind of the background voices shouting, GO HOME, GO HOME, GO HOME. In Dickens the good, without fail, look into the fire and see the faces of the ones they love. But when the villains look into the same flames they see just hell and doom. I see nothing. It's as if I haven't yet decided which I'm going to be.

As I retreat down the central aisle, I'm aware that I no longer have a choice. I HAVE TO GO HOME; go home and face the music for the crimes I did not commit.

Someone taps me on the shoulder. I hate being touched, and make a concerted effort not to shrug the paw away.

It's the woman from the top of the church. She says, 'How are you, Mary?'

'I'm great. Thanks.' I smile a friendly smile. I have no idea who she is.

She senses this and says, 'We have met before.'

'We have?' I tactlessly ask.

She reddens but struggles on with, 'You look so great. Always. I so admire you. So many people do. We're always saying it. So elegant. You're… what's the word? *Sophisticated.* Suppose you're going home now?'

'Yes.'

Her eyes go far away. 'It's always good to go home.'

I don't bother arguing with her.

Exiting the portico, back into the night and my life and all its crises, I almost run from the church. I miss needing God. I wish I could return to religion – it would be a nice excuse for everything I find difficult to deal with. In this life, people generally find what they need. Eventually. It's amazing how often the drunk finds her bottle, and the gambler stumbles across a deck of cards. Isn't it about time I found what I needed? It's nice to imagine that I can feel a presence. Maybe I don't believe in heaven. But I do believe in hell. I have to. Otherwise I'd want to die. Hell is something to avoid for as long as possible.

Getting into the car, I stare back at the church for one last time and then drive home.

A motorcycle flashes by on the inside lane, doing over one hundred, a chainsaw roar in the dark. And then, just as suddenly, a petrol station whizzes by, bright as the vault of a refrigerator. I can't close my eyes but I do let the road blur into the background as I picture my masseuse rinsing her hands in the wooden basin before opening her box of bottles like she's about to cast a spell. Oh, the smooth heat from the fingers, their diligent firmness that is almost painful.

Finally, I turn into St Catherine's Hill and number 13 is up ahead. But I don't turn the wheel. Instead I'm slowing down and pulling into the pavement across the road from my house and the Kellys next door and the bungalow on the other side.

I can't go into my house. Not yet. But I know what I have to do. In the past it was easy – no matter how I felt or whatever I may have known, I had to keep it all to myself and carry on with things. Because that's what people like me have to do. I have to be all right even when I'm not all right.

But this time the pain I feel doesn't want to be contained in just me. It grows and fights to leap onto another person. It wants me to be the virus that shows the pain where to go.

CHAPTER TWENTY-TWO

CONNOR

He stood in the corner of his patio listening to the muffled voices that carried from the opened door of Mary's kitchen and out into her garden. The house next door was noisy with stories but he couldn't make anything out. It was just another family drama. Everyone had them. Connor himself had the usual handful of memories of his parents together, ignoring one another, silences in the room, sighs between mouthfuls of food; the same few instances of his brother humiliating him over his speech impediment and then filling the house full of mayhem and noise.

But then there were other images too. Christmas Day and Easter. The big TV movie every Saturday night. All four of them sitting on the sofa, the box of chocolates being passed from one end to the other; Connor, Frank and their father picking out the toffee barrels and hiding them until their mother bemoaned how Cadbury were putting in fewer of her favourites, and they'd all surprise her by flinging the little gold barrels into her lap. She'd loved the Bond movies. So had their father. Connery and Moore. *Mam loved Connery. Dad Moore.*

Connor's sudden feelings for his lost family – the gut-wrenching absence – alarmed him. *Imagine if Frank and I were alike in so many ways but neither of us knew. And neither of us would ever know.* Connor placed his fresh drink on the rail and stared down into the vodka and orange. Damp patches had blossomed under his arms. The collar of his shirt itched his neck.

Connor walked back inside, undoing his shirt buttons as he went. He finished undressing in the bathroom and stepped into the shower. As the hot water powered down, he thought, *wash it away. Wash it all away.* Then the lights went off and the water immediately ran cold. But just for a few seconds. Long enough for Connor to curse and spin round, whacking his elbow off the glass. It felt like the house was doing it; as if St Catherine's Hill had turned cold on him, showing him its displeasure at his presence.

As Connor dressed in a fresh shirt, he hesitated over the last button and then quickly went ahead and fastened it. Returning to the patio where his drink was waiting, the ice had melted and the glass was warm from the humid evening. But he sipped it anyway.

Across the gardens, Zachery was out on his balcony. His elbows were resting on the banister as his hands loosely drooped towards the ground. Hs head was lowered and his hair hung down.

Where's Brona?

Connor checked out the long kitchen window, the upstairs bedrooms, the skylight. There was no sign of her. He returned his attention to Zachery. With his back now to Connor, he took a sip from a bottle of beer. *Prick drinks just like a lady. It must take him an hour to down a pint.* Then Zachery appeared to purposely drop the bottle to the balcony floor where it surely smashed.

'Jesus,' Connor muttered.

Zachery upturned his hands and stared down into their palms. Connor squinted. Zachery's palms were smeared with something dark, as if he had cut himself open. Rubbing his hands together, he seemed to make the mess messier. Then he walked into the kitchen, flicked the lights on and ran the island tap. For a moment Zachery seemed to marvel at the water pressure before scrubbing his hands beneath the powerful stream.

Where the hell is Brona? A man on cocaine; a man with no self-worth; a man whose lover tore his heart out like a weed; what was that man capable of?

I'll call around to them. Why not? It's not as if he had anything to lose. He'd insist on Brona coming to the door. If Zachery had hurt her – or worse – he'd never forgive himself for having done nothing. *There's literally blood on Zachery's hands. He'd stated his fantasy about killing. He's unhinged and high on a class A drug. What the fuck am I waiting for?*

Connor grabbed the car keys, stepped out into his drive, cursed himself for not getting the back window of his Saab fixed and thought how embarrassing it would be to drive around St Catherine's Hill in a vandalised car. Then he noticed something next door. Andrew's Land Rover was there but his wife's SUV was missing. In its place, it was as if someone had thrown a bunch of old clothes onto the driveway. He leaned over the wall. A dark, moist stain was spreading beneath a body lying prostrate on the driveway.

Connor said, 'Jesus – are you OK?'

PART THREE

CHAPTER TWENTY-THREE

THE NIGHT OF

CONNOR

Connor was crouched next to the dead body. He clutched the wound in his side and fought against the instinct that was telling him to run and run and run. *Stay calm. Make a smart decision.* A scummy glaze was already forming on the blood next to his feet. There were footsteps further down the road. Bairbre from next door had shouted out to the neighbourhood. Lights were illuminating houses that were usually dark at this time. His stab wound throbbed.

Looking down on Finbarr's pale, smooth, adolescent face, Connor wondered why he'd tried to stab him. Had the young man truly hated him after all? Or in his dying state had he imagined that Connor had been his murderer? No one would ever know.

Connor stared up at the sky. In his peripheral vision the roofs aligning the road framed the stars.

This is the time to listen to your instinct. Run. You've been set up. Bairbre Kelly has seen you with the knife, with the body. Who else is watching too?

Gritting his teeth, Connor straightened and stepped away from Finbarr's corpse. The pain from the knife wound was outside. Not inside. He had to convince himself that that was a good thing. There was something soft beneath his foot – Finbarr's cap.

You've got to run. They think you've been sending hate mail. The world has seen you attack this dead boy out in the garden in broad daylight.

He scanned the nearby windows. One by one the rooms lit up in the Kellys' house.

This is the careful destruction of your entire life. Don't let it happen. There's still time.

And suddenly Connor was running. Down the driveway, onto the road and down St Catherine's Hill. There was something rattling in his jacket. Car keys.

Turn back. Get in your car. It's the only thing you've left.

But there was just one road in and out of St Catherine's Hill. The police would be already coming, intent on adding him to their annual haul of 'bad guys stopped'. He wouldn't get beyond a mile of the house before they'd have him – especially with the back window smashed to pieces. And while the police would be processing him, Zachery would be getting away, destroying evidence, perfecting his story, gold-plating his alibi. Because it *had* to be Zachery. Zachery had already wrecked his career, his reputation, his finances. Now he was obliterating what remained of Connor's existence while also realising one of his life's desires – experiencing the kill.

Connor knew what he had to do. He had to get to Zachery. Stop him before he left. Get him to admit it. Get him to hand himself in. And maybe Brona was in danger, too? Maybe this final act of Zachery's plan wasn't as flawlessly conceived as the rest. Maybe he'd lost it completely and was going to kill her. But he could save Brona; if she wasn't dead already.

As he moved, building speed, Connor felt all used up inside. But simultaneously, his body surprised him, as if it were a separate creature that he was observing. Running at speed now, he was suddenly aware of every second passing. Connor was so grateful for the next minute of his life, thankful for it, feeling that he could make an hour out of it. But then he thought of Finbarr and all the life he should've had left to live, and his brief moment of positivity felt like the most selfish thought he'd ever had. In the distance were sirens. Already.

Unlike his brother, Connor had never run from the police before. Flight is what they called it. One part of it was fear: intense, head-melting terror. But the other part of it was the greatest excitement he'd ever known. He was free from time, from who he was, from everything he'd ever done. He darted like a fish away from the hook, like a cat outrunning a hound.

Someone was on the far side of the road. A teenage boy – no older than Finbarr – was returning from football training with a sports bag thrown over his shoulder. He clocked Connor's hobbled run, his hand flat against the wound in his side. For a moment the teenager's eyes flickered at him and then he carried on, not wanting to get involved. People prefer not to see these things.

Remember where you're going. Remember what you have to do.

About ten houses along from his bungalow, Connor veered off the road into a tree-lined driveway. It led to another fine triple-storey dwelling. As he jogged up the tarmac, a security light blasted Connor with a white beam, blinding him. That wasn't good. Connor knew that the reason why 99 per cent of criminals were caught was *not* because of ingenious detective work, not by snitches, not by turning themselves in – they were caught on CCTV. Most of these houses had cameras.

He kept going down the side passageway. It was the only thing to do. He replayed the advice he'd offered his dynamic, overachieving clients when their usually bulletproofed confidence had taken a hit and all seemed lost: *winners always know exactly what to do if they lose a throw of the dice – they simply double their stake and roll again.*

And then his feet were thudding across the decking of the house, then the spongy quiet of the lawn. Another security beam lit him up but he kept going until the darkness at the garden's end swallowed him up. He needed the relief of the shadows. The wound in his side was beginning to bypass the pumping adrenaline and had started to ache badly. It felt like a bone had been displaced – probably a rib.

As he slipped across one lawn towards the next garden, he stuck close to the tall, deep greenery at the end of the properties. He barged through hedges, squeezed between bushes and climbed over walls. Above, the branches of the trees seemed twisted, low and misshapen, as if they'd been combed by decades of storms rather than painstakingly fashioned and planted by landscapers. From these back gardens, St Catherine's Hill seemed almost uninhabited – as if the entire area was a security-gated waiting room for God: big, beautiful houses all occupied by the nearly dead. And suddenly he noticed something in the dark, something circular on stilts – Finbarr's trampoline.

'I'm home,' Connor muttered, looking over at his darkened bungalow: the monument to his great folly. He turned away from Mary's so he wouldn't see what was going on inside. There would be tears. There could be police. Quickly he worked out where Zachery had made his way through the hedge to get back to his own pad. And there it was – a split in the end of the hedge. With a push, Connor was through to the other side.

Ahead of him was Brona's. Wooden steps led up to the balcony and the opened kitchen slider. But Connor ignored that. He would be in full view of Mary's house if he took that route, and the police were probably there already. Instead Connor moved along the side passageway to the front of the house.

A door slammed. Connor lunged to the side and into the bushes aligning the front winding driveway. Someone was coming, and Connor moved through the undergrowth away from Brona's house. Behind him the warning lights of the parked BMW flashed orange. Zachery, with a holdall thrown over his shoulder, got into the car, started it up, did a quick three-point turn and accelerated away down the driveway. As it sped past, Connor was stung with the abrupt realisation of how, in the end, after everything he'd just been through, Zachery had already escaped.

He looked down the drive as the BMW turned and disappeared into the darkness. Brona's side of St Catherine's Hill was even more exclusive than Mary's. There was more space between the houses, even more greenery and coverage from the road created by rows of tall Irish junipers. But still, what if the police had followed him here? What if they were watching him even now? Did they have marksmen ready? As far as they were concerned he'd killed a teenage boy. If they knew he was lurking in these bushes, they'd surely try and take him out. If they were out there in the dark, then right now Connor was nothing to them but just a green humanoid blob in their infrared vision: dead meat in the reticle of their telescopic sights.

He pressed the doorbell and heard silence. Had it rung? He pressed the bell again. Nothing. Was Brona even inside? Was she alive? There were more sirens in the air, no doubt coming from outside Mary's. With the flat of his hand, Connor hammered against the solid oak door. It was loud but the house and its land was expansive, so hopefully not loud enough to alert neighbours. Suddenly the door popped open and light came onto the darkened steps like the silver steel of a blade.

Then two things immediately happened. Brona's furious expression changed in a second to one of amazement, and the house alarm began bleating its countdown.

'Turn it off. Please, Brona. Turn. It. Off.'

'Yeah, no problemo,' she breezily said, retreating a few feet into the hall. Flicking open the cover of the alarm pad, she keyed in the code. The bleating stopped. 'Sorry, I always have it on when I'm home alone.'

'Thank you,' Connor muttered, looking back into the driveway, making sure that there were no blue lights approaching. He looked down to his side – beneath his jacket the blood spotting through his shirt looked black in the dim shadows.

Without waiting for the invite, he stepped into the hallway and closed the door behind him. 'We need to talk.'

'Is everything OK?'

'No. Nothing's OK.'

'Come on through. You need a drink.' She walked on into the house. 'Well, this is embarrassing – you've obviously heard all about it when Zach called over via your back door. Jesus! Yep, you're a part of it now; the mess and mayhem of our lives, rich embarrassments that should only happen behind closed blinds. But… ya know, that's life. *Real* life. If people want to teach the world to sing in perfect harmony, then they can just buy a Coke. Know what I mean?'

Connor was barely listening as he followed her past expensive lamps, a red bass guitar nailed to the wall (*the vainglorious prick*), a chaise longue and a huge, original Tara Brown painting that hung opposite the staircase.

Brona was saying, 'Sorry you've been dragged into it all. But it was now or never. And if it was never, then… in a few years we'd be just like my sister and Andy. And they're like a threat.'

The cat was on the counter and its eyes widened as Connor entered the bright kitchen. Brona petted it and said, 'Look who it is – your hero. What do we say, Kitty-Kat? We say "*Twank wu*". Yes we do, honey-bunny.' She raised Kitty-Kat's white paw, waved it at Connor and repeated, '*Twank Wu!*' Then she gestured to the kitchen island where there was a steaming bowl of soup and a perfect hill of white rice. 'See, Connor? My life will go on. I *will* get back to normal immediately. I won't be sucked into his drama.'

With the lights on inside and it being dark outside, Connor couldn't see out clearly but knew *they* could see in. Immediately he began closing the three large sets of blinds. While doing so, the sirens came into the kitchen through the opened slider. In the space between his bungalow and Mary's, he noticed a blue light reflecting on the side walls.

Brona watched him with curiosity and a wry smile. 'The voyeur really does hate being watched, doesn't he? So, what's going on out there? One of your elderly neighbours checking out?'

'We need privacy.' Connor stayed away from the exposed slider. 'The whole world is out there.'

'Whatever makes you feel at home, dude. Look, Connor, I don't want you to feel that you're in any way responsible for all this. Sure, you influenced my decision. But it had already been made. I just hadn't realised it. You helped me explore my feelings. Recognise them for what they were.'

'Brona, listen to me. Zach, he—'

'He took coke again. I know. Cocaine! What was he thinking? And it doesn't suit him. It never suited him. It doesn't suit anyone. Jesus. But with Zach, each time he goes off the rails it's a battle royal between him and coke – which coke wins each and every time. Idiot.'

'Jesus, no. I mean—'

'I was going to wait till morning. But... I told him it was over. He took it bad.'

Connor grabbed her arms and pulled Brona towards him, taking in the fading smear of blood on her cheek, the drying red stains on her white shirt. 'Jesus – where did he hurt you?'

'Hurt me? He didn't.'

Connor softly touched her cheek. 'Brona – where did he hit you?'

Her eyes widened. 'I'm not a victim defending her abuser. He didn't hurt me and he didn't hit me. I hit him!'

'What?'

'I said we both needed our freedom. It's run its course. He's a weak man. Weaker than I ever knew. I mean, it's the twenty-first century – *so what* if I earn more than him? *So what* if my career is… God, for want of a better phrase – *bigger* – than his? I mean, because of his attitude, Zach has chosen to have no life, no sense of usefulness and is wasting away growing more envious and bitter. He'll be happier free. He needs to get back Stateside. Some big scene. Some big glass city where he'll find some bubblegum kid straight of out college who'll go, "Oh wow, Zach, you're *so* amazeballs!" and he'll be happy until she grows up and cops on to him. Leaving New York was like walking off the map for Zach.'

'I saw blood. Blood on his fingers.'

'I'm getting to it. I told him, "I'm letting you go." That's exactly what I said. And he said, "Like I'm some expendable employee?" And then he raised his fist and he came at me. He wasn't going to stop. Coke makes him a dumb animal. He grabbed me by the throat. The throat! Dragged me across the kitchen and out into the hall. And I don't know what I was thinking – I *wasn't* thinking, I guess. But I headbutted him.' She mimed, in slow motion, moving her head forward. 'And bam! Blood from his nose. All over his face. And me. It took about ten seconds to realise I'd done it. It made him sorry, though. It made him cop on. He was horrified with himself. Actually crying. And he went upstairs without me telling him – and he packed. And he left. Look at me. What must you think?'

'Jesus…'

Connor looked towards the opened slider and out into the darkness. He could've sworn he'd seen something move. *I'm losing my mind.* Everything was utterly wrong. Finbarr was dead. Someone had killed him. Brona has dried blood on her face. What if Zachery had actually killed Finbarr and she knows? Is this an act? Is she covering for him? She's so normal. But when is normal abnormal? Especially after apparently breaking your boyfriend's face with a headbutt.

'Ah, sweet Connor, you came to rescue me.' She leaned forward and kissed him hungrily. Connor stood there and let her. He was tired – radically tired. It was as if his energy was spilling out and pooling onto the floor.

Jesus – did she kill him? He remembered some of the things she'd said about Finbarr. She'd called him a shark. She'd wanted him 'taken off the shelf'. Getting right up close and knifing someone – it appealed to the most primal fears and frailties. It was the purest assertion of 'I am right and you are wrong'.

Connor pushed her away and quickly looked down to her hands as if expecting them to be holding a weapon.

Brona was embarrassed. 'Damn. I'm sorry. I don't know what I was thinking. Look, it's not like I don't see what Zach's going through. I know it's tough and horrible when a relationship breaks up. I mean, I'm the one who ended it, and I saw his hurt up close and then I kiss you, but it's not like I struggle with basic empathy. Look... he lied about my professional status. Think about that. Think about what he would prefer me to be. I'm not cruel to want a partner in my life who supports me, encourages me and just maybe is proud of me. And I'd like a partner who I could also feel the same way about.'

Connor's mind was churning through the facts. He'd seen Zachery on the balcony with blood on his hands but had never seen his face – he'd been either looking down over the railing or had been in the kitchen with his back to the bungalow while washing his hands. Therefore Connor hadn't been able to see Zachery's bloodied nose.

Brona said, 'Oh God, I tried to kiss you. Just after kicking my boyfriend out. I'm a cliché. Everything about me is. Look – a TV-dinner. My favourite drink is champagne but I'll rarely order it because I believe in delayed gratification. I don't have a daily newspaper because "suffering" depresses me... Instead I get the stories that interest me from Facebook and Twitter... like every other thirty-something busy singleton.'

It couldn't have been Zachery. Of course it wasn't Zachery.

Brona was petting Kitty-Kat again. 'I mean… the fact is, I might want a family. I'm thirty. *Thirty*. I'm not in love, have no plans and I'm getting to that awful stage in a woman's life where I'm too old to sell my body for sex and too young to sell it to science.' She laughed as she opened the fridge, took out a beer and put it on the counter before him.

Connor was staring at her, his pulse beginning to escalate. If Zachery didn't kill Finbarr, then who did? Had someone else set him up? He remembered Mary's neighbour screaming down from her window. It had been like hearing the voice of the entire planet.

Brona was still talking. 'Fine, he's immature like most artists and musicians. That can be endearing. But his talent is just that – talent. He's not driven. It's not like he *had* to play because he reckoned the only way to come to terms with his mortality was to create something that would outlive him.'

Listen to her. So controlled. And it all comes from her strength. Her common sense. Of course Brona didn't kill Finbarr or cover up or help. What's the matter with me? Think. Your time is almost out. Think!

Connor pictured the knife on the driveway, stained with Finbarr's blood and his own. Had it been a military knife? He couldn't remember. He could only see the steel. Had the handle been green? Was it the same knife that Andrew had threatened him with? Andrew, who had killed in the Lebanon. Andrew, who was trained to inflict maximum damage. Andrew, who walked around like a time bomb.

Brona looked down to his side and pulled back the flap of his jacket. 'What *the actual* hell? Are you bleeding?'

'Don't worry about it. It's fine. Look, we need to talk. Now.'

'It's a wound. A *real* wound. What are you thinking, just coming in here and saying nothing about it?'

Connor didn't tell her what he'd been thinking – that for even a moment he'd entertained the preposterous thought that she'd killed a seventeen-year-old boy.

'Shit,' Connor said, realising that he'd given Andrew time to do whatever he needed to do to set him up – because that's what he *had* to be doing. Andrew had blamed him for sending anonymous hate mail. What type of man pulls a knife over a neighbourly squabble? A knife! *Of course it's Andrew! I was too busy focused on Zachery and how he'd ruined my life to see what was right in front of my face.* But still… why? Why would Andrew kill Finbarr? It still didn't make sense.

I'm out of options. There's only one thing left to do.

'Brona – you have to phone the police.'

'Yeah. Of course. Were you attacked? Where?'

'Just phone the police.'

'In a minute. Show me the wound. What happened?'

He placed his hands on her shoulders, stared into her face and said, 'Finbarr's dead. *Dead.* I found him.'

She didn't react. Instead she remained still and expressionless.

'In the driveway. Mary's driveway. He was stabbed. With a knife. Andrew's knife. I'm sure of it. From the army. I thought it was Zachery. I thought he was setting me up. I thought he had lost it. He'd been talking about killing people. Killing you, even. And before finding Finbarr, I saw Zach attack you. It made sense. But… But it's not Zachery. It's Andrew. Brona, you've got to call the police.'

'No. I can't.' Brona was pale and – for the first time – frightened. 'I'm so sorry. But it's too late.'

Connor felt like she'd slapped him. He focused all his attention on her.

'*Why?*'

'Because the killer is right behind you.'

CHAPTER TWENTY-FOUR

MARY

Across the road is my house. I don't think I've ever viewed it from this specific angle. If I'm out walking I'm always on my own side of the street. Extra lights from the surrounding houses are switching on while the front room and hallway of my own home have also lit up. The entrance door is open. Meanwhile on the driveway, it's as if there's a play being produced.

Finally, I get out of the car – me – the only person on the planet who knows exactly what has just happened. For a second it feels good; like I'm special. As I cross the road, I still don't know how I should look for this catastrophe. Should I go inside and change my clothes? Should I brush my hair? Should I have messed it up – made myself more dishevelled? I know what I'm about to do but it never occurred to me until now how I should look while doing it. But then a crushing reality smashes into me like a solid blow. There is something intrinsically black in the nucleus of my core. Otherwise how could anything to do with the conclusion of Finbarr's short, muddled life even for a second make me feel good, proud, special?

The screaming has stopped. But there's shouting.

'Get an ambulance.'

'It's coming.'

'Where's the police?'

'They're coming.'

'Dr O'Brien from seventeen is on his way. Look! There he is. Is that him?'

'Come on! Come on!'

I walk up the drive. Besides Finbarr, there are five people there. Bairbre Kelly from next door is being held by her husband. There are two men from further up St Catherine's Hill talking animatedly into their phones. And then there is my husband.

Andrew is cradling Finbarr, like he's holding the body of his own son. I never would have imagined it. He lowers Finbarr's handsome blond head to the ground and leans over him like he's mid-operation, his white shirt stained like a surgical gown.

I can see the wound. Clearly. Finbarr is certainly dead. It seems wrong to have all these people around him; all this emotion, this concentrated spectacle. It's disrespectful. The dead shouldn't have to be present with all the bawdy aliveness of the living. Various voices continue to chatter in the night. I make out, 'Finbarr's gone.' One thing I know for certain from being reared a Catholic is that the best word for 'dead' is 'dead'.

Towering over Andrew, I stare down on Finbarr's corpse. It's like a waxwork. When a body's dead it doesn't bleed. The blood stops moving and quickly congeals. No one seems to wonder where I've appeared from. Everyone's still in shock. I do wish Bairbre Kelly would shut up. She's too loud. Her crying is almost like a baby's, demanding all the attention you can give it, as if she's the most pressing emergency on this driveway.

Beneath Bairbre's noise, I zone in on my husband's weeping. It occurs to me that he never cried at his father's funeral. Until now, the only time I'd ever seen him shed a tear was at the end of *Logan* – an absurd superhero film. And even then, it was a single drop he'd slyly wiped away.

Andrew notices me and for a moment forgets about his grief, the aching loss, the frustration, the unfairness of the hand that Finbarr was dealt. And he looks up at me, reaches out, and I ignore his hand. Almost disbelievingly he registers my rejection of him in this, of all moments. He's hurt; hurt for selfish reasons. But this is his future now. Our future. No one walks around holding hands forever.

Crouching beside my father's cast-off cap, I flatten Finbarr's blond hair. It's something I usually only did when he was sleeping. Then I stand again. There's a weight in my hand. I grip it tightly – the knife – forcing myself not to drop it, to not throw it away. I've never cared for knives. Never felt safer when I had one in my hand. I slip it inside my jacket.

Someone's approaching. Have I been spotted? It's Bairbre. She's crying and in between her sobs, she's saying, 'The police are coming. The police are coming,' over and over as if their arrival will mean that all of this can then be reversed. But the police won't be able to fix what has happened here. They'll never understand it. They'll just clean it up. Hide it all from view.

Bairbre grabs my elbow. In the background, her husband tries to pull her away but she twists free of him and says, 'Mary, I have to tell you something.'

'Hmmm?' I reply. It's a polite sound, distant, warning that this is not the time to broach anything of importance.

Her eyes are welling up again. She inhales and begins, 'It was us. Tony and me. Tony and me… we…'

'You *what?*'

The tears begin streaming again, decorating her terrible confession. 'We are so, SO, sorry. We can't imagine… we never would've thought—'

Her husband interjects, 'For God's sake, Bairbre!'

'It was us. We sent the letters. The letters from the neighbourhood. I wrote them and Tony put them through the letterbox when he left for work, before anyone was up. We are so sorry. We just wanted… it doesn't matter why now… it was nothing… poor Finn. Poor Finn.'

I actually feel pity for her. She is so out of her world. Bairbre's like an astronaut cut loose in space, drifting away into endless darkness, away from the light and warmth and blueness of earth. She's never known anything outside of being a school-run mummy, occupied with her children as if by an army, hiding behind them making tedious small talk. I've lived next to her for a decade and in all that time having a conversation with her has not been possible; her children have made her entire life a zone that forbids adult exchanges.

As her husband places an arm around her while avoiding my eyes, I realise that finally Bairbre can be useful. I cover my mouth with the flat of my hand, turn away and quickly make towards the house and the remaining privacy of my life within that door.

'Mary,' a voice calls. It's Andrew. I throw a wave behind me, as if to say, 'Give me a minute', and then I'm through the hallway, across the kitchen, out onto the patio, down the steps and it's like arriving in another country on a faraway continent. It's quiet – dead quiet – and peaceful, with no hint of the sinister mayhem only fifty feet behind me on the other side of the rooftops. I'd like to sit, feel the grass, kick off my shoes and earth myself to the land. But then the sirens sound, nearer and nearer. Here they come. I have to keep going. This has to finish tonight. Soon there will be no time left if my plan is to work.

Walking through the garden, passing Finbarr's trampoline and into the darkness of the trees, it occurs to me how unfair it is that Finn's death occurred out front on the concrete drive rather than back here in the garden where he could be himself. I wonder how long will they leave him lying there before they wrap up his body and shove it into the ambulance like bread into an oven. Already the lights of the arriving police cars out front cut through the air and flash high on the houses, sticking icy blue along their slanting roofs. How peculiarly beautiful Finbarr's blood would now look under their strange shine. Echoing between the buildings is the crackle of police radio, while above, between the trees, a helicopter chops up the air like a gigantic metal dragonfly. It's most impressive, all these luxuries of destruction. No wonder the fall of Berlin in '45 and its accompanying horrors eventually became such a gothic masterpiece.

Tick.

The helicopter has moved a block away in the direction that they think Connor-the-murderer has run. But they're wrong. I saw from my car exactly where he went and which house he dodged into, and no doubt he's down here now somewhere in the gardens, hiding like a rodent. I can't picture a man like him shrouded in bushes. It would be an interesting, humorous sight.

Tick-tick.

I have to put him out of my head. It's the killer that counts. Only the killer. And what the killer wants. And where the killer is. Squeezing through the gap in the hedge, just like Zachery had done earlier, I'm suddenly in Brona's garden and heading up to her house with the brightly lit kitchen half-shielded by the pulled blinds – which is odd because she never does that. But this is an unusual night.

Tick-tick-tock.

I climb the steps to Brona's patio and stand outside the opened slider. Remaining in the slanting shadow of the kitchen's overhanging roof, it's as if I'd melt if electric light fell on me.

And inside there's an unpleasant surprise. Connor's not hiding in the weeds where he should be. He's in there too: pale and wounded, bewildered by all the dark mysteries he can't solve.

And there's Brona, standing next to Connor; experiencing a world of responsibility, of restrictions, of high emotional stakes that is usually only reserved for me, her oldest sister, the one who ensures that her carefree life up to now has been clean and simple. Poor Brona. She's the type of person who keeps a gratitude journal and spends forty-five minutes a night filling it in before telling everyone about it, without irony, on Facebook: 'Tonight after writing my journal, I find that I am so grateful for…' You spoilt, horrible bitch.

And both of them face the killer.

Emer – standing before them, with deep-socketed eyes, their circles looking like purple teabags, sunken cheeks and hair clinging like oily ropes. Her white sneakers are sockless and filthy. The grey tracksuit bottoms are too loose on her, the top stained with mud and blood. She's alive and well; like all killers are after they've done what they've been born to do.

The calls and texts from the hospital weren't what they'd initially seemed – to report that she'd killed herself. They were to say that she'd escaped. Though, of course, they didn't say 'escape'. They'd said, 'Left without permission or official discharge'.

I'd pulled in across the road from my house, not yet able to go home. And there she'd appeared, Emer, walking along St Catherine's Hill, stopping at my driveway, looking in, no doubt noticing that my SUV was missing and having no idea it was directly behind her across the road.

I was about to get out and rush over but then the front door opened and Finbarr had emerged, wearing Dad's cap, marching towards Andrew's Land Rover, holding Andrew's knife, and his intention had been clear – to leave it back where it belonged: in the boot of the car. Emer had hidden herself along the side of the Land Rover as Finbarr had lifted the boot. As he'd done so, Emer had emerged from her crouched position. He saw his mother and she him and they both froze in time for a few lovely seconds. Finbarr with Dad's cap pushed back on his forehead, looking so like his grandfather, was still holding Andrew's knife with one hand, the long blade pointing away from him at his mother, the street lights reflecting on the steel. He then dropped it into the boot before his arms spread to greet his lost mother – she'd always been the only human he'd willingly allow to smother him with touch. It was then that Emer grabbed the knife from the opened boot, and, stabbing from below, the knife lunged upwards through Finbarr's stomach, the blade inside, ripping its advance to his heart.

Finbarr had staggered backwards, until his side rested against the back of the Land Rover. Then he suddenly reached out and grabbed Emer with both hands by the throat. He tried to pull her in, but the knife's handle was still protruding from his gut. And so, keeping her at arm's length, he squeezed and squeezed, and just as Emer's legs threatened to buckle, Finbarr released her and collapsed to the ground.

Emer had stared down on her son, her hands by her sides. I wonder what she was thinking then. Finbarr was holding the handle of the knife, protruding at an angle from his stomach and then suddenly he'd ripped it free and dropped it next to Dad's hat beside him. He made to get back to his feet but found that he couldn't, that the blade's removal had not made everything better; that it had perhaps made everything worse.

Just as I had managed to push aside the shock and been about to get out of the car to see if anything could be done for poor Finbarr, the door to the bungalow opened. Connor stepped out, his back to my sister as he locked up. And so, with Finbarr dying on the drive, the strangest feeling came over me. That this was meant to be. That everything that had happened over the last few days had built to this and it was all for the best. There was a definite plan in my head. A clear vision of the future. I knew how everything could finally be put to right for us all. So I stayed where I was and watched Emer walk into the opened door of my house like an invited vampire and drift through the hallway into the kitchen; all the while my oblivious husband was hiding down in his dungeon. From my car, it had been like looking down a brightly lit tunnel. I could see Emer getting smaller and smaller as she'd kept walking, following her nose and disappearing out through the opened slider onto the patio and then down, down, down the steps to the garden.

On Brona's patio, I quickly light up a cigarette and take a single pull. Dropping it to the decking I don't bother stomping on it. Without further ado, I enter the kitchen, walking by Emer without looking at her mess. Stopping halfway between both parties, I nod at Connor and Brona.

Connor is pale and clutching the side of his suit jacket. The wound obviously isn't deep but it must hurt like hell. His expression is one of bafflement and exhaustion – but there's a sense that these emotions are mostly directed inwards, as if he can't quite believe that a situation has arisen in which the combined power of his professional toolkit is completely redundant.

Brona widens her eyes at me, like she's trying to communicate something private and personal between us; like we're friends, like we're close. Emer hasn't even acknowledged my presence.

Now what happens? I can barely even remember my plan. Why am I even here? Did I come to stop Emer doing any more damage? To somehow fix everything? I wish Father were here – marching into this room. I can see him. Before me. Before us all. Taking control. Knowing what to say. He had the gait of a leader. A general. I so loved Father's beard – thick and rich and full of religion. He didn't know what doubt was.

Emer looks up, hurt, her eyes lingering. Then slowly she lowers her gaze again, giving it the full Princess Diana.

'Emer,' Brona says. 'What have you done?'

Emer immediately switches tack and sighs, like she's just examined a leaking tap, and says, 'I really wish he'd stop bleeding.'

'Oh, God,' Brona says. 'You did it. You really killed him.'

Emer straightens and asks, 'Do *you* think I killed him?'

Brona has no words, so I say, 'You stabbed him. Didn't you?'

'I… I think so, Mary-Contrary.'

'Well, Emer, that's how you kill people.'

I feel something. A force. I turn my head and ten feet away meet the blast of Brona's glare.

'For fuck's sake, Mary,' she snaps.

Emer's gazing into the room, but at nothing in particular. 'The blood. It poured out of him. It gushed.'

'Oh Jesus,' Brona says. 'Emer, what have you done? You've stabbed him to death?'

Emer asks, 'Why was he wearing Dad's cap? He looked so like him. It was like seeing Dad again through warped glass – young and old. But I also knew it was Finn. And I… I just wanted him to stop suffering.'

So Emer thinks she did it to stop her son from suffering. But the way she did it, he suffered more than he'd ever done in his entire life.

Emer hugs herself, demonstrating that grief is an absence that takes up space. She then faces me straight on, turning her body like she's in pain – all plank-like, deficient in neck and shoulder mobility. It's hard not to look away, she's so wretched-looking.

She asks, 'Mary – do you know what I was doing in there?'

'Where?'

'The home. The institution. The place in which you put me away.'

'I didn't put you—'

'*What* I did in there… what I did to get peace, the only peace I got, the only respite, was when I went out to the grounds in the morning. I'd put earplugs in to block out all sound. No birds or leaves swishing. All I could hear was my own pulse and my own breathing and… behind that a perfect empty space of silence, and do you know what that silence is?'

She waits for a reply. When none comes she shouts, 'I asked you a question! Do you?'

'No,' I answer.

'That silence is the sound of God.'

I notice a slight flicker in Connor's white expression. Emer does too and switches her attention to him. 'Who's this?'

'My friend,' Brona says.

Emer bares her teeth 'Who. Is. He?'

'I'm Connor,' he says feebly, but polite, like he's just been pulled over by the police. His chest is rising and falling with laborious breaths and I think he's going to faint. His hand is tight and flat over his ghastly wound.

Emer says, 'Umm… You don't even know me and you still need to demonstrate, even in a minuscule way, how you consider religious discussion so far beneath you that—'

'What? No… I'm just trying to focus—'

'*That* you consider it no different from someone talking about UFOs or Big Foot.'

'I'm sorry you think that.'

'It's a modern conceit on a par with an evangelical's boundless proselytising. Don't you realise that? *I* realise that. I'm sure Mary realises that. She knew Dad as well as me. Brona doesn't, though. She never got to know our dear dad.'

Emer has more energy out here in the world than she ever had inside the institution. It's not just the fact that the drugs have worn off. It's something else, like a burden has been lifted, like a strap has been loosened around her chest. It must be so hard to breathe with all those people around worrying about you all the time.

'Let's forget about the past,' Brona says. 'Let's deal with the now.'

Emer ignores her. 'Mary, you put me in there.'

I'm done with trying to tell her that she put herself in there – her life choices, her weaknesses, her myriad of inabilities. But I still want to give my sister something; the only crumb of support I'm capable of offering.

'Remember, Emer, "Their angels in heaven always see the face of my Father in Heaven".'

Emer's lips twitch with the suggestion of a smile. 'What a clever girl you are to be able to think of that.'

What a clever girl you are to be able to think of that. I feel a rush of cold rage.

Emer adds, 'Yes. It's amazing how Matthew 18 verse 10 always has the right words of comfort. If God exists, He sympathises.'

And yet if He exists, He also punishes. And then it occurs to me, the words that Emer has just spoken. 'What do you mean, "*if*"?'

'Mary, did you never notice the way that when Dad started talking about Jesus he always ended up talking about Satan? Know why? 'Cos to Dad, and all those like him, he was way more interesting.'

'He was just scared of the devil,' I said. 'It's different from being interested *in* him.'

'Umm,' Emer says, not sounding convinced. 'I think that an upside-down cross is still a cross. That's what people don't realise. But *he* did.'

I say nothing.

Emer continues, 'All those days in that home you put me in, sitting in the gardens, the plugs in my ears, listening to the sound of God, thinking, thinking, thinking until it became so clear that the truth is obvious – like everything that is true and proven is – I finally realised that good is the exception. Evil is the rule.'

'You've lost your religion?' Brona says. There's something in her tone hinting that this was possibly a good thing, that a breakthrough had been made, albeit a little late for Finbarr. I'm not so sure. In becoming deradicalised, Emer has clearly deprived herself of something useful to her, no matter how grotesque.

'You've got to go,' I say, becoming aware once more of the chopper hovering nearby over St Catherine's Hill. 'I'll bring you to them before they come to you.' It isn't over for Emer yet. She still has a chance. I can give it to her.

'Not yet.'

'Why?'

'Because you owe me.'

'I don't owe you any—'

'You know you do. Just admit it. Just tell me. Face up to it. What you did. What you didn't do.'

Emer has decided to waste her final chance, instead focusing on this nonsense. I look at Brona. It's time for her to be useful. 'Call the police.'

'No, Mary, I will not.' There was an edge to Brona's voice. She clearly hadn't liked my tone – the assumption that her eldest sister always gets her way.

It's time to put Brona in her place. 'You will. Call the police, or—'

She laughed – a false, bitter sneer of a sound – before saying, 'Or you'll do *what*, exactly?'

Even though Connor is clearly fighting against passing out, he's also had enough of our mad family. He says to Brona, 'Mary's right… the boy's dead… his mother killed him. Jesus, she's standing here in your fucking kitchen.' He looks at me, then at Emer and finally back to Brona. 'What is wrong… with you people?'

But even Connor can't get through to her. Instead Brona takes a step towards me and says, 'This is the time, Mary.'

'Call. The. Police.'

'You'll never have another chance.'

'Call them.'

'Say it aloud. You owe it to her.'

'Shut up, Brona. You always speak when no one wants to listen. And you know why? Because your tone is one that believes whatever it's saying must be important. But it isn't. Poor Brona. I think that underneath your desperate urge to be relevant and your need to be heard the loudest, and to get your fair share, to be first in the queue, to be praised for helping everyone and everything – underneath all of that huge egotism and self-regard I truly think that you *still* really believe that you're doing the right thing.'

'Mary – do you want me to say it?'

'For once in your mollycoddled life, shut up. In fact, let someone who knows you the best – better than everyone in this room – let *me* give *you* some sound, honest, advice: people like you should listen to your instincts and then do the exact opposite.'

'Fine then, *I'll* say it.'

Brona just never lets it go. She sees what lies behind the eyes. She hears what's said in the spaces. It's why I've always found it unpleasant to be in her presence. I've always tried to twist my dislike of her into shallow reasons – her youth, her exciting career, her freedom and looks. All her self-satisfied buoyancy. But the fact is, she's just a torch shining into my special box of secrets. I've always found it oppressive to spend too much time around someone so immediately in tune and perceptive as Brona.

She takes another step towards me. So does Emer.

Brona says, 'Dad raped you.'

They are awaiting a response. Brona's basically holding her breath as if she's just offered me a revelation as important as splitting the atom.

Does Brona actually think I don't remember it all? Is she that stupid, that immature, that ridiculous that she truly thinks I, too, suffer from some mental disorder? I remember *everything*. Every last great, terrible detail. No one can take their memories and throw them out, dismiss them from reality like they're old, forgotten stories told before the existence of the written word. When I was younger, when it had been happening, and when it had finally stopped happening, I thought, thought, *thought* about it to death. So much time I've wasted trying to understand his motivation for that type of behaviour. But the fact is, it's impossible to find his motivation.

'You're mad,' I say. 'He didn't touch me *or* her.'

'He raped you,' Brona repeats.

Sex with your father makes you an orphan – but I wanted a father, and I still want the memory of one. You can't force yourself to forget. But you *can* force yourself to fantasise, to play make-believe. When something happens that causes my memories to boil and bubble, I don't picture Dad's bicycle shed opening out onto the back laneway. I picture the church laneway. I don't examine the memory of being alone with Dad at the end of the garden. I picture one of those young men waiting around for Dad to finish oiling their bike chain, tightening the shiny new wheel-fork, balancing out the replaced gear change. That's one thing I've never been able to incorporate into my make-believe – a specific face for my rapist, even an approximate age. Because Dad's regulars ranged from schoolboys to postmen. I find it impossible to choose just one and stick to him and use him as the patsy to Dad's violations.

I say, 'You shouldn't listen to Emer. Jesus – look what she's just done.' I gesture out to the patio and the sound of the sirens and all those voices echoing from over the rooftops two gardens away.

Brona says, 'When you got too old, he eventually moved on to Emer. You know this. And you let it happen.'

Now that Brona has spoken the unspeakable, I'm embarrassed. I'm mortified. My make-believe just seems so twee, so ineffective against the harsh reality that my little sister broadcasts into the room like a shout into my face. It's not fair – because it had been something that worked for me. It's not easy to make the past leave you alone. It's not easy to beat it. It's not so simple to remain unscathed. But I did my best. I did better than most of the rest. Look at Emer. Look at all the others in the papers and on the news and writing their books and crying to talk show hosts. I did better than the lot of them. And I'm not going to let Brona take that from me because she wants to feel even more fantastic about herself – Brona: the wonderful sister who finally brought truth, balance and calm to her turbulent family. She. Is. Pathetic.

I say, 'You're as mad as she is. Dad didn't do anything.'

I know what I'd felt like back then. It hasn't totally left me. My body can still mutiny in such an anti-erotic manner. I still experience that carnal foreboding. Dad turned sex into exploitation, decadence into degeneracy and orgasm to oozing disease.

Brona says, 'I've always known, Mary. Emer told me long ago what happened to you. And then, later, what happened to her. And it would've happened to me if he hadn't died. Because Emer would've been gone, cast out with her baby – our dad's baby, our fucking *brother*. The only person who could've stopped him getting at me would've been you. And you'd already abandoned Emer and run away to get married the earliest you could. You'd have hardly helped me. So, tell her. Admit it. And… maybe apologise.'

'You've listened to a madwoman.'

I don't want to feel it again, and not just the physical aspect of it. I relive that regularly – the pain, the dirt, the disgusting human vapours. I can deal with that. It's the other thing – the mental thing, that I can't, or rather, *won't* suffer again. It's something people, if they must, should only face once. Like Andrew's experience of killing a man. I know it tortures him. I know he regrets it and I understand how he'll never ever speak of it to anyone – not even his old army friends. But part of him treasures it – whatever 'it' is – that morsel of secret knowledge. By the time I was seventeen, I had experienced true despair while the most interesting girls I knew had only read about it from their favourite authors. So as far as I was concerned, I possessed a rare knowledge.

Brona takes another step towards me. I put out my hand like a traffic cop.

'Please,' she says. 'Think about it. Think about Emer. Think about what she has left, about what has just happened, about Finbarr. Think about it all. Do the right thing, Mary. Please.'

Part of me – no, all of me – craves to talk about this: to tell them what had actually happened, to finally give words to the mute voice within me. But still, I can't. And it's a simple reason that stops me. If I tell Brona and Connor, I can't *un-tell* them. And no matter what, I will not have my life being entertainment for others. For people like me, the world doesn't want to know us. The world just wants to know *about* us.

Emer moves towards me. Again I put up my hand to halt any further advance but the hex I can weave over Brona is ineffective against *this* witch. She continues until there's only six feet between us.

Emer says, 'You could've stopped him. You knew what he was going to do. He was done with you for a few years before he started on me. But you ran. You left and got married. You were twenty-one. I was thirteen. That was when he started with you, wasn't it?'

I shake my head.

'And he finishes up with you about fifteen.'

I fold my arms.

'But he messed up with me. Got me pregnant. He was only able to live with himself for a while. Once it began to show, that was it. I was disowned and then he had a heart attack. Dead in his sleep. So, so fucking easy for him. And once he was gone, you still didn't make amends for not protecting me. You were just like Mum.'

Brona asks, 'If he'd lived, you'd have let him have his go with me. You're our big sister. You were meant to be there for us.'

'"For us"?' I snap. 'Nothing happened to *you*. Nothing. You've never had to deal with anything of importance in your entire spoilt life.'

Brona shouts back, 'And you just can't bear that, can you? You're actually so messed up, you believe the fact that Dad never molested me makes me spoilt? You deranged—'

And suddenly everyone is quiet. I'm holding the knife. Andrew's charming blade. The steel dulled with Finbarr's dried blood. Or is it Connor's juices that have darkened its twinkle?

'Jesus,' Brona says as Connor weakly tries to pull her back towards him, like he thinks he's some sort of wounded, dying superhero like the ones my husband likes.

But I'm not about to threaten anyone. Instead I throw it to Emer's feet. It lands with a metallic clang.

Connor straightens on his stool when Emer picks it up. There's a brief puff of colour in his pale exhausted face. I know what he's thinking. He's probably thinking that in a certain way, murdering poor Finbarr was an impressive act. Because Finbarr isn't – *wasn't* – a young man to be taken lightly. Finbarr, when adrenalised, was immensely strong, fearless and unbalanced; a formidable combination of traits. He'd been invincible until the day he wasn't. And that day was the day his mother came home. Connor is probably thinking, *what else can this mental patient do with a knife before the police arrive?* So am I.

Brona says, 'Put down the knife, Emer. Please. For me.'

'Why?'

'I don't want you to hurt yourself. Or anyone else.'

'Too late for that.'

Brona tries again. 'Put the knife down and I promise you everything will be OK. You will pull through this. There is another side to it all. And you'll see that soon. This is just the lowest point. The road will rise now. I promise. You'll see.'

What is Brona trying to convey? That the road shall rise before Emer? Only if that road leads back to the institution where her stay will no longer be temporary but will be for the rest of her life. How could it be anything less? They can't put Emer in jail, because she's mentally unwell. They can't let her out because to the *Daily Mail*'s public she'll always be the drugged candy, the razor in the apple – a child trap.

'Emer, you're amongst your sisters,' Connor gasps, trying to stagger off his stool but failing to leave it behind because he now needs it for support. 'The only family you have. *Family*. Your sisters are your friends... and friends don't lie to each other or threaten one another.'

She ignores him. And she ignores Brona. Of course she does. This is just about Emer and I. It always was. It always has been.

Emer says, 'Finbarr was wearing Dad's hat. You gave it to him. He was already growing into our father. He was the spit... and you gave him his hat. And when I saw him in the driveway... and the knife was there... he should never have existed. If you could go back in time, would you have stopped his conception? If I could go back, I would. So what's the difference, Mary? And... you gave him the hat...'

'He deserved something of his grandfather's. He was family.'

Emer's face widens, enlarging to contain its wonder. And then she sees the weakness in me light up in all its obviousness and she smiles. Yes – Emer knows what happens to weak girls.

She points the knife at me. 'Do you now accept what I said?'

I say nothing.

'Do you acknowledge the past?'

I say nothing.

'Do you believe you should've helped me?'

'You got the knife – so you get to tell the truth.'

'That's not enough.'

'It's all you're getting. Now do it – I give you permission.'

'The only permission man or woman needs is that granted by their heart and by God.'

She remembers so much of what Father said. We have so much in common.

Emer then adds, 'And since I now know that there is no God...'

I say, 'Then you must listen to your heart. It's all there is. It's all you have left.' And with that, I'm satisfied with my last words.

She raises the knife and marches towards me. I unfold my arms and lower them to my sides. *I've had enough. Come to me.* My eyes close. There's darkness. But something else too. Something within the darkness. Something I would never have expected. Is it God? Is it Dad?

CHAPTER TWENTY-FIVE

TWO MONTHS AFTER

CONNOR

It was Friday evening and the autumnal sun had almost set. On the patio, Connor fastened his jacket against the chill and raised the coffee to his nose. He loved its brassy smell and the creamy head that was so perfect he was reluctant to disturb it. Above the lip of the kitchen, the clouds had darkened, becoming knotted and gnarled as if trying to blot out the world. But they won't. They'll just rain on it.

It was quiet. Gloriously quiet. Or maybe, possibly, too quiet? Over the hedge, Finbarr's trampoline remained a permanent fixture, like a mausoleum interning his absent energy. Connor felt sorry for Andrew. He would often see him walking down his garden and standing before the trampoline, hands on hips, pondering something. Sometimes the army man would be there for ten minutes before, head down, he returned to his hollow house.

The sight of Finbarr dying in the driveway – it still woke him. He'd lie there at 3 a.m. wondering what the boy had thought, if anything, as his own blood had oozed between his fingers, pumping hard with each pulse. Had he known that the stream weakening had been bad in the worst possible way?

I wish I could stop thinking about that night. I wish I could just focus on the other things. The good things.

And there were good things. When the media discovered that he had been a key participant in the drama of Emer's tragic escape, some serious investigative journalism plus a background check by the detectives had finally pieced together the truth of what had happened that afternoon between Connor and Finbarr in the garden – truth which was quickly made public in several newspaper articles, absolving Connor of all malicious intent against the tragic boy. When it became clear that the media had cleared Connor of all wrongdoing, key figures from the Health Board had been most eager to meet with him and pick up where they'd left off. So his role as head of the Committee of Mental Health and Noise Pollution was very much on the cards again.

Connor gulped down the coffee in two swallows and returned to the kitchen, feeling suddenly alone and adrift. But, of course, he wasn't. Because there she was at the counter, making drinks. He wasn't yet totally used to the new situation of having moved in with Brona. But he liked the fact that he always got home first from work, and that each time she arrived after him, he felt the childlike surprise and excitement of finally being alone with a favourite secret pleasure that he kept totally to himself.

'Surprise again,' he said, drolly, as he entered the kitchen.

'Make yourself at home,' she replied and then, after a beat, added, 'And by make yourself at home I mean take off all your clothes. Actually, wait till I've fixed us a drink. It's our new Friday ritual. What goes in this again? Galliano, juice and… how much vodka?'

A double. A triple. 'Just a shot.'

'How did the Health Board meeting go?'

'Well, now it's official – the contracts are signed and the money transferred.'

'How generous?'

'Six figures – per year.'

'Oh wow, I think I just had a money-gasm. So, the Milky Bars are on you? I'll have to start charging you rent.'

Brona's energy and enduring brightness had continued to amaze him over the past month or so. Considering what she had been through, it wouldn't have surprised him if she'd retreated to a spa for a long stay or at least locked herself away indoors for a month with the blinds closed. However, it wasn't as if she'd dealt with everything – or indeed, anything.

Brona continued to insist that it was too early to talk about what had happened. The few times he'd tried to push it, Brona had accused him of trying to 'fix' her, of trying to scrutinise her. But the fact was, Brona had never got what she'd wanted from Mary that night. And as for Emer – no one on the planet had wanted what she had offered.

Connor rubbed his eyes. He needed to stop thinking about Mary and the weirdness of Brona's family.

Brona rounded the counter and, holding both drinks, leaned in and kissed him. Then she took a few steps backwards, made a funny leering face and nodded towards the bedroom. 'C'mon, I've had a long day at the office. I need my therapist to analyse me in his special way.'

'Wait a sec. Look at that...'

Over the hedge, Andrew could be seen dismantling the trampoline. The two corner poles were quickly removed and the entire construction tilted to the side like a listing ship. In a few minutes, it would be gone forever.

Brona muttered, 'Finally...' She then picked up something from the counter to show to Connor. 'Look what I bought today.' It was a small but powerful pair of travel binoculars.

Outside, rain had begun to blow against the windowpane as if being flung at it in handfuls. Connor sipped his drink. It was too weak but he smiled as if it was perfect. He said, 'I'm so glad to be out of that place. I don't even like being able to see it from here.'

Brona put the lenses up to her eyes to survey the empty bungalow. 'Yeah – houses are like cats. They never forget the bad things that happen to them.'

Slowly she moved her view towards Mary's and looked to where the upstairs windows had no light behind them and just reflected the falling night. Brona then scanned the middle floor: the raised decking space, the hanging flower baskets, the sprawl of glass window, the shadowy kitchen inside, the telescope.

Brona adjusted the focus dial. What was the telescope doing on the ground floor? But there it was, on its tripod, pointing directly at her.

Connor said, 'I wish someone would come along and just knock that bungalow *and* next door to the ground. Start again. Put up something new. As if they'd never been there.'

Brona understood how he felt. It wasn't nice to be locked outside of knowledge, and Mary's house was a totem to clandestine history. It was a constant reminder that everyone had secrets. Even God had secrets. He had secrets that he kept from his angels.

Suddenly someone stepped out from the darkness of Mary's kitchen and walked up to the telescope.

Brona watched as the person lowered their head to the single viewfinder, closed one eye and peered through it. For a moment each watched the other.

Brona lowered the binoculars. Then she carefully said, 'About that bungalow…'

'Yeah?'

'There's something important I've been meaning to tell you…'

CHAPTER TWENTY-SIX

MARY

I won't back down first. So I keep my eye to the lens until Brona lowers the binoculars and steps away from her kitchen window to judge me in private with her latest lover. However, the sight of my sister spying on me is like a mocking neon sign: You Tried to Die.

I remember my arms spreading to welcome the spike of the blade. Emer was lunging for me. My eyes closed. And then they opened. Because Connor was behind her after somehow finding the strength and energy to jolt across the kitchen and save my life. He'd grabbed Emer's wrist – as thin as a sparrow's ankle – and with his other hand around her waist, lifted her as if she were a bundle of sticks before he collapsed to the ground, unconscious. Emer crumpled on top of him. How did he do that despite his wound? And why would he have wanted to, after everything that had happened? But in the end, Connor saved me and that was that. Not long after – minutes – the kitchen had filled with police.

I don't know where it came from, that sudden urge to die; to let Emer do what she had truly wanted to do. But over the past few weeks, I've been walking along Dublin Bay at sunset where there is something harmonious about the soft falling waves hitting the sand that speaks to me of an enlightenment beyond mere words. I don't know exactly what it means to me but I find it oddly consoling how all those waves come from far away just to die on the shore, as if that is their sole point.

There's a bang – the front door closing. So Andrew is finally gone after doing his last ever chore for me – disassembling the trampoline. He didn't even say goodbye. That's thoughtful. Neither of us like awkward moments. And it's not as if I'm going to change my mind, or that Andrew was going to suddenly produce a silken line that made everything OK or at least made sense of things – he's hardly morphed into a genius overnight.

It's fitting that he left behind his telescope. As I've said, the one thing our relationship did have, right up until the end, was Andrew's capacity to interest me. I admire the fact that he didn't take the one thing I would have thought he'd have definitely packed. And I appreciate how he's set it up for me, here, in the kitchen, by the window, pointing in the right direction and even focused correctly. I just have to look and see. Simple.

My estranged husband is gay and has always been gay. But had he been lying to me when he'd also been lying to himself? Do both those lies cancel each other out? Plus, there's the remaining fact that I don't like to consider; that my desire was fake, as was his. The fact is, being chained together had almost been as bad as being alone. *Almost.* I may have hated our life together, but it was a life. However, in the end, I have left him. Or rather – I threw him out. I don't need him any more and one day soon he'll realise that he doesn't need me.

My husband over the last decade has taught me what it's like to be ignored. But only recently have I begun to experience from the world what it's like to be not noticed. They're very different experiences. I'm forty now, but I look damn well even for St Catherine's Hill. I'm going to join the gym. I used to work out. Now I don't even own any nice gym clothes. It was a shock to realise that. I – Mary Boyd – suddenly have many great plans.

I look through the telescope again – just to be sure I'm not being watched. Yes – Brona is gone, her lover drooling after her, one supposes. Connor and Brona won't last, of course. Already she's lying to him, keeping things from him, putting her dysfunctional family first – as needs be. When he was moving out of next door, I'd briefly spoken to him on the driveway and it was obvious that Brona still hadn't told him about her plans for the bungalow. That was two weeks ago. I would wager that she still hasn't told him. That's no foundation to build a relationship on. Brona will break his heart fast enough.

The thing about Brona is that she's always believed she's been looking for a perfect father to head her future family. But the family she truly wants will soon be right outside her window. She knows it, unconsciously – that's why she came to live in St Catherine's Hill in the first place. That's why she'd pretended to like me, why she'd wanted to be close to me, wanted to spend so much time with me. Brona had always wanted to come home. Just like Emer wants to come home.

I'm still dreaming of Finbarr almost every night; I see him lying on the driveway with no one there. Not even me. I'm just watching from another dimension: a type of omniscient narrator. Then flies rise off his body like claps of dust and I wake. It always takes so long to get back to sleep, and when I'm drifting away I hear my father's voice and the words he used to say whenever someone we knew had died: 'He's gone off to join the majority.'

But at least all the attention and its attendant local scandal has almost totally faded into the past. I wasn't sure how much longer I could've taken the intrusion. I'm not like Brona. She's always loved being stared at, having a camera pointed at her, people looking and whispering. For her, it's like having her soul warmed with love.

Surprisingly, I was totally done with the police at an early stage. Five different interviews; two different detectives. But they never pushed me on the facts – never tried to slip me up and test the veracity of my character. They were simply making sure that there was nothing I'd forgotten as to what had occurred that awful night. As far as they were concerned, everything I'd said was the truth.

So only I know what really happened.

And Emer.

Brona pretends she doesn't – the truth wouldn't fit her view of the world, her sparkly view of herself. For the third time in about five minutes I look through the telescope and see the empty kitchen where it all happened – and I see it happening again.

Connor's unconscious on the ground. Emer is hauling herself off him. Brona is kicking the knife away to the other side of the kitchen. And a plan that had begun to take shape the moment I'd seen my sister kill Finbarr from my car, now, piece by piece, in rapid succession, forms into a whole, very doable, masterpiece. It's like what I imagine an artist must experience when struck by sudden inspiration.

I say, 'Emer, why are you acting like this? You didn't kill Finn on purpose.'

Emer is back on her feet next to Brona. Both my sisters stare.

I say, 'I saw everything from my car. You don't have to be frightened. I witnessed it all. I saw what Finn did.'

Brona asks, 'What? What did Finn do?'

I say, 'Finn was bringing Andrew's knife back out to his Land Rover. He'd put it in the boot. When Emer showed herself to him, he attacked her. He grabbed her by the throat… look at Emer's neck… see the marks? He was choking her. I was… I was frozen. I couldn't believe what I was seeing. But he *was* strangling her. Both hands. He was going to kill her. It was obvious even from where I was. And then, before I could get out of the car, she… well, you know what she did.'

'I took the knife?' Emer asks in barely a whisper.

'You took the knife,' I answer.

'I took the knife and stabbed him.'

'Yes. Because you had no choice. You were about to black out. You were about to die. That *is* what happened.'

'Is it?' Emer looks at Brona.

Brona swallows. 'Mary saw everything.'

I say, 'It was self-defence.'

Brona nods. 'Mary is the witness. It was self-defence if she says it was self-defence. He tried to strangle you.'

There are men moving through the garden. I say, 'Here they come. Just tell the truth. It *was* self-defence. Tell the truth, and I will too.'

Brona says, 'Yes. You *both* have to tell the truth.'

I straighten behind the telescope. No wonder Andrew loved this thing – I don't think I'll ever tire of looking through it. I remember the police piling into Brona's kitchen like we were all on a film set. Brona told them that poor Connor, in his weakened semi-conscious state, had thought Emer was about to stab me, when in fact she'd been simply handing me back the knife for safekeeping. Later, when Connor was getting stitched at the hospital, he told the police that he could've sworn Emer was going to attack me, but also admitted that he had been very confused and could barely see straight at the moment she'd approached me with the knife. Upon hearing Brona's version of events he'd immediately accepted that as the real truth, and later even dropped me in a note of apology for unintentionally adding to the drama of that terrible night.

Emer immediately told the police that it had been an act of self-defence. And even if she'd sounded uncertain at first, she soon got to grips with our new great family historical event. The police's scepticism soon faded – she was after all an escaped mental patient in shock, deeply depressed and suffering withdrawal from her meds that she'd managed to *not take* for a week. Who could blame her for being initially confused after being attacked by her son and then stabbing him in self-defence? The marks on her throat from Finbarr's dying grip were pronounced and painful. Amongst other facts the police were fully aware of was Finbarr's chequered history of violent delinquency and that I – the witness – had been his caring minder and, as the woman in the church had implied, a well-known member of the St Catherine's Hill's exclusive community. Even Bairbre Kelly turned up unannounced at the station the next day to offer the detectives unsolicited anecdotes as to my unrelenting care of Finbarr over the last few months.

I told the police how I'd arrived back from the church to see the mayhem unfold in my driveway – Finbarr trying to kill his mother, Emer stabbing him because there was nothing else she could do to defend herself and then Connor's nightmare begin to unfold around him. I told them how I'd sat in my car doing what I'm good at – seeing everything – but frozen with fear, shock and disbelief. When I'd finally crossed the road, I'd picked up the knife because it was just lying there and I didn't know what to do with it. Anyway, Bairbre Kelly had been hysterical and causing chaos so I wasn't thinking as I'd shoved it into my jacket. I told them that I saw my hall door open and I'd instinctively continued on down the garden to find Emer and to tell Brona what had happened.

They got me to repeat the story again and again, just as they did with Brona and Emer. But when you come from a special family like ours, one of the first skills you inherit is how to get your story right.

The fact was, the police had seen it all before – just another family tragedy. But not murder. And that, in the end, is all that counts. Thankfully our family history was not mentioned in any of the media reports during our few days in the limelight. Besides the obvious, the stories just focused on the stresses and lack of support that families – particularly single mothers – suffer when cut adrift with a severely troublesome child. The police weren't even that interested in the childhood abuse that Connor had mentioned – especially after Brona and I reduced it to something 'long ago' that Connor in his wounded state had picked up on and blown out of all proportion. The police, of course, focused on Finbarr's paternity issue as a biological reason for his violence – which, of course, suits everyone. Again, they'd heard it all before and were as eager to put this ugly mess to bed as we were. However, they did thoughtfully offer counsellors to Brona and I, which we both turned down.

Externally, Brona is perfectly at peace with it all. Perhaps even internally she's convinced herself that my version is the real story. I wouldn't put it beyond her. Brona is the type of woman who would choose to believe whatever narrative, no matter how ludicrous, suits her self-image. As for Emer, she's now making great progress back at the institution. Despite her piousness, she had never been a dull, stupid girl. Anything but, in fact. And now that religion has left her, what remains is a sharp, undiluted, undusted intellect, honing itself for practice.

I light up a cigarette – there's no one to stop me from smoking indoors now – and check my phone messages. There are none. I was hoping for another missed call from Emer, and therefore a voicemail full of her words. Despite now having restricted access to phones, she's still managed to call me from the institution on someone else's mobile. Just yesterday I'd been walking on the beach and had answered the unknown number. Her calls affect me deeply. A phone call makes Emer so near and yet so far out of reach; as if it were possible to be simultaneously separated by miles and by nothing at all. It scrambles me emotionally. When she'd hung up, the silence had killed the phone in my hand in such a mild way that I'd placed it gently away in case any sudden movement disrupted the lingering hint of Emer's farewell.

In her calls, she picks apart every flaw in my character like a dry scab – I'm self-absorbed, controlling, a liar. But she doesn't understand that I'm just a big sister. However, she will one day. Soon. When she gets out and moves into the bungalow next door. Then it'll be just the two of us – side by side – and Brona tagging along at the end of the garden… as always. Until then, I will cherish these harsh judgements Emer sends me whenever the opportunity arises. It means she's thinking of me. And it means that despite it all, Emer cares what I think.

So, while Emer tries to convince herself that she hates me, the fact is I'm the best friend she has in the world. Brona does her best. She always did. But she doesn't have our bond. She was just too young when it happened. And that's why she can do nothing real for Emer except the one thing I've asked her to do – in a text, of course – which is to keep the bungalow for Emer's release in about a month's time.

I so want Emer home. I'm afraid that if my sister wastes much more time in there then the world will have passed us by and the only future that will await us is one of pure loneliness. But I have to remind myself that even if the worst happens, I have no doubt that we can deal with it. For what is loneliness? It's just boredom, fear, homesickness, being unwanted, excluded. It's nothing to be afraid of. My sister must be brave. But I'll be waiting for her; waiting for her to come home.

I tip the ash in the sink and return to the glass. There's too much to see. I always seem to be looking out of windows or looking in them or have people behind windows watching me. But I'm not nervous about my future here in St Catherine's Hill. In fact, I'm almost overwhelmed at how comfortable I feel.

Being surrounded by family means that we can all press 'reset'. I think of all the events that shaped our lives – Emer killing Finbarr, Finbarr coming to live with me, Emer being committed to an institution, Emer having a teenage pregnancy, spoilt Brona avoiding her real responsibilities, me being raped in the church laneway – and I wonder what it is we learned from them. For me it was a teaching in fortitude; a lesson that, if it doesn't fracture you, it will make you so much greater. It was an insight into myself that few are afforded. Therefore, it was knowledge and knowledge, by its very nature, *must* make you wiser.

A LETTER FROM
S.D. MONAGHAN

Dear Reader,

Thank you sincerely for choosing *The Family at Number 13*, as it's the reader that brings a book alive. If you want to keep up to date with all my latest releases, just sign up at the following link. Your email address will never be shared and you can unsubscribe at any time.

www.bookouture.com/sd-monaghan

I've followed, with much appreciation and interest, my readers' insightful perspectives on Amazon, Goodreads and my own Facebook, Twitter and Instagram feeds. Therefore, I would be very grateful if you could write a review. I'd love to hear what you think, and if you've enjoyed the novel, then like-minded readers will too. Thank you to all those who have left reviews and been supportive so far.

Until the next story begins, take care.

S.D. Monaghan

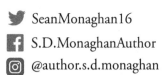

SeanMonaghan16

S.D.MonaghanAuthor

@author.s.d.monaghan

ACKNOWLEDGEMENTS

I would like to thank:

Anne Hughes, first reader and initial editor.

My agent, Zoe Ross, at United Agents.

The amazing team at Bookouture who have all been a pleasure to work with. In particular, I'd like to thank my brilliant editor Abigail Fenton, for her keen expertise and infinite enthusiasm. Thanks also to Kim Nash for always being available and to Noelle Holten for all her unwavering support, advice and resourcefulness.

And finally my parents, Carmel and John, and my sisters, Pat and Teri.

CPSIA information can be obtained
at www.ICGtesting.com
Printed in the USA
BVHW041938210921
617214BV00020B/318